Praise for Catherine Bybee

Wife by Wednesday

"A fun and sizzling romance, great characters that trade verbal spars like fist punches, and the dream of your own royal wedding!"
—Sizzling Hot Book Reviews, 5 Stars

"A good holiday, fireside or bedtime story."
—Manic Reviews, 4½ Stars

"A great story that I hope is the start of a new series."
—The Romance Studio, 4½ Hearts

Married by Monday

"If I hadn't already added Ms. Catherine Bybee to my list of favorite authors, after reading this book I would have been compelled to. This is a book *nobody* should miss, because the magic it contains is awesome."
—Booked Up Reviews, 5 Stars

"Ms. Bybee writes authentic situations and expresses the good and the bad in such an equal way . . . Keeps the reader on the edge of her seat."
—Reading Between the Wines, 5 Stars

"*Married by Monday* was a refreshing read and one I couldn't possibly put down."
—The Romance Studio, 4½ Hearts

Fiancé by Friday

"Bybee knows exactly how to keep readers happy . . . A thrilling pursuit and enough passion to stuff in your back pocket to last for the next few lifetimes . . . The hero and heroine come to life with each flip of the page and will linger long after readers cross the finish line."

—*RT Book Reviews*, 4½ Stars, Top Pick (Hot)

"A tale full of danger and sexual tension . . . the intriguing characters add emotional depth, ensuring readers will race to the perfectly fitting finish."

—*Publishers Weekly*

"Suspense, survival, and chemistry mix in this scintillating read."

—*Booklist*

"Hot romance, a mystery assassin, British royalty, and an alpha Marine . . . this story has it all!"

—Harlequin Junkie

Single by Saturday

"Captures readers' hearts and keeps them glued to the pages until the fascinating finish . . . romance lovers will feel the sparks fly . . . almost instantaneously."

—*RT Book Reviews*, 4½ Stars, Top Pick

"[A] wonderfully exciting plot, lots of desire, and some sassy attitude thrown in for good measure!"

—Harlequin Junkie

Taken by Tuesday

"[Bybee] knows exactly how to get bookworms sucked into the perfect storyline; then she casts her spell upon them so they don't escape until they reach the 'Holy Cow!' ending."

—*RT Book Reviews*, 4½ Stars, Top Pick

Seduced by Sunday

"You simply can't miss [this novel]. It contains everything a romance reader loves—clever dialogue, three-dimensional characters, and just the right amount of steam to go with that heartwarming love story."

—Brenda Novak, *New York Times* bestselling author

"Bybee hits the mark . . . providing readers with a smart, sophisticated romance between a spirited heroine and a prim hero . . . Passionate and intelligent characters [are] at the heart of this entertaining read."

—*Publishers Weekly*

Treasured by Thursday

"The Weekday Brides never disappoint and this final installment is by far Bybee's best work to date."

—*RT Book Reviews*, 4½ Stars, Top Pick

"An exquisitely written and complex story brimming with pride, passion, and pulse-pounding danger . . . Readers will gladly make time to savor this winning finale to a wonderful series."

—*Publishers Weekly*, Starred Review

"Bybee concludes her popular Weekday Brides series in a gratifying way with a passionate, troubled couple who may find a happy future if they can just survive and then learn to trust each other. A compelling and entertaining mix of sexy, complicated romance and menacing suspense."

—*Kirkus Reviews*

Not Quite Dating

"It's refreshing to read about a man who isn't afraid to fall in love . . . [Jack and Jessie] fit together as a couple and as a family."

—*RT Book Reviews*, 3 Stars (Hot)

"*Not Quite Dating* offers a sweet and satisfying Cinderella fantasy that will keep you smiling long after you've finished reading."

—Kathy Altman, *USA Today*, "Happy Ever After"

"The perfect rags to riches romance . . . The dialogue is inventive and witty, the characters are well drawn out. The storyline is superb and really shines . . . I highly recommend this stand out romance! Catherine Bybee is an automatic buy for me."

—Harlequin Junkie, 4½ Hearts

Not Quite Enough

"Bybee's gift for creating unforgettable romances cannot be ignored. The third book in the Not Quite series will sweep readers away to a paradise, and they will be intrigued by the thrilling story that accompanies their literary vacation."

—*RT Book Reviews*, 4½ Stars, Top Pick

Not Quite Forever

"Full of classic Bybee humor, steamy romance, and enough plot twists and turns to keep readers entertained all the way to the very last page."
—Tracy Brogan, bestselling author of the Bell Harbor series

"Magnetic . . . The love scenes are sizzling and the multi-dimensional characters make this a page-turner. Readers will look for earlier installments and eagerly anticipate new ones."
—*Publishers Weekly*

Not Quite Perfect

"This novel flows extremely well and readers will find themselves consuming the witty dialogue and strong imagery in one sitting."
—*RT Book Reviews*

"Don't let the title fool you. *Not Quite Perfect* was actually the perfect story to sweep you away and take you on a pleasant adventure. So sit back, relax, maybe pour a glass of wine, and let Catherine Bybee entertain you with Glen and Mary's playful East Coast–West Coast romance. You won't regret it for a moment."
—Harlequin Junkie, 4½ Stars

Doing It Over

"The romance between fiercely independent Melanie and charming Wyatt heats up even as outsiders threaten to derail their newfound happiness. This novel will hook readers with its warm, inviting characters and the promise for similar future installments."
—*Publishers Weekly*

"This brand-new trilogy, Most Likely To, based on yearbook superlatives, kicks off with a novel that will encourage you to root for the incredibly likable Melanie. Her friends are hilarious and readers will swoon over Wyatt, who is charming and strong. Even Melanie's daughter, Hope, is a hoot! This romance is jam-packed with animated characters, and Bybee displays her creative writing talent wonderfully."

—*RT Book Reviews*, 4 Stars

"With a dialogue full of energy and depth, and a twisting storyline that captured my attention, I would say that *Doing It Over* was a great way to start off a new series. (And look at that gorgeous book cover!) I can't wait to visit River Bend again and see who else gets to find their HEA."

—Harlequin Junkie, 4½ Stars

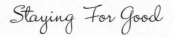
Staying For Good

"Bybee's skillfully crafted second Most Likely To contemporary (after *Doing It Over*) brings together former sweethearts who have not forgotten each other in the 11 years since high school. A cast of multidimensional characters brings the story to life and promises enticing future installments."

—*Publishers Weekly*

"Romance fans will be sure to cheer on former high school sweethearts Zoe and Luke right away in *Staying For Good*. Just wait until you see what passion, laughter, reconciliations, and mischief (can you say Vegas?) awaits readers this time around. Highly recommended."

—Harlequin Junkie, 4½ Stars

Making It Right

"Intense suspense heightens the scorching romance at the heart of Bybee's outstanding third Most Likely To contemporary (after *Staying For Good*). Sizzling sensual scenes are coupled with scary suspense in this winning novel."

—*Publishers Weekly*, Starred Review

Fool Me Once

"A marvelous portrait of friendship among women who have been bonded by fire."

—*Library Journal*, Best of the Year 2017

"Bybee still delivers a story that her die-hard readers will enjoy."

—*Publishers Weekly*

CHASING
Shadows

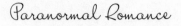
Paranormal Romance

MacCoinnich Time Travels

Binding Vows
Silent Vows
Redeeming Vows
Highland Shifter
Highland Protector

The Ritter Werewolves Series

Before the Moon Rises
Embracing the Wolf

Novellas

Soul Mate
Possessive

Erotica

Kilt Worthy
Kilt-A-Licious

CATHERINE BYBEE

CHASING
Shadows

BOOK THREE IN THE FIRST WIVES SERIES

Montlake
Romance

Text copyright © 2018 by Catherine Bybee
All rights reserved.

Published by Montlake Romance, Seattle

www.apub.com

Amazon, the Amazon logo, and Montlake Romance are trademarks of Amazon.com, Inc., or its affiliates.

ISBN-13: 9781503903432
ISBN-10: 1503903435

Cover design by Letitia Hasser

Cover photography by Regina Wamba of MaeIDesign.com

Printed in the United States of America

For Tanya.
Strong women are the cornerstone of my life.
You, my dear, are one of them.

Chapter One

Left, right, cross . . .

Avery met each punch with a counter and waited until the fourth strike to move in.

Two hits in, Avery shoved her assailant's nose into her knee and then fell to the left when a second attacker swooped in from nowhere.

Next thing Avery knew, she was on her back.

She froze.

Her head flew to the right.

The left.

"Stop."

Her breath came in short, quick pants.

A boot to the face.

The pain . . .

She shot up to a sitting position. "I'm good."

Brenda pushed in and knelt down on the mat. "Your hands were down. Your legs were free . . . you froze."

"I didn't." The denial was quick on her lips.

"The sooner you realize you're wrong, the faster you're going to end this fear." Brenda's German accent cut through Avery's muddy brain.

She pushed Brenda out of the way, pulled her headgear off, and threw it onto the mat.

Leslie, her opponent, had been studying krav maga for three years. Avery had a measly ten months under her belt.

The fact that Brenda was correct in her observation of Avery's freeze only added to her anger.

At herself.

At the world.

At the dead asshole who made her freeze.

Emotion welled up inside and forced her feet to move. She pushed past her instructor and beelined to the locker room.

"Is she okay?" Avery heard Leslie ask.

"She's fine."

Avery let the door slam behind her.

Alone, she moved to the sink and turned the water on cold. She splashed her face, attempting to cool the hot anger swimming inside, and looked in the mirror.

Her flushed features were evidence that she'd exerted herself. The bloodshot eyes were a combination of lack of sleep and frustration. "Get a grip," she cautioned herself.

A sharp knock on the door spiked her blood pressure.

"Are we doing this or not?" Brenda yelled from the other side.

Avery glared at herself in the mirror and shoved away.

"Yeah."

An hour later she stood under the hot stream of the shower, nursing a stinging shoulder and a bruised ego.

Leslie had efficiently handed Avery her ass. Brenda had obviously coached Leslie to get her on the mat repeatedly. Twice Avery had started to freeze, and twice Brenda had yelled something in German that Avery knew was both offensive and condescending. And when their session ended, Brenda's praise was nothing but a half-baked smile that lasted all of a second. If Avery had blinked, she would have missed it.

"You were slow, and your legs should be used for more than screwing."

It was as close to a compliment as Avery could expect. Most of the time Brenda had a never-ending diatribe of faults that Avery needed to work on. To only have two roll off Brenda's tongue was a rarity.

Leslie turned off the water in a neighboring shower, reminding Avery that she'd been standing in the hot water for ten minutes. She quickly rinsed the soap from her hair, turned the water off, and grabbed a towel from the peg outside the stall.

She padded into the locker room and kept herself from looking at the naked woman running a hand through her wet hair.

"Thanks for the workout."

"I'm not sure how much of a sweat you managed, knocking my ass into the ground every five minutes."

"Every opponent brings a new challenge." Leslie reached for her underwear. "How come you don't come to the group classes?"

"And let several people witness my humiliation?"

Leslie cocked her head to the side, her short hair falling in her face. "Brenda told me that you didn't think you were any good."

"Did she?" Avery tossed her towel to the side and turned her back. "What else did Brenda say?"

"That you were good."

Avery glanced over her shoulder. "That's a lie. Brenda never hands out praise."

Leslie winked. "Yeah, I made that up. But you are. Good, that is. You should join us sometime."

"I'll think about it." *And then dismiss the idea.* This was a thing she did under the radar. The fewer people that knew she was studying krav, the better.

Leslie pulled a light sweatshirt over her head and hid the tattoo that covered the entire right side of her body. She didn't put on a bra. Dressed in black, with her dyed red hair spiked, she looked a lot more badass than when covered in protective gear.

"Wanna grab a beer?"

3

Avery thought about what waited for her at home. Nothing.

"Sure."

"Cool. Meet you outside."

It was early fall in Southern California, which meant hot, dry, and windy. Most of the time that meant fires in the foothills and poor air quality in the city. Tonight the sky was clear and electricity seemed to snap in the atmosphere.

Leslie leaned against the brick building, her cell phone in hand, when Avery walked outside the studio. "We can walk. It's not far."

Pug's Pub was a dark lit bar with three men for every woman. The jukebox played old rock and roll from the seventies, and the bartender appeared to have made a lifetime career out of pouring drinks. Overweight and out of shape, the guy blended in and wasn't dressed to earn tips from his customers. From the limited selection behind the counter, Avery assumed the man's talents were limited to Jack and Coke and whiskey, straight up.

"I wouldn't suggest the beer on tap. Safer to ask for a bottle," Leslie suggested.

"Good call."

A handful of men sitting on beaten up barstools watched while they found a high table with a couple of empty seats.

"Hey, Keith." Leslie waved to the man behind the counter, put two fingers up in the air.

"You come here a lot?"

"After a class, some of us come here to decompress. Hard to go home and go to sleep with all that adrenaline swimming inside."

Avery could attest to that.

She sat at the table and winced at the pain in her side. As much protective gear as they used, there was still some pain involved when practicing the fine art of kicking the shit out of someone.

Keith made his way to their table and put two longneck Stellas in front of them. "New friend?" he asked.

"Avery, this is Keith."

"Nice to meet you."

Avery smiled and put out her hand. "A pleasure."

Keith smiled, wiped his fingers on a towel, and reached for her palm. "You class the joint up just by walkin' in the door."

Avery grinned.

"That wouldn't take much," Leslie teased.

"Hey, watch it." He smiled, unoffended. "Where is the rest of the gang?"

"Just us tonight." Leslie tilted her beer back.

"Let me know if you need anything else."

"Gotcha."

Keith walked away, and Avery let the cool liquid roll down her throat. Yup, this was exactly what she needed.

"So what's your story?"

"My story?" Avery asked.

"Yeah. Why krav? Why now? Why do you forget everything the second your back hits the mat?"

Avery took another swig of her beer. "Nothing like easing into a conversation."

"Ease isn't my style."

"Okay . . ." She took a deep breath. "A dirtbag ambushed me last year. I barely knew what hit me before I was waking up in the hospital. Lived in the ICU for a week and got a nose job out of the whole thing. Once I recovered, I decided to take up krav instead of a polite form of martial arts."

Leslie listened without emotion. "What happened to the dirtbag?"

"Dead."

Her eyebrows lifted.

"It wasn't a random act. And it's a long story. So I put the alarm in after I was ripped off, so to speak. I figure the next time someone tries to put me in the hospital, I'm not going without a fight. Fool me once, shame on you and all that, right? Besides, the stronger I felt taking krav, the less frequent my nightmares kept me up."

Leslie leaned in on her elbows, peered closer.

"What?"

"What did your nose look like before?"

The question made her smile and helped lift the heaviness that sat in her chest anytime she thought about that time in her life. "What about you? What's your story?"

It was Leslie's turn to pause and take a drink from her beer. "My daddy liked little girls. I was the closest little girl he could get his hands on."

Avery swallowed, the levity of a moment before gone. "Jesus."

"Nope, Jesus wasn't a part of it. Anyway. I did the high school drop-out thing, ran away. Blah, blah . . . then I met this guy, total douche, but he didn't believe in hurting women. He taught me a few things about fighting. Firearms. Got my GED."

"How long ago was that?"

"Six years. Took up krav a few years back, right as I was getting out of the Army."

"You were in the service?"

"Four years."

"Wow," Avery said.

"Wasn't a career for me, but it was exactly what I needed at the time."

"What do you do for a living now?"

"I design video games."

Avery stared in disbelief. "Get out."

"True story. What do you do?"

Avery played with the condensation on her beer and was happy to be able to say she actually had a way of earning a living. "Estate sales."

"Yard sales for rich people?"

She laughed. "It's a little more complicated than that, but essentially."

"We probably never would have met in the real world."

"I've met a lot of good friends that way."

Leslie lifted her beer to Avery. "To new friends."

❧

Liam kept himself ducked in a back corner of the bar, his eyes trained on the one woman in the place who didn't belong. He'd been staring at her so hard for twenty minutes, it was surprising she didn't feel the heat of his eyes.

Blonde wasn't normally his thing, but he could see making an exception for her. He couldn't see the color of her eyes, but he did notice how much they took in everything around her. Guarded or observant? She leaned against the cocktail table, listening to the woman she was seated by, and while she looked at home tilting the beer back, he found himself watching small details others wouldn't catch. Like how she picked up the bar napkin and wiped the edge of the table before leaning against it. Or how she kept her foot on the strap of her bag, which sat at her feet. She wore designer jeans, and the watch on her wrist glittered in a way that said it wasn't cheap. High cheekbones and a body that wasn't shy on curves.

Liam wondered just how fast he could make her smile.

He couldn't remember the last time he'd picked up a woman in a bar, but maybe he needed to try his hand and see where it led.

The blonde's companion stood and motioned toward the bathroom and then waved toward the bar, which was now packed with customers vying for the bartender's attention.

As the friend left toward the toilets, the blonde walked three steps in the direction of the bar while keeping an eye on the bags left at their table.

Liam watched as the bees started to swarm.

He wasn't the only one in the room attracted. He wondered if he should cut the others off before anyone stepped in before him. Before the thought managed to leave his brain, competition was already sliding in.

The blonde turned toward a customer who opened a conversation. Even though Liam couldn't hear it, he could read the woman's thoughts by how she eyed the man up and down and shook her head before looking back toward the bartender.

As Liam started to push his chair back, a second man pushed right up against her and said something close to her ear. Liam glanced at the lack of personal space between them and noticed her flex her hands. She took a small step back, and the admirer said something over her shoulder to the first guy she'd turned away. With her somewhat caged between the two men, Liam thought it was as good a time as any to step in and make the men stand down. He could see the stiffness of her jaw from two yards away.

Then, without warning, the man on her right slid his hand onto her hip. In a blur, the woman wrapped his unwanted arm in hers, came up over his shoulder, and effectively buried his head in the bar.

All conversation stopped.

"If I wanted your hand on my ass, I would have asked for it." She pulled up higher on his arm. The man moaned. "Got it?"

"Got it, lady."

"You okay, Avery?" the bartender asked.

She shoved the man away.

Several men at the bar started to chuckle.

"I'm fine. Just looking for another round."

Liam stood rooted in place. She could have easily broken the man's arm, even though he was a full head taller and had at least fifty pounds on her.

This was a woman he wanted to know.

She glanced around the audience she'd attracted by defending her space. Her hazel eyes landed on him and paused.

His fingers tingled.

She stared.

She blinked and turned back to her table. There, she grabbed her bag from underneath and pulled what looked like a fifty-dollar bill from her purse. She went back to the bar, dropped the money, and hiked her bag onto her shoulder. "Tell Leslie I had to go."

It took less than ten seconds for the man she'd humiliated, and what appeared to be his friend, to get up and follow her.

Liam stepped in. "Can I help you?"

They eyed him as men do. As expected, they stood back. "Just getting some air," said Contestant Number One.

He took a step as if walking around.

Liam lifted a hand to the other man's chest, stopping him. "Well then, you can just wait a few minutes, can't you?"

Mr. Humiliation eyed the door and drew in a deep breath.

"Fuck."

"I think you two should go back to the bar and have another drink. That fresh air will be there later."

The men looked at each other and receded.

By the time the room calmed, the blonde ninja was gone.

Her friend returned from the bathroom a few minutes later and eyed their table. "Hey, Keith, where did Avery go?"

Keith wiped his hands with a bar towel before tossing it over his shoulder. "Said she had to go, right after she just about broke this joker's arm for hitting on her."

The smile on the other woman's face had Keith chuckling.

Liam felt laughter growing in his gut.

"Never underestimate a woman."

"Yeah, it was classic."

"What do I owe ya?"

"She took care of it."

The short-haired woman lifted a hand in acknowledgment and grabbed her bag. As she walked out, Liam noted the graphic on what looked like a gym bag. *Power Up Krav Maga.*

He laughed.

All the pieces fell into place.

Chapter Two

Adrenaline built like a charged circuit just waiting to fry something.

She gripped the steering wheel of her Aston Martin and turned onto the interstate instead of taking the route that would bring her home.

Driving fast was the recipe she needed to calm her nerves, and since it was close to ten, the highway cooperated. She put the car in sport mode and pressed down on the gas.

Slowly, a smile crept onto her lips. The image of shock on the face of the jerk that had grabbed her ass would live with her for a long time. She flexed her hand as if repeating the move she'd learned in class and started to laugh.

She hit the wheel. "Hell, yeah!"

God, she felt good.

Better than she had in quite a while.

It wasn't until she kissed the coast that she started to come down.

She pulled over in an empty parking lot and stepped out of the car to lean against the hood.

Wind blew toward the ocean. The air was warmer than normal, another by-product of the Santa Ana winds.

She pulled her hair back and looked up at the starlit sky.

A tiny twinge of pain hit the bridge of her nose. A barometer of sorts since it had been brutally broken. The weather was shifting. She didn't need an overtanned meteorologist to tell her that.

She closed her eyes and recalled the bar as it had gone silent. Although she'd had a rush that had filled her ears with a roar, the bar had gone quiet.

Then he stood there.

He was as tall as he was broad. Amusement swam in his piercing eyes.

Her body responded to the stranger in the split second they held eye contact.

He wasn't her type.

Too big.

Too hard.

Much too difficult to take down.

So why was she thinking about the stranger now?

The muscles deep inside her started to wave frantically. Oh, yeah . . . she was thinking about the well-cut stranger because it was the first time her body had heated in nearly a year.

She let the image of him fade. "Guess it's good to know I'm not dead inside," she said to herself.

Her phone buzzed in her purse.

A reminder she'd set for herself.

Go To BED! Appointment in the morning. 8 AM.

With a heavy sigh, Avery pushed away from her car and opened the door.

Adulting really did have its drawbacks.

∽

"We can't have the First Wives meeting next month. I'll be swamped with last-minute wedding preparations. The bachelorette party doesn't count, cuz that's all about me," Trina whined on the phone. "And we missed last quarter for Lori and Reed's wedding."

Avery tapped the pen she was holding against her open calendar. "It isn't like we don't all see each other, with everyone getting married every five minutes." At least that's what it felt like with two out of the four women in the club tying the knot within the same season. It was ironic, considering the basis of their club hinged on the fact they were all previously married and either divorced or, in Trina's case, widowed.

"Oh, wait a minute. What are you doing next Thursday?" Trina asked.

Avery glanced at her schedule. "Nothing. I fly out Friday to Seattle to meet a client."

"Perfect. I know Lori is in town. We just need to catch Shannon."

"You're coming to LA?"

"Yeah, Wade and I need to sign the prenup."

Avery leaned back in her chair. "How does Wade feel about that?"

"He insisted. And it's just smart. Not that there is any question that I'm not marrying him for his money or vice versa. It's just too much money to leave in question should something happen to one of us."

"Sounds like you're drawing up a will instead of an agreement before you get married."

"We plan on doing that once we're back. Life was easier when I didn't need to check so many boxes on my tax form."

Avery rolled her eyes. "You're marrying Mr. Country Western Superstar whose last single was number one for how many weeks?"

Trina laughed. "A few."

"More like six, but who's counting . . . and you're so loaded, presidents call you to see which way you're voting, and would you mind holding a fundraiser?"

"That was a governor, not the president."

"Splitting hairs and you know it."

Trina's laughter grew. "God, I miss talking with you all the time."

Yeah, Avery missed her friend, too. But since she became the other half of Wade Thomas, Trina was a little more preoccupied than when she was single. "It's okay. The newness will wear off and I'll be here."

"God, I hope not. The sex is so good."

"Now you're just bragging."

"It's nice to have something to brag about. Seems like the only one who knew they had a functioning vagina was you."

Avery looked at her dormant lap. "Glad we all have something to talk about, then," she lied.

"Oh, is Shannon finally dating?"

"I don't think pigs have learned to fly." Avery leaned forward and circled Thursday. "I'll call Shannon when I hang up with you."

"Perfect." Trina sighed. "Can you believe I'm getting married in a month?"

"I hope so, since I have a maid of honor dress hanging in my closet."

"I'm so excited."

And for the next thirty minutes, Trina relived every exciting moment so Avery could catch up.

$\sim$

The silence between the occasional noise of a fork touching a plate, or glass clinking against a table, was the only thing Avery could focus on.

Adeline sat across from her, perfectly alert, back straight, shoulders squared . . . fake smile in place. The proper English tea was her mom's idea of a good time. They'd been meeting every other week for six months. Somehow, a friend joining them made enduring the two-and-a-half-, sometimes three-hour purgatory better. Today it was Margaret. Not Maggie, not Mags . . . Margaret. The stick up her ass was nearly as large as the one up Avery's mom's. Two women who lived in the same galaxy of one-upping the other would make most people squirm. Avery was simply happy the focus was off of her.

At least it had worked in the past.

"It's been positively forever since I've seen you, Avery."

Avery leaned in for the air kiss to the side of her cheek before the waiter tucked Margaret's chair under her.

"My wedding, I think."

Margaret's fake pout was almost as bad as her phony smile. "Oh, yes. Such a shame about that divorce."

"Oh, well. Have to get the first one out of the way sometime," Avery said.

Adeline shot her a nasty look.

"I'm happy you're so well adjusted with the situation. Bernie seemed like such a nice man."

Avery was fairly certain that Margaret's only barometer for judging Bernie's character would have come from the two-second handshake at the receiving line during the reception. But like most of Adeline's friends, people with money were quickly referred to as *dear friends*. It only took a season or two for those new friends to become old friends.

Margaret's husband was a partner in an investment firm, and good ol' Maggie herself was a domestic engineer that employed a housekeeper, a cook, and a driver. In short, Mags spent her time memorizing the names of the "important" people in her husband's social circle and had high tea at the Waldorf as often as she could. The reason Avery knew so much about Margaret was because the woman was a mirror image of her mother.

Adeline had never held a job, although she did have a liberal arts degree. A piece of paper she waved over Avery repeatedly while she was in college, doing her best to flunk out. The problem was Adeline did nothing with her degree other than brag that she had one.

"I wouldn't give up hope on Bernie. He's still in love with Avery," Adeline told Margaret.

"I wouldn't bet money on that," Avery said.

"He would take you back in a breath."

The waiter took that moment to walk up to the table. "Ladies?"

He was tall, young, and very cute.

"Champagne," Avery spat out before her mother could order them all tea.

"Avery, please. It's teatime."

The waiter kept his smile in the corner of his eye. He'd obviously seen women like her enduring tea with their mothers before.

"Fine." Avery smiled. "I'll take some tea with that as well."

The waiter tried not to laugh.

As expected, her mother ordered all the fancy proper tea bullshit without asking anyone's opinion. By the time the wine came to the table, Adeline and Margaret were deep in the gossiping world of who said and did what.

"And did you hear that Avery is the maid of honor for her dear old friend Trina Petrov and Wade Thomas's wedding?"

"I do think I heard about that. Isn't he someone famous?"

Avery didn't even try to open her mouth and get a word in. Adeline felt she had a name to drop, so she did.

"Only the wealthiest country music singer out there."

Avery wasn't sure that was true, but again, she just sipped her champagne and let her mom gossip.

"Maybe you'll meet the right man at the wedding," Margaret suggested.

I'm not looking!

"Never know," Avery said instead. The conversation about Avery's future husband had started at birth. *Men want educated wives. You'll never find a proper husband if you continue to be outspoken. Polite women find proper husbands.* That had been Adeline's constant diatribe at every family dinner, every school visit. Howard, Avery's dad, chimed right in with the expected "Yes, dear" and "Listen to your mother." It was no wonder that Avery fostered temporary friends with benefits over relationships her entire adult life. The last thing she wanted to do was become what her mother wanted her to be. *Polite, respectable Avery Grant* were words that would never pass anyone's lips.

The tiers of finger food arrived at the table to help soak up the liquor. She reached for the sandwiches at the same time her mother did.

"What happened to your hand?"

Avery glanced at her krav maga battle scars. Her knuckles were purple and blue after her sparring match with Leslie.

"You should have seen the other guy."

Adeline sucked in a breath. "That isn't funny."

"I accidently hit it against the wall, Mother. Relax."

"You should be more careful. Men don't like women who are bruised and broken." Her mother dismissed all concern for her hand with her retort.

"Good thing I'm not looking for one, then."

"Don't be ridiculous. Of course you are."

Avery bit into the tiny cucumber sandwich, which tasted a lot better than it sounded, and then washed it down. "I'm working, Mother. Making good money and have a purpose other than being another man's possession. You might want to get used to the idea."

"You're working?" Margaret turned her attention toward Avery.

"It's a silly little hobby she picked up last year," Adeline jumped in.

"A full-time hobby that is making me six figures a year. Without being shackled to anyone." Especially her parents.

"Grant women don't work. This is just a season."

"Sure, whatever you say, Mother."

The stiffness in Adeline's upper lip displayed her displeasure with the entire conversation.

"Are you serious about not wanting to marry again?" Margaret asked.

"Been there, done that . . . got the check. I'm doing fine on my own."

Adeline started to grumble before Margaret jumped in.

"I don't understand why you bothered with plastic surgery, then. Isn't the whole point of those things . . . to find or keep a man?"

Avery blinked a few times. "What are you talking about?"

Margaret lowered her voice and leaned forward. "Your nose job, dear."

Inadvertently, she lifted her hand to her face. Her blood started a familiar beat in her head. "That wasn't a choice."

"We should just drop it, Margaret. Avery is very sensitive about her surgery."

Avery pinned her mother with a look. "I'm sensitive about *why* I had surgery. I don't give a crap about the nose job."

"I don't understand. I thought you said Avery was fine-tuning her face to attract another man."

The confusion started to settle in Avery's mind. "So you told Margaret that I had surgery but didn't tell her the truth behind why?" she asked her mother.

Adeline blinked several times and kept her chin up. "I didn't want you to be embarrassed, darling. Everyone has nose jobs. It's not a big deal."

Avery placed both hands on the table and leaned forward. "Someone rearranged my nose on my face with the bottom of his boot, Mother."

Margaret drew a sharp breath. "Oh, my."

"I'm not embarrassed, because it wasn't my fault. But obviously you're ashamed to tell people the truth." God, this was pathetic.

Her mother's resolve started to crumble. She kept her voice low and looked to her left briefly before saying, "We are not the kind of women who get into fights."

The muscles in Avery's forearms tightened.

"I'm so sorry to have brought this up," Margaret apologized.

Avery stared her mother down. "On the contrary, I'm glad you did. At least now I know how my own mother feels about the subject. You honestly think I brought this on myself." She pushed back her chair and grabbed her purse.

"Avery, sit down. Don't be overly dramatic."

When she was a teenager, her mother's cue of calling her dramatic would have resulted in a loud tantrum that would grab the attention of every patron in the room. If she were honest with herself, she wanted to do just that. Instead, Avery kept her voice cold. "Tell Daddy I won't be able to make our Sunday dinner next week." She turned to Margaret. "Lovely seeing you again." *Said no one, ever.*

With a turn of her heel, Avery offered her mother a view of her back as she left the restaurant.

Chapter Three

"I just wish she liked me."

Trina took center stage of their First Wives Club meeting, but that was to be expected, since she was on the verge of joining a Second Wives Club.

"Vicki likes you," Shannon argued.

"When a future mother-in-law wants you to marry their son, she doesn't go out of her way to be around every weekend. Wade and I seldom have the opportunity to be alone."

"A future mother-in-law should be thinking of grandbabies."

Everyone turned to Lori.

She jumped. "No. I'm not. I'm just saying . . ."

"You want a baby." Shannon voiced what they were all thinking.

Lori shook her head. "Of course not. I'm too old."

Trina started to laugh. "I'm sorry . . . Do you still have a period?"

"That's a stupid question."

"Then you're not too old," Shannon said. "Has Reed talked about kids?"

Lori stood and walked to her kitchen and grabbed the open bottle of wine they were working on. "He might have mentioned something the other night."

"What kind of something?" Avery asked.

"About what our kids would look like." Lori leaned her trim figure along the counter and stared beyond the three of them. "Would our girls have his brown hair and my smile? Would our boys be lawyers or join the Navy SEALs . . . you know, stuff like that."

"Someone's biological clock is ticking." Avery leaned back on the sofa and stared at her friend.

"It's not."

"It is!" Trina said. "Nothing wrong with that. You're married to a man you love and trust. You're young enough to go there. It isn't like the first round, where you knew you were married to Mr. Wrong."

Of the four of them, Lori was the only one who had married her previous spouse for love and forever. Avery, Trina, and Shannon were all temporary, hired brides who entered matrimony for a predetermined amount of time and left their marriages several million richer. And for Avery, that was exactly how that played out. Trina, on the other hand, dealt with her late husband allegedly taking his own life and then found out he was offed by his own father. Cue the music for *Days of Our Lives*. And Shannon fell in love with her temporary husband and never got over it. Hence the cobwebs growing in her vagina.

To have one of them talking about having kids was a plot twist in itself.

"I totally want kids," Trina told them.

All the attention fell back on her.

"Soon?"

"I wouldn't say no if Wade suggested it. He's going to be a fabulous father."

"I think we should get you married first," Shannon suggested.

The four of them laughed.

Avery pondered for a few minutes. "Maybe that's why Vicki doesn't like you. You're going to make her a grandmother. Since she was practically a baby when she had Wade, she isn't ready for the title."

They sat in silence and considered the thought until Shannon spoke up. "I want a baby."

Avery's jaw dropped. "You have to have sex in order to have a baby."

Shannon narrowed her dark brown eyes. "Yeah, I took the class."

"Seriously?" Lori asked.

"I'm older than all of you, and I know I want to have a kid."

"Older by less than a year from me," Lori reminded her.

"Still counts. I never considered how my life would be without kids. So if Mr. Forever doesn't come along, I'm just going to do what I have to do to have a child."

"Sperm bank?" Trina asked.

"Maybe. I don't know. Maybe I'll have a one-night stand."

Avery choked on her wine. The harsh taste going down into her lungs had her sputtering for several seconds.

Trina patted her back and Lori handed her water.

Once she got ahold of her breath, she squeaked out the words, "Shannon Wentworth does not have one-night stands."

"Well, maybe it's time she does," Shannon defended herself.

Avery shook her head. "They will eat you up and spit you out." Worry over her friend jumping into that kind of lifestyle made her skin tighten.

"I think that's kinda the point, Avery," Lori said.

Shannon smiled and sat farther back on the couch. "It isn't like I haven't had a one-night stand."

"I don't think college counts," said Trina.

"Of course it does."

"I support the idea."

Avery stared at Lori. "The attorney is supportive of Shannon getting knocked up by a complete stranger and then never seeing him again?"

"A man knows the risk of any one-night stand. If there aren't phone numbers or real names involved . . . I don't see the big deal."

"Isn't that risky? What if he's a sociopath, or has some health issue, or really bad family genes?"

Trina chimed in. "Since when is Avery the sound of reason and Lori is on the sidelines flashing pom-poms and cheering on team impropriety?"

"Think about it. Shannon hasn't had sex since Jesus was in diapers, and we're going to encourage her to dive into just anyone's bed to procreate? There's a lot of shitty men out there." Why was Avery the only one thinking logically about this absurd idea?

"Maybe jumping into bed, anyone's bed, is what triggers the buttons to add some romance to her life," Lori argued.

"Excuse me." Everyone turned toward Shannon. "I'm sitting right here, and I think I'm adult enough to make this decision on my own. I said I considered it, and in truth, haven't ruled it out . . . but I'm not taking ovulation tests to see when is the best time to hit the bar. So everyone can stand down."

That made Avery feel marginally better. "Take me with you . . . when you hit the bar. You need backup. I think we can all agree on that."

Lori nodded and Trina voiced an affirmative.

A few hours later, once Reed and Wade returned from their guys' night out, Shannon and Avery excused themselves to her condo in the same building as Lori's. Even though Shannon's home was only a twenty-minute drive outside the city, she'd planned on staying with Avery to avoid driving or needing to call for an Uber after a few glasses of wine.

Avery peeked her head into the guest room. "Do you have everything you need?"

"You're sweet. Yes, you've thought of everything."

Avery paused. "I meant it when I suggested you have me tag along if you go daddy scouting."

Shannon scooted over on the bed and tapped the space beside her.

Taking the cue, Avery shuffled to the bed, jumped up, and leaned against the headboard.

"Are you okay?" Shannon asked.

"I'm fine. You're the one searching for something you don't have."

"Mm-hmm . . . you see, the thing about being the silent one in the group is that no one knows when I'm watching them. And I've been watching you."

Tension formed at the base of her neck.

"Normally I would expect Trina to catch on to your change in behavior, but she's a bit preoccupied, taking on the title of wife. And Lori . . . yeah, same thing. But I'm not in the same sexual haze as our friends, and you, my dear, have changed."

"I haven't." The denial sounded weak even to her.

"Please don't underestimate me. It's insulting."

After thirty seconds of silence, Shannon read her mental list. "Your knuckles have been bruised every time I've seen you in the last six months. You never brag about your sex life anymore. You just allude that it's there, say something expectedly trashy, and wait for someone to change the subject. Your smile isn't as bright, and your laughter doesn't come as much as it did last year. Something happened with your mom this week, but you didn't open up to us . . . Why?"

Avery knew her mouth was gaping open. "I didn't know you had a crystal ball."

"Talk to me. Isn't that what we're here for? Isn't that the point behind the First Wives Club? Cut the crap and talk about the trials in our postmarriage lives?"

Avery's chest lifted with the oxygen she needed to open up. "I won't be the one to kill Trina's buzz. She deserves to be happy."

"Good thing I'm not Trina."

Avery glanced at her lap, noticed her bruised knuckles. "I had three guys on rotation before New York." She didn't need to explain the reference to New York. Everyone in their little club, along with bodyguards and detectives, were knee-deep in the drama surrounding the violent attack that changed her life. "I cut them all off when I returned."

There was silence.

"Why?"

Avery had asked herself that question many a night since. "I think the easy answer is I didn't feel safe anymore. But that's not completely it. I've changed. The doctors said that a personality change after a head injury is normal. I didn't question it very much. Sometimes I feel like my old self."

"But not all the time."

"No. Most of the time I feel like an imposter."

"Is there anyone?" Shannon asked quietly.

Avery shook her head.

Shannon placed a manicured fingernail on Avery's bruised knuckles. "What's up with this?"

Avery closed a fist, turned to look Shannon in the eye. "Trina doesn't need to know. Not yet. She'll blame herself." Considering it was Trina's late father-in-law that hired the thug who attacked her, it was safe to say she'd suck in any blame for Avery's issues and change in lifestyle.

"I'm the silent one. Secrets are my thing."

Avery lifted her hands in the air, turned them backward and forward. "Self-defense class."

Shannon released a short breath. "Oh, thank God."

"What did you think I was doing?"

"I don't know, punching walls. I read up on head injuries, too, and I didn't rule anything out."

"You've been thinking about this a long time."

"A few months. And you're right. I think Trina would take it to heart that you're feeling the need to bulk up on survival skills."

Avery smiled. "Listen to you talk like a badass."

"You went through hell last year. I think you're incredibly smart to empower yourself. It's what changes a survivor into a warrior."

"I like that."

"I'd love to take credit for it, but I'm sure I read that somewhere."

Avery leaned her head against Shannon's shoulder.

"What about your mom?"

She squeezed her eyes closed. "Is there a class for dealing with self-absorbed mothers?"

Shannon's shoulder shook as she laughed. "Sign me up if there is."

Fifteen minutes later, after delivering the CliffsNotes version of her Adeline high tea, Avery fell into bed and closed her eyes. It felt good to have the validation of one of her friends. There wasn't a thing wrong with the direction she was taking in her life.

She was a warrior.

Which was a hell of a lot better than being a victim.

Chapter Four

He was a contractor, not a freaking handyman. So why was he nailing racks to walls in a gym like an apprentice?

Oh, yeah . . . that's right. He'd started going down this fork in the road once he realized that the blonde named Avery didn't take the group class. He'd told Brenda, the owner of the studio, that he had to work for her after his normal working hours to give her the deal she needed. And when the group class turned up empty of his target, he might have seen the schedule on Brenda's desk when it "accidentally" fell open on the floor. After flipping a few pages, he saw Avery's name and insisted that Tuesday or Friday was the only time he had to finish his contracted job.

A voice in his head suggested that his motivation was a tinge too close to a stalker's.

He was good with that.

The door from the locker room to the studio slammed.

"You need to get this door fixed, Brenda!"

Liam didn't turn around.

It was her. He could tell by the way the hair stood up on his arms.

"Your warm-up is on the board," Brenda yelled from her open office.

"I hate burpees."

Liam felt his lips split into a smile while he lifted his level to the rack he'd just attached to the wall.

"I haven't seen you in a week. You're weak and pathetic," Brenda sneered.

Avery's displeasure was voiced under her breath. It was then that Liam glanced over his shoulder.

Oh, damn.

He was in trouble.

She was taller than he remembered. Or maybe it was the spandex she wore that seemed to add inches to her frame. Her hair was pulled back in a ponytail. No makeup. Curves.

Rail-thin women did nothing for him.

She noticed him for the first time.

Her eyes narrowed. "Hello."

"Hey." Yeah, he was playing it cool, like a damn teenager. *Hey? Who said hey?*

"Do I know you?" she asked.

Liam started to shake his head.

"Ignore him. He's working. Fifty burpees. One-legged. Twenty-five each side." Brenda took a breath. "Stretch first."

"Brutal," Liam said quietly.

Avery rolled her eyes before lifting her hands over her head.

Liam swallowed.

Hard.

Spandex. He loved spandex.

She caught him staring and waited for him to stop.

"Sorry." *So not sorry.* He turned around.

"One," Avery called out. "Two, three."

Liam made the mistake of looking over his shoulder on *ten.*

One leg up, her shoulders peeked out from under her skintight shirt, making his mouth go dry.

Since when did a woman's shoulders make his dick stir?

He closed his eyes, shook his head, and turned around before she could catch him staring a second time. *Get it together, man.*

On forty-seven, Brenda walked out of her office, past him, and stood over Avery.

"You're not sweating," she said once Avery announced she was done.

"I am."

There was a pause.

"Ten more!"

Avery grumbled. "I hate you."

"As long as your check clears, I don't care."

Liam laughed. He couldn't help himself.

"Are those shelves done?" Brenda asked.

"Almost."

Brenda turned and focused on Avery as she did her last ten burpees.

"Damn, that hurt," she said as she collapsed on the mat after the last one.

"That's because you missed Friday."

"I had to leave town."

"Yes, I know. But take your workout with you and it won't hurt as much when you return."

Liam finished screwing in one of the brackets and moved on to the next, all the while eavesdropping on the conversation as much as he could.

"Today we're starting with punches."

Out of the corner of his eye, he saw Avery twisting on a pair of boxing gloves while Brenda placed pads on her hands to catch Avery's swings.

For five minutes Brenda yelled out a series of numbers: One, two. One, two, one. One, two, three, four, one, two. Jabs, cross hits, uppercuts. He had no idea krav had so much boxing involved.

Avery was sweating; her rapid breathing accompanied the grunts that would occasionally follow her efforts.

Brenda broke them off. "Get a drink. The next round is on your back."

Liam had never worked so slowly in his life. Once Avery caught her breath, she lay down on the mat, and Brenda straddled her. He was pretty sure he'd seen something like this before. Only the women were wearing bikinis and were covered in mud.

"Left, right, until I call it."

Avery started punching. Each slap of her boxing gloves to the mitts the instructor wore cracked the room with noise.

Brenda called time and instantly told Avery to force her off the domineering, if not slightly erotic, position she held over her.

For a brief second Avery sighed and acted as if she were going to just lie there, then, in a blur, Brenda was knocked off to the side, and Avery was two feet away and on the balls of her feet with her hands in front of her face.

"Holy shit."

Brenda shook off her mitts and wiped her forehead with the back of her hand. "Don't be impressed."

For an instructor, Brenda didn't seem to have a lot of motivational skills.

"I'm impressed." Liam met Avery's eyes.

"She refuses to spar with others."

"I was with Leslie last week."

"You have ten pounds on her. And she kicked your ass."

Avery didn't argue.

"You need more of a challenge. There is only so much I can teach you one-on-one. One of these days a man his size is going to challenge you, and you won't have the skills to get away." She pointed to Liam.

He placed his hands in the air. "Don't look at me. I don't attack women unless they ask for it." He was pretty sure he smirked.

Avery rolled her eyes. "I could get him off of me."

He laughed and sized her up. "I'm twice your size."

Brenda glared. "Size means nothing."

"Do you study krav?" Avery asked him.

"No."

Avery turned to Brenda. "Then I could get away."

"You *think* you can get away, but you've never tried. How do I know if anything I'm teaching you is useful if you don't exercise it?"

"You'd be surprised at what I exercise."

Brenda narrowed her eyes. "I know about the drunk at the bar."

"What?"

"Leslie told me. In group. Right after she fought off two—not one, but two—of my best male students. So you can put a drunk into his drink. Good. I'm glad I taught you that much."

Liam watched the women arguing in silence until that moment. "If you can't teach her any more, then why do you keep taking her money?"

Both women turned to him as if they'd forgotten he was in the room.

"So I can pay you to stand around."

"If I can get him off of me, will you let this go until I'm ready?" Avery pointed toward him.

He was pretty sure she'd just suggested that he straddle her while she tried to squirm away. This idea he could get into.

Brenda cocked her head to the side and shook it. "Too much liability."

"I won't hurt her."

Brenda looked at him like he was an idiot. "Not her. You!"

Liam laughed.

That had both women glaring.

Without words, Brenda stormed into her office and returned with a piece of paper. She shoved it in front of his face and handed him a pen. "Sign this."

"What is it?"

"Waiver. You get hurt? You don't sue."

He was cocky enough to think the blonde in spandex wasn't big enough, fast enough, or strong enough to get him off of her. He was cautious enough to know he could lose a nut in the process.

He signed the paper. "I might wanna have kids one day."

Brenda walked across the room and produced a jockstrap.

He held no shame in strapping on the ball barrier on the outside of his clothes, which was what this one was designed for.

The whole time Avery watched with her hands on her hips, determination in her eyes.

When he was ready, Brenda pulled him onto the mat. "You." She pointed at Avery. "On your back."

Liam had to admit, this was a first.

Avery lay down.

A hard-on in a jockstrap is probably not the best idea, Liam.

Talking to himself was a thing. And this time the voice told him he was an idiot.

Brenda knelt on the ground. "You remove him three times and I won't harp on you for six months. No punches to the face. He doesn't have padding."

When she stood, she patted Liam's chest. "Straddle her. Don't let her up."

Yup, definitely a first.

Liam puffed his chest out and smiled. Only that cockiness subsided as he knelt beside her. A combination of annoyance and vulnerability lurked in her eyes. And while Liam had no problem attracting women, he never purposely hurt them. "You okay with this?"

She motioned with her hand to climb on up.

The moment he straddled her hips, his dick waved. She was hot, sweaty, and flushed from her workout, or maybe that was the anger. One pass by in the bar a week ago and he'd already thought about this moment.

Well, maybe not this exact moment, but one with her under him with the aforementioned thoughts swimming in his head.

He clenched his jaw and waited for some signal to hold her down.

There wasn't one. He counted to maybe three, and Avery was on the move.

Liam attempted to squeeze her with his thighs and instead found her knee in his chest, his balance thrown off, and she was two feet away on the balls of her feet, and he was on his back.

"How the hell . . . ?"

"I said hold her down."

It was Avery's turn to smirk while looking at her fingernails.

"Okay, Princess. I see how this works." Liam jumped to his feet and motioned to the floor.

Brenda stood back.

He admired the swagger in Avery's hips as she moved to the same position on the mat.

This time when he positioned himself on top of her, he immediately grabbed her hands and pinned them to the ground.

She went limp as if giving up, and then, like a cat who was done being petted, she bucked with strength he didn't see coming. He braced himself with one hand to keep from falling off of her, and she used it to her advantage. She wrapped her leg around his, and then she was on her side, his arm in a hold that threatened to bend it backward.

He'd like to say he didn't cuss in that moment, but he'd be lying.

She let go and jumped to the balls of her feet.

"You know, the last time I was beaten up by a girl, it was my sister, and titty twisters were involved."

Avery laughed and Brenda scowled.

"That is your problem. Avery isn't your sister. She isn't someone you protect and let win. She is having a seizure, and if you let go, she will fall off a cliff into the Grand Canyon. Hold. Her. Down."

Brenda slammed her hand on the mat beside him.

Liam pulled himself together as he stood. He had half a foot on Avery. He easily had fifty pounds over her.

But damn, she was fast and cunning. He was pretty sure the pain on the left side of his body was a bruised rib from her knee providing the space she needed to escape.

Seizure.

He could do this.

She took her position and he took his.

He pinned her hands and she bucked. Only he was ready for that this time. He flattened his body against hers. Would have enjoyed it if she wasn't trying to head butt him. He dodged what would have been a headache for both of them.

She attempted to use her leg to wrap his. He pushed away until he could capture it under his. His distraction gave her the opportunity to get out from under one of his hands. She attempted to leverage herself and twist him off.

He held her tight.

When he had her pinned again, Brenda hit the mat.

She moved two inches from Avery's face. "You cannot beat strength with strength. There will always be bigger opponents than you out there."

Liam lifted his hands from Avery's arms.

She was breathing hard, her jaw set in a firm line. Vulnerability overtook the anger in her eyes.

Liam stood and backed up when Avery squirmed away.

"Whatever!" Avery released the tie that held her hair back and shook her head. She stormed out of the gym and into the locker room. Liam found his feet following.

"Leave her alone."

Yeah, Liam wasn't one to follow orders.

Chapter Five

With both hands on the lockers and her head hanging between her shoulders, Avery attempted to push back her anger.

She had him.

Twice.

She shoved her fist into the locker, accepted the pain that came with it.

"Hey."

It was him, the man who proved Brenda right. "Girls' locker room. Or can't you read?"

He didn't respond and didn't leave. She could feel his eyes staring at the back of her head.

"No one likes a sore loser."

Avery twisted on her heel. "I took you."

He hunched his shoulders. "Surprise is something you can only use once."

"Twice."

He chuckled.

The anger inside of her started to ebb, and she voiced what she'd been thinking since she saw him watching her warm up. "Were you at the bar the other night?"

Was that a smile? "What bar?"

"One block up?"

"Pug's Pub?"

"Yeah."

"I've been there. You don't seem the type to go to Pug's."

She closed her eyes and turned her back to him. "And what type is that?" She twisted the combination on her lock and pulled her bag from the locker.

When he didn't immediately answer, she looked at him.

"Let's see . . . the women at Pug's haven't had a manicure in a long time, therefore the color of their nail polish would be red. Yours is beige. Highlights in your hair . . ." He glanced at her bag. "Is that Gucci?"

"I don't know a lot of heterosexual men who know Gucci from Walmart."

He winced. "That would hurt, except I have a Gucci-style sister and I'm as hetero as they come."

She turned toward the locker, removed her Prada handbag, and stuffed it into her Gucci duffel. Heat boiled in her veins.

"I came in here to see if you were okay."

She lifted a hand in the air without turning around. "I'm fine."

"Oh, hell . . . Did I do that?" He took a step closer and touched her arm.

Avery twisted like a cornered cat and nearly struck out.

Mr. Handyman stepped back and stared at her arm.

Tiny purple bruises emerged where he'd pinned her hands to the mat.

"I'm fine." She pulled her hands away. "Part of the deal with these classes."

He shook his head. "Years of my mother telling me not to hurt girls makes this everything *but* okay. I was here to put up shelving, not manhandle the students."

She took one step toward him and looked up. He did have half a head on her. "Well, be sure and tell your mother that you're keeping your promises."

"I'm obviously not."

She considered him for a brief moment, his size, the actual concern in his eyes. "Did you let me win?"

He pointed a thumb behind him at the closed door. "Back there?"

"Yeah. Did you hear your mother's voice and let go?"

He shook his head. "Much as I hate to admit it . . . no."

At least she had that.

"But Brenda's right. I wasn't trying to hurt you. And my guess is, the only kind of man you'd have to use those moves on isn't trying to be your friend."

"Yeah, I get that."

"So what's the issue? Why not practice with men twice your size more often?"

She closed her eyes, thought of the recurring dreams she'd had ever since her face had met the bottom of someone's boot. "I have my reasons." She reached for her bag, hiked it up on her shoulder, and closed the locker behind her.

"Then why did you let me join in?"

"Because you don't look like—" Avery stopped short and quickly diverted her eyes. *Him.*

"Oh . . ."

"It isn't what you think."

"I call bullshit."

Avery shook her head. "Usually I know the people insulting me or calling me a liar."

"I haven't insulted you. But you are lying and you know it. Which is why the defensive hair is probably spiked on the back of your neck."

"So you're a therapist and a handyman?"

"My sister is a crisis counselor. I guess some things wear off at our family dinners."

Avery wondered what it felt like to have a weekly dinner with someone she admired enough to pick up some of their habits. "Well, you'll forgive me for not paying for your little session here." On some level Avery knew she was channeling her inner bitch and taking it out on this hulk of a stranger. The corner she felt herself being pushed into was as uncomfortable as wool in summer.

She took a step toward the door, and he stood in front of her.

Her feet froze.

"My name is Liam. Let me buy you a drink."

She blinked several times. "Are you trying to pick me up?"

"An hour ago I would have said yes."

Her brain couldn't process what he meant. "But not now?"

"The protective part of me wants to erase that look in your eyes."

"The angry, pissed off look?"

He smiled. "Sure, that, too."

"Well, Liam. Thank you, but no thank you." She brushed past him and stepped out the door.

Halfway across the gym floor, Brenda called out from her office, "See you Friday."

Avery knew she'd be back.

⁓

Sometimes addictions took time to become the compelling habits that often debilitated a person. Then there were times those addictions happened overnight.

Liam was pretty sure he was on the latter half of that thought.

That's why he was standing in a group krav maga class with a bunch of strangers on a Wednesday night. Brenda made it clear that he could train in her studio for free as long as he gave one day a week to Avery. Actually the conversation hadn't quite happened that way.

As he was leaving the studio after Avery stormed out, he approached Brenda about returning to spar with her problem student. Brenda allowed it on the condition that he take classes with her group.

The class started with a warm-up that reminded Liam that he didn't spend time in a gym. He never needed to in his profession. Yet as his crew had grown to twenty or so men doing most of the heavy lifting, Liam had softened up in the past couple of years.

Brenda paired him off with Craig, one of her trainers.

"Have you ever boxed?"

Liam shook his head.

"Weight lifting?"

"Do two-by-fours count?"

Craig had Liam's height but not his broad shoulders or natural girth. That wasn't to say the man was thin—he wasn't.

Liam looked around the gym at the other men. Lots of them were on the thin side, but most of them seemed to punch like demons were talking in their ears.

"Sports?"

"High school, but that was a long time ago."

Craig nodded. "Okay, let's start with some basics."

An hour and a half later Liam pulled into the driveway of his single story bungalow and put the truck in park. He looked at the backs of his hands.

Purple.

He thought of the bruises on Avery's wrists and how they didn't fit her perfectly manicured fingernails.

Liam jingled the keys to the front door and was greeted by Whiskey barking from the other side. He opened the door and braced himself.

His lab was sixty pounds of energy that should be reserved for puppies, but at seven years old, it was obvious she wasn't going to settle down because of age.

He knelt down and let the dog crawl all over him, her tongue lapping his cheek.

"Did you miss me?"

"Your dog is crazy." Michelle peeked around the corner from the kitchen, dish towel in hand.

"Uncle Liam."

Liam knelt and caught his niece as she ran into his arms. He swung Cassandra up in the air to a chorus of giggles.

"You spoil her."

He settled the spirited five-year-old on his hip and pinched her nose. "That's my job."

Whiskey barked at his feet, tail wagging, tongue hanging out. He stepped past the dog and into the kitchen. It smelled like his childhood home. "Pot roast?" he asked as his stomach approved with a growl.

"Mom's recipe."

He kissed his sister's cheek. "You're too good to me."

"We live here rent free. It's the least I can do."

He'd heard that before. "Well, I appreciate it."

Cassandra placed her hand on his cheek and pulled his attention away from her mother. "Uncle Liam, do you wanna see what I made in school today?"

She'd started kindergarten in the fall, and every day it was the same. From pictures colored with crayons, to watercolors, to plants growing in egg cartons that sat in the kitchen window, to decoupage plates with his pixie nosed niece smiling at the picture placed in the middle.

"Wash your hands."

"Yes, Mom," he teased his sister.

"I was talking to Cassie, but you should, too."

He set Cassandra down and took her tiny hand in his. "You heard your mother."

"Washy, washy . . . happy, happy."

Liam laughed. "Where did she get that?"

Michelle shrugged. "Someone at school says it."

"Mrs. Steel says germs are the enemy, and soap and water are the weapons."

They walked into the bathroom, and Cassandra marched up on the two-step stool that put her at the right height to wash her hands on her own.

"I like Mrs. Steel."

"She's married. So you can't like her too much."

He laughed. "Good to know."

Liam helped her with the soap dispenser and lathered his hands along with hers.

"Uncle Liam?"

"Yes, Pipsqueak?"

"When are you getting married?"

Not anytime soon.

"I don't have a girlfriend, so I can't get married."

Cassandra considered him through their images in the bathroom mirror.

"Why don't you have a girlfriend?"

Liam considered changing his nickname for her to Twenty Questions. Or Twenty-Q. "I'm a little too busy for that."

"Mommy says you're working extra hours and that makes dating hard."

"Your mom is right."

"What about when Mommy and I move out? Will you get a girl-friend then?"

He turned off the water and grabbed a towel. "I don't know." It would certainly be easier to get naked with a woman.

"Who will cook for you if you don't get a girlfriend?"

Liam lifted her off the stool and placed her little butt on the counter. "You know, I did cook for myself before you and your mom moved in."

"Mommy says frozen dinners don't count."

He lowered his voice. "One of these days you're going to go to college, and you'll realize they do count."

"You guys coming or what?" Michelle yelled from the kitchen.

Liam made a face at his niece. "I think we're late."

Easily amused, Cassandra giggled, and Liam lifted her up and tossed her over his shoulder. She held on to his back, her head closer to the ground than her feet were, and laughed all the way to dinner.

Thirty minutes later, Liam was on his second beer, and the pot roast was a pleasant memory. Cassandra left to go play in the room she shared with her mom.

"Are you still okay to watch Cassie tomorrow night?"

"My social schedule hasn't changed."

"Would you tell me if it did?"

"Family first. Always. We've been over this."

Looking into his sister's eyes was a lot like looking into his own.

"You seem more restless than normal."

"Busy, not restless."

"Did you pick up another job?"

He sipped his beer and set it down. "Why do you ask?"

"You've been coming home late."

He picked up his plate and hers and took them to the sink. "I worked late before you moved in." She'd been there for a year. Slippery Scott, her slimy ex-husband, had left her and Cassandra a month before they moved in. Michelle had started taking classes after Cassandra started preschool so she could earn her degree. Scott couldn't handle being a dad longer than a few hours at a time, so when Michelle needed to pull a few nights working the crisis hotline as a class requirement, Scott couldn't deal.

According to Michelle, he picked a fight one night, packed a bag, and left. Come to find out he hadn't paid their rent on the apartment for two months. If Scott had stayed in town, Liam would have happily pounded some sense into his brother-in-law. But the coward moved to Atlanta, denying him the chance.

Liam was there to pick up the pieces.

"You're working extra for me."

"I'm the boss. I'm working late because that's what being the boss means."

She brought the other dishes from the table to the sink while he filled it with hot water. "Sit down. You cooked."

"I can help."

"Chelle!"

"Okay, okay." She sat down and took a drink of his beer.

"So what's Cassandra's obsession with me having a girlfriend?"

"I think it has to do with her new friends at school. She started talking about a baby brother or a sister, and somehow she's concluded that I can't give her that since Scott is gone."

"But I can? That's a stretch."

"She's five. What can I say?" Michelle sighed. "He sent a check."

Liam looked over his shoulder. "Who?"

"Scott."

He almost dropped the dish he was rinsing off in the sink. "You're kidding."

"Four hundred dollars."

Considering the man had ignored his child support bill ordered by the divorce court for the past five months, the amount was laughable. "Big spender." Liam went back to the dishes.

"He says he finally got a job."

"Did you talk to him?"

"No. There was a check in the mail with a note. He said he would send more." Michelle sounded hopeful.

"I wouldn't count on it."

"I won't."

He dried his hands on a dish towel and turned to his sister. "You don't need him."

She sighed and offered a weak smile. "I know. But she does."

"Cassandra has me."

"It's not the same."

"I know. It's better. She can depend on me. Forever and always."

Michelle walked over and wrapped her arms around him.

Liam kissed the top of her head.

"Love you."

"Love you, too."

Chapter Six

Thankfully, Brenda didn't harp when Avery showed up for her lesson. The woman was painfully quiet, and thirty minutes in, Avery figured out why.

The door to the studio opened and he walked in.

Big shoulders. Thick biceps. *Liam.*

"What are you doing here?"

"Right on time," Brenda announced.

Avery shifted her gaze between the two of them. "What is this? An intervention?"

Brenda shook off her boxing gloves. "He agreed to spar with you."

That was comical. "I don't remember agreeing to spar with him."

"You did last week, and I don't look like your demons." He dropped a bag on the floor and walked farther into the room.

When he was damn near nose to nose with her, she looked up and held her ground. He didn't look anything like her demons. The fact that he knew she had them was a little unsettling.

Avery weighed her options.

Stay and spar with Handyman Hulk, who didn't know krav from a bar fight, or find another instructor.

Brenda didn't have a warm and fuzzy bone in her body. It was one of the reasons Avery liked working with her. She didn't ask questions, didn't offer a shoulder to sob on. She slapped Avery into place and pushed her out of her comfort zone.

That zone was just pushed a little further.

"Fine."

Liam's whole face changed when he smiled. Even now, with a smirk that resembled a cocky teen's, he looked completely different.

"All right. Let's get started."

Most of their lessons before Liam showed up had consisted of practicing the moves Brenda taught Avery in the past and building on them. In the past few months there were times Brenda would attack Avery without any predetermined moves. She didn't tell her she was going to attempt to choke her or grab her from behind. She just did it and Avery needed to respond.

They rewound the tape, and now Avery was back at the beginning.

Brenda would do the move first, have Avery respond, and then have Liam be the aggressor. This time, he wore more than a jock. He barely fit in the padding needed to protect his head. The first time he wrapped his arms around her as if he were snagging her off a street corner, she barely felt his strength before she dropped her weight, pulled him off balance, and started elbowing his face from behind her.

He let go.

Once Brenda explained the moves Avery was doing, Liam attempted to adjust his attack to challenge her from escaping. Anytime she struck just shy of his junk, he hesitated. In reality, she knew he would do more than pause if someone boxed his goods. After a while, he learned to keep his hips far enough away, or too close, to avoid being a target.

There were times Avery got away . . . and there were times Brenda stopped their sparring when it was obvious that Avery wasn't going to win.

As much as Avery hated to admit it, when they were done she felt stronger, even in light of the weakness she demonstrated in Liam's shadow. The fact was she did manage to get away from him several times. Like when she'd taken the guy down at the bar, she felt empowered.

When they were done and Avery was wiping the sweat from her shoulders with a towel, Brenda approached her. "Liam agreed to come every Friday."

Avery glanced at Mr. Hulk. He sat on a bench, water in hand. "Works for me," he told her.

Avery nodded.

"Good. This was good. You're better for it, Avery." Brenda turned away. Avery knew surprise was written on her face.

"That was almost a compliment."

"I take it those don't come often from that one."

Avery grinned. "Never." She had questions. Lots of them. "About that drink we didn't have last week."

That little-boy smirk on that big-boy face peeked out. "I don't know . . . I have a lot to do."

Was he turning her down? "Suit yourself."

He stopped her halfway to the showers.

"Meet you outside in fifteen."

She didn't turn around. Smiling, she waved a hand in the air, felt the heat of his eyes on her ass, and disappeared into the locker room.

Pug's was busy, it being Friday night and all. They found a small table tucked in the back, away from the majority of people.

Liam grabbed a couple of bottles of beer and sat across from her.

He'd barely sat his ass in the chair and she was asking the questions that had been swimming in her head for hours. "Why? Why are you doing this?"

He struggled with his answer for half a second. "I'm attracted."

Avery should have been prepared for his answer.

She wasn't.

"That's the short answer."

She took a drink from her beer. "And the long answer?"

"I need a challenge, a change in pace. Something tells me pursuing my attraction isn't going to be easy. Not from a woman who has no problem kicking my ass . . . repeatedly."

She forced her lips from smiling but knew her eyes lit up. "All this for a date."

"That's why it started." He leaned on his elbows and stared. "Now I'm genuinely fascinated. Who is this beautiful, guarded woman, and what drove her to master a class in kicking someone's butt?"

He blinked a few times as he spoke, and a voice told Avery that he was well practiced in throwing women off his scent of seduction. "Do women fall for that? The 'fascinated' line followed by a compliment and a smile?"

He lifted his eyebrows, leaned back. "Yup. All the time."

Avery laughed and grabbed her drink. "I think I might have written a book on lines that get me what I want from a man. So you're going to have to do better than that."

He lifted his beer in the air in a silent salute. "I'll work on it."

⌒⊙

"I don't want any of it."

Avery took in the dark hall of family portraits professionally painted on canvas. "Not even the artwork?"

Sheldon Lankford considered the paintings and shook his head. "My parents waited until they were fifty to adopt me. I never met any of these people. I was raised by a series of nannies and knew my parents through weekends and the occasional summer vacation." Sheldon kept looking up at the vast walls that filled the room, which hosted thirty-foot ceilings. "Did you ever go to boarding school?"

Avery sighed. "Yes."

Sheldon focused on her as if surprised. "Then you know."

At thirty-five, Sheldon inherited his parents' wealth with the passing of his mother.

His father had died eight years prior from a sudden heart attack. His mother had lived out her years in a mausoleum of a home with a full-time nurse and a truckload of medication. From what Avery knew, Sheldon made sure his adoptive mother was being cared for and that no one was squandering the accumulated wealth of the Lankford family fortune.

And it was quite a sum.

Sheldon had learned of her services through her ex-husband. When Bernie heard that she was working, he offered to cut her another check. As tempting as that sounded, Avery liked that she was providing a service and being paid for it. Since most of her clients were in the upper ends of the tax bracket, her payday matched her spending habits . . . or it was getting there.

"Family photographs?"

Sheldon shook his head. "I've already taken what I want."

"Okay, then. A house this size will take some time to go through. I have a questionnaire."

Sheldon frowned. "Homework?"

She smiled. "People collect crazy stuff in their lives. I need to know what your parents held value in. Did your mother collect art? Did your dad have a habit of buying antique flasks or pens? I'll bring in the experts needed to place the pricey items in the correct auctions. You're paying me a percentage to take the burden off of you. A few questions and I'll make sure the overlooked frame old Grandma Beth is in isn't discarded. Once I've farmed the stuff of known value, I'll hold the estate sale."

Sheldon nodded. "What about the house itself?"

"You're selling?"

"Could you live here?"

Dark, dingy . . . full of spiders—she cringed at the thought it was the exact opposite of how she lived. "Do you want to sell as is or get top dollar?"

"Are you suggesting remodeling?"

"I don't think dark paneling and dated kitchens sell homes. But the location would bring in investors and people who can't afford to come into the neighborhood at a high dollar. That said, it is Brentwood. You'll make millions walking away, regardless."

Sheldon took a breath and Avery cut him off. "But since you're hiring me to go through the interior, I would urge you to get as much as you can from the home itself."

"I don't want to deal with any of it," he confessed.

"Then we sell."

"I'm also allergic to work."

Avery grinned. "Let me come up with a couple of contractors and bids for the basics. Do you have a Realtor in mind?"

Sheldon shook his head.

"I'll find a couple . . . get an idea of what we're talking about. Money invested, time . . . and bottom line, money in your pocket."

"What do you charge for that?"

"I can't say I've done it before. So nothing. I have to be here to sift through a lot of stuff, so inviting a real estate agent or two over to give their opinions on things isn't going to take any more time from me. You'll have to pick who you like and what you ultimately want to do."

"You're obviously not allergic to work."

"I used to be. Then I bored of spending money . . . or more importantly, I realized that I needed to work in order to shop the way I wanted to. Growing up in a world of boarding schools and pretentious parents made this job perfect for me."

Sheldon turned on his leather loafers and tugged on the silk sleeves of his two-hundred-dollar shirt and looked her up and down as if for the first time.

For a brief moment, Avery felt a chill.

"How long is this going to take?"

"You want it done right or fast?"

"Right."

"It's an eight-thousand-square-foot house with fifty years of living." She set out a timeline they could both work with, taking into consideration the smaller estate she was working with in Seattle that she was wrapping up. At least Brentwood was closer to home.

By the time Avery left the Lankford estate, she had the keys and a signed agreement for her services. Services that apparently now included obtaining a Realtor and a contractor. It was time to start hitting the networking circuit and finding contacts.

Chapter Seven

"I used to hate these things," Shannon told Avery as they walked into the mixer wearing professional, *I'm more than just arm candy* attire.

Of course the designer shoes, clothes, and attitude completed their professional yet high-class facade.

They approached the reception desk and gave their names. The intern wrote each name on a standard sticky label and handed it to them.

Avery looked at the tape disguised as a name tag. "This is Chanel."

Shannon laughed. From her purse, she produced a magnetic name tag that she attached to her dress jacket without tape or a pin.

"That's cheating."

"Good thing I had one made for you, too."

Avery wadded up her paper name tag and tossed it in a nearby trash can before placing the nondestructive tag on her blouse.

"So how do we do this?"

"It's a mixer. We mix."

"Looks like everyone is just standing around drinking."

Shannon led them to the bar and asked for two glasses of chardonnay. "One glass, and make it last all night."

Avery dropped the glass from her lips. "So it's a prop."

"Yup. If you're not holding it, some will think you're a recovering alcoholic, if you're overindulging, you're going to be labeled as one."

"Critical group." Avery pointed to an elderly woman dressed to the nines and well into her wine. "What about her?"

"That's Mandy Wilson. She doesn't count. She's not here to drum up business."

"Then why is she here?"

"Probably to find a future ex-husband. C'mon, let me introduce you."

Mandy Wilson looked to be in her late sixties. Yeah, it was apparent she'd had the usual cosmetic surgeries wealthy women did in order to hold back Father Time, but that was something Avery was used to looking past.

"Well, look who is here."

Shannon smiled at Mandy as she leaned in for a kiss on the cheek. "Mandy, I want you to meet a friend of mine."

She made the introductions, and Avery accepted the thorough once-over from the older woman.

"What brings you two uptown women here? Looking for a husband?"

Avery shook her head and Shannon laughed. "We'll leave that to you. Any prospects out there tonight?"

Mandy scowled. "Sadly, the place is shy on men. Too many liberated women joining the workforce."

"Some of us like to make our own money," Shannon teased.

"Don't start that with me. Your divorce was public record. Unless of course you've blown through it all already . . . have you?"

"What a juicy bit of gossip that would be. I like being busy."

"The right man keeps you busy at night and has enough money to afford all the pampering and fluff a woman needs during the day." Obviously this was Mandy's philosophy.

"So what brings you here?" Mandy addressed Avery.

"Not a husband. I'm with Shannon on that." She glanced around the room. "Realtors, contractors. I'm in estate sales."

"Selling dead people's stuff."

Avery had said that to herself on more than one occasion. "That would be it. Rich dead people."

This particular networking mixer was put on by an exclusive company that offered discounts for things like private air travel, high-end cars, memberships to exclusive golf courses . . . all for an annual fee, of course. Not just anyone could get in, and therefore people in entry-level vocations weren't there.

"I can't say I know of any contractors here, not for residential real estate, at least. Bowman." Mandy pointed to a short, balding man talking to a small group of men. "He's the mayor of . . . oh, what was the name of that town? It doesn't matter. Mayor and a broker. He might be able to help you. Although he's a bit pompous even for me. I'd suggest you find out if anyone has recently purchased or sold."

"Thank you."

Mandy smiled and turned to Shannon. "And you? You're still taking pictures?"

"That I am."

"Mavis Ellendale said something about her daughter expecting a proposal. First marriage."

Shannon tilted her head. "You're a gem, Mandy."

"Yes, I know. Be sure and tell me if you find any ill eighty-year-olds. Rich, of course. But that goes without saying."

Mandy turned away, and Shannon and Avery moved deeper into the room.

"She's a riot."

"Two divorces and one funeral," Shannon said.

"You'd think she'd be set."

"Oh, she's set. She just likes the chase. Her profession is finding a rich man who isn't put off by the fact that she's searching him out. At seventy-five, you'd think she'd take a break."

Avery did a double take over her shoulder. "Wow, I want to know who her plastic surgeon is."

"Thirty years from now when you need him, he'll be gone."

Two hours later, long after Avery had poured out her glass of wine because it became too warm to drink, she'd determined that Bowman was a pompous ass and the small town where he held a position as mayor was nowhere near the league of Brentwood real estate. She did pick up one lead from a financial adviser that sounded promising.

Shannon had planted the seed of her professional photography business to Mrs. Ellendale and her friend. Both of them had daughters in their midtwenties who were in serious relationships.

They worked their way to a sky view restaurant in the heart of LA, where they ordered a proper bottle of wine, intending to drink it.

"How many of those things are out there?" Avery asked once they ordered and were sipping wine.

"More than you can imagine. Paul dragged me to most of the political ones. The problem with those was there weren't very many spouses that had any form of a job outside of being a wife."

"None of them had kids?"

"They had kids, they just didn't raise them. There were very few new mothers that showed a picture of their children, and the older moms spoke only of which school their children were attending or what college they'd been accepted to. It's a cold group. Not all of them, but most. I plan on raising my children."

Avery paused. "You want to have more than one?"

"You're an only child. How did that work out?"

Shannon had a point.

"You have a younger sister, right?"

"Angie."

"You never talk about her."

"I never see her. She joined the Peace Corps after two years at Stanford. My parents were furious."

"She didn't finish school?"

"She did, only while she was in Spain. My parents cut off her funding, but that didn't stop her from going after what she wanted. It takes a lot of guts to go from how we grew up to living in places that most people avoid. Last I heard she was educating women and tutoring English somewhere in some remote town in Brazil."

Avery leaned back. "And our rebellion was divorce from what our parents assumed was a perfect life."

"That's because our parents were the kind that married for status and stayed that way, happy or not. I think in my head I thought they'd let loose once Paul and I split."

Avery understood that. "My mother is worse. It's all about what I'm doing to find a replacement or how I can get Bernie back."

"I never understood why money makes so many people assholes."

Avery buttered a piece of bread and savored it. "And unhappy. I wonder if it's true what they say about people without anything being the happiest."

Shannon shrugged. "I'm not willing to flush my money away to find out."

"Me either."

∽

"You're late," Liam announced when Avery showed up ten minutes past the hour. Wearing a pencil skirt and high heels, she tapped across the gym floor and straight to the locker room.

"Yeah, sorry. Give me five minutes."

He admired her hips as she ran by and sighed in relief. For ten minutes he'd wondered if she'd show up at all.

Their after session drink the previous week had ended with a smile and a *see you next week*. But he hadn't managed to get her phone number or get her to see him outside of the studio.

Truth was, he didn't ask for either.

She wasn't ready to give them to him.

Avery was wrapping her hair into a ponytail when she emerged from the locker room. She glanced at the warm-up on the whiteboard and sat down on the mat and proceeded to tie her shoes.

"I thought I'd scared you away."

She grinned. "Last minute meeting that went late." She folded over her legs in a stretch.

"What do you do for a living?"

She opened her mouth only to be cut off.

"Less talking, more working." Brenda emerged from her office and pointed at Liam. "You . . . I'm sure you can squeeze out another twenty push-ups with those guns."

"Yes, ma'am."

After ten he glanced up and noticed Avery dart her gaze away.

At least she wasn't completely oblivious to him.

There were a lot of basics Liam had yet to learn in the krav world. So far, he'd been asked to hold Avery down, grab her from behind, and attempt to choke her. All with direction. Each time he filled the place of Brenda, he celebrated the fact that he could get close to Avery. That party didn't last long. She worked hard to get away, and most of the time she did. Today's session, Brenda wanted him to be more aggressive.

"Hitting women goes against every cell in my body."

Brenda's deadpan stare told him to get over it.

"You won't actually hit me. Just come at me."

"Slowly at first. We'll pick up the pace once you get the feel for it."

Yeah, right. His mother would kill him.

Still, Liam did as asked and oftentimes found he was the one at a loss for moves.

Avery would wrap his arm and come up short with what would be a punch to his face or an elbow to the back of his neck.

On her third shot of wrapping his arm, he managed to get away by bear-hugging her waist.

She lifted her knee and stopped short of his groin. He bucked out of the way, and she squirmed again, her elbow tapping his neck. With his arms still holding her, he lifted her off her feet.

"Ahhh!" She started to laugh.

Liam set her down.

"No way you'd be able to do that after I smashed your balls."

Brenda stood with her arms folded over her chest. "Probably not. But someone high on drugs . . . maybe. We'll start next week where we left off and work on counters."

Avery looked at the time.

"We're done?"

Brenda didn't blink. "I have plans."

Silent, Avery peered closer. "You're wearing mascara. Oh my God, you have a date."

Liam hadn't noticed any makeup.

Brenda didn't smile or nod or anything . . . but she did blush.

Avery's jaw dropped. "Give it up, sista. Who is it?"

Brenda turned toward her office. "See you on Tuesday."

Avery glanced at Liam, a sneaky smile on her face. "C'mon, Brenda. I won't tell anyone."

"You don't know him." Brenda slammed her office door.

Avery turned to Liam. "Him?" she said in a rough whisper.

Yeah, Liam wasn't all that sure of Brenda's sexual orientation either.

"I'm going to want details on Tuesday!" Avery yelled out.

Brenda met her comment with silence.

"You're never going to get details out of that one."

Avery looked at him like he was an idiot. "Don't underestimate me."

They parted at the locker rooms.

"Meet you outside in ten?" was all he asked. Hoping to make a habit out of an after session drink.

She narrowed her eyes. "Okay, but it isn't a date."

"Of course not." *Yes it is . . . kinda.*

She walked out of the gym wearing the clothes she'd run in with.

Liam looked at what he was wearing. Jeans and a pullover shirt.

"I think Pug's is a bad idea in this," she said, indicating her dress.

Liam knew he wouldn't be the only one admiring her curves if she walked into the dingy bar.

"Do you have another suggestion?"

"A few blocks away."

He looked at her feet. "I can drive."

She smiled. "I was born in heels. C'mon."

"I thought Brenda was a lesbian," Avery started with once they'd rounded the first corner outside.

Liam thought about that for a few seconds. "She scares me."

Avery laughed. "Yeah, I get that. She knows her shit, though."

"Total respect."

They stopped at an intersection and waited for the light. "It would take a strong man to take her on. Can you imagine their sex life?"

Liam squeezed his eyes shut. "I really don't want to think about her that way."

"Headlocks and takedowns."

He took hold of Avery's elbow when the light changed and conveniently didn't let it go. "Brenda's sex life is not the image I want in my head, thank you very much."

"No, really. What kinda guy is into someone like her? He either has to be a total sub to her dom or so completely badass she can just be a girl."

Liam knew Avery hadn't clued in that he was wrapped around her arm as they walked down the street. And like a teenage boy who felt he was getting away with something, he just grinned and didn't let on. "You've given this a lot of thought."

"Not until tonight. Brenda's gettin' lucky." Avery did a little dance.

"You're really excited about this."

"I am." They walked another block. "And if you think I haven't noticed that you're holding my arm, you'd be wrong."

Liam nearly stumbled.

"But I'm a little cold, so I'm going with it."

He kept silent and kept walking.

Chapter Eight

Avery took him to Bailey's. It wasn't upscale or a dive. It was just a neighborhood place that the locals knew about that wasn't frequented by tourists or bums. For a bonus, they could get food. Since she'd missed dinner, a meal was necessary.

She led Liam into the bar and sat at an empty table in the middle of the room.

She dropped her gym bag under her feet and Liam followed suit. "Unlike Pug's, it's safe to order a drink here."

It wasn't long before the waitress walked up to the table. "Hey, Avery."

"Hi, Nikki."

"I haven't seen you in a while."

Avery looked at Liam. "I've been busy."

Nikki took Liam in . . . from head to toe. "I can see why."

Smiling, Avery shook her head. "Vodka martini, Grey Goose."

Nikki winked. "And for you?"

"Maker's Mark."

"Neat or on ice?"

"Ice."

"You got it."

Liam turned to Avery. "You know the waitress?"

"I live close by." As in one block over and one block up. If she looked hard enough, she could see her condo from the street.

"I didn't realize you lived in the city."

She lifted her hand in the air. "Central to everything, lots of restaurants."

"Krav."

"That, too."

"How long have you lived here?"

"About a year and a half. What about you? Are you in the city?"

He shook his head. "Atwater Village. Still central but far enough away."

Low-key, nothing too fancy. Not seedy. Funny how savvy Avery had become since she'd joined the working world.

"And you're a handyman?"

Liam paused. "Kinda."

"What does that mean?"

"I'll do side jobs, like the ones that Brenda needed, for extra cash."

"So what's your day job?"

He didn't answer right away. "I'm a contractor. Currently working on a loft space here in the city."

"You're kidding."

"Why would I kid you on that?"

"You're a licensed contractor?"

"Yes."

So why was she wasting her time at mixers when the man who was tossing her around on a mat did the very thing she needed advice on?

"Do you work on single-family homes?"

"That's where I started. Still do on occasion . . . why?"

She rested her head in her hands.

"Avery?"

Her head shot up at the sound of a female voice calling her name.

"Lori?"

Oh, damn . . .

Avery leaned close to Liam's ear. "She doesn't know about krav. I'll explain later."

She scooted closer and painted on a smile.

When Lori was at their table, Avery detached from Liam's side and stood for a hug. "What are you doing here? Where's Reed?"

Lori eyed Liam while she answered the questions. "Reed's on his way down. We're going out to dinner. Wanted a drink first."

What were the chances of Lori excusing herself before Avery was forced to make an introduction?

Lori reached out a hand toward Liam. "I'm Lori."

Liam stood; a broad smile matched his broad chest. "Liam Holt." Once he released Lori's hand, he pulled out a barstool. "Sit, we just ordered drinks."

Avery wanted to elbow his ribs.

Instead, she smiled.

Liam signaled for Nikki.

"Liam, huh? Avery hasn't mentioned you."

He pulled Avery's chair closer to his and waited for her to sit. "We haven't known each other long."

Lori sent a questioning look to Avery. Instead of adding to Liam's explanation, she sat beside him and acted like they had a more personal relationship than partners in a krav class. Lori would expect nothing less and ask fewer questions than if Avery and Liam appeared to be just friends.

"I've known Lori for a few years. We live in the same building."

"What do you do, Liam?"

Small talk . . . Is that what this was going to be?

Lori signaled Reed when he walked in the door. "This is my husband."

Avery laughed. "You love saying that, don't you?"

Lori nodded.

"They're newlyweds," Avery explained.

Once again Liam stood when Reed approached the table.

"Look who I found," Lori said.

Reed kissed Avery's cheek. "I haven't seen you here in a while."

"That's because you two never come up for air," Avery teased.

"This is Liam . . . Avery's *friend*." Yeah, Lori wanted more details. The men shook hands.

"Have I ever met one of your *friends*?" he asked.

Avery glared. "Smooth, Reed . . . really smooth."

Lori nudged her husband's arm. "Stop teasing." She turned her focus on Liam. "Avery keeps her private life private."

Avery tried not to flinch when Liam placed a hand over hers. "I've figured that out recently."

"How did you two meet?" Reed asked.

Avery said "The gym" at the same time Liam said "A bar."

Lori's lawyer radar spiked. Avery saw it in her eyes. "Those two things are worlds apart."

She caught Liam's hand and squeezed.

"The first time I saw you was at Pug's. I approached you at the gym."

"I knew it. That *was* you at Pug's. How did you figure out where I worked out?" She'd been asking herself that question for over a week.

"That wasn't hard. Leslie had a gym bag."

"Who's Leslie?" Lori asked.

Avery didn't look away from Liam. "A friend. So your job at the gym wasn't on accident?"

"I might have approached Brenda about a side job so I could meet you."

Avery's jaw dropped.

"Who's Brenda?" Reed asked.

"The owner of the gym," Avery and Liam said at the same time. "How did you know I was there on Tuesday and Friday nights?" She wasn't sure if his actions were exciting or scary.

"Appointment book. Brenda's office is always open."

"Wait, wait, wait." Lori placed a hand between the two of theirs. "You see Avery in a bar. You search out the location of her gym, follow her to it, get a job there, and now you're both here having drinks?"

Liam offered a brief, unapologetic nod.

Lori grabbed Avery's hand. "How well do you know this guy?"

Avery liked the gleam in Liam's eyes. "He's safe."

"What he just described is a little too close to stalking for my taste."

Reed placed a hand on Lori's shoulder. "Simmer down, Counselor. If Liam had an ulterior motive, he wouldn't have told us all that."

"I wanted to meet you," Liam said.

"Yeah, well, you've met her." Lori wasn't happy.

Nikki showed up with Avery's and Liam's drinks.

"My usual, Nikki," Lori told her.

"Hon, our reservations are in thirty minutes. Maybe we should go."

Lori looked at Reed like he was crazy. "We aren't leaving him with her. He could be a sociopath."

Liam smiled, his eyes crinkling with amusement. "I'm not."

"That's what they all say."

Avery put a free hand in the air. "Chill, Lori."

Avery realized that her other hand had somehow ended up back in Liam's. His thumb stroked the underside of her wrist in a strangely calming way.

"Do you want a drink, Reed?" Nikki was still standing there, watching the four of them.

"No, thank you. We're leaving."

Lori pushed back her chair. "We're going to talk about this later," she warned Avery. "And you . . . just so you know, I'm an attorney, and my big, burly husband here is in private security. He has even bigger friends."

Liam reached into his back pocket and removed his wallet. From it, he pulled out what looked like a business card. "I have nothing to hide."

Lori glanced at it briefly before Reed snatched it from her fingertips. "C'mon. Let's leave them to their date."

Liam stood again and shook Reed's hand before he ushered Lori out of the bar.

"That was intense."

"My friends are protective."

"Understatement."

"You really went through all that just to meet me?"

Liam picked up his drink for the first time. "Worked, didn't it?"

Avery let loose his hand and lifted her glass to his. "Yes, it did."

Avery had moved a little farther away after her friends left. But her rapt attention told him she was interested.

"So you don't introduce your dates to your friends?" Liam picked a few things out of their conversation with Lori and Reed.

"My dates, as you call them, aren't usually around long enough to meet the important people in my life."

He'd ordered a steak and she'd ordered fish. He cut into his dinner while he spoke. "Should I be flattered?"

She paused, her fork halfway to her mouth. "We were ambushed tonight. It isn't like I brought you to a plus-one event."

"A plus-one what?"

"You know, an invitation that leaves it open for you to add a person . . . plus-one."

"Do you ever take someone to a plus-one?"

She considered him for a second. "If you want to know about my dating life, just ask."

He started to do just that before she cut him off.

"And don't judge when I deliver answers you might not want to hear."

He set his knife down. "Now I'm really curious."

She chewed her food and didn't add anything.

"Okay, Avery . . . tell me about your dating life."

She sipped her drink and said, "I don't."

"Date?"

"Yeah, I don't date."

"You don't seem like the hermit type."

She placed a hand on the table. "Dating is holding hands and long walks on the beach, fancy dinners and midnight phone calls that may or may not include dirty pictures. Dating is attempting to go somewhere." She lifted her fork and dug back in. "I don't do that. I meet guys, flirt, have a good time, and move on."

He wasn't expecting that. "Sounds like a man."

She shook her head. "No. Men don't admit that they are players to the women they hook up with. Me? I'm honest about it. Makes it a whole lot easier to avoid that plus-one thing."

"And if the guy wants more?"

Avery smirked. "I haven't met him."

Liam was silent until she looked up.

"Yes, you have."

Chapter Nine

Her skin itched, like it was a suit she wasn't used to wearing or it was made of wool and she was poolside in Palm Springs.

Liam had taken the power away with one sentence and one look. And when she couldn't come up with anything to force the ball back into her court, he started a conversation about his work. He was a contractor. Legit, with a crew of twenty guys he kept employed most of the time. While he spelled out a day at work, Avery gave up eating her dinner and proceeded to order a third cocktail. She was more than a little tipsy, which became evident when it was time to leave the bar. "I'll pay." She reached for the bill.

Liam managed to grab it before she could. "Not in this lifetime."

"Oh, please. You're not one of those guys."

"What kind of guy is that?"

"The kind that think a woman isn't capable of paying a bill."

"If you live in this neighborhood, I'm pretty sure you can pay the bill. But you're not buying my meals."

She reached for it again. "Then we split."

"Avery, stop. I got it. Let me be the guy my mother raised."

She wondered what kind of mother that was.

"The stubborn one?"

"Him, too," he said, laughing. He handed his credit card to Nikki, who processed it quickly.

Liam hoisted his gym bag and hers over his shoulder once they were outside.

She chilled instantly and wobbled on her high heels.

He used his free arm to steady her and didn't let go.

"We're not holding hands," she told him.

"No. I'm holding your elbow. Which way?"

She pointed at her building.

They crossed the street and walked up one block.

The doorman opened the door before Liam could do it for them.

"Good evening, Ms. Grant."

"Hi, James. This is my friend Liam."

"Of course, Ms. Grant."

Avery pulled on Liam's arm until they were in the elevator.

He was strangely quiet for the first time all night.

Outside her door, she opened her purse and removed her keys and cell phone to disarm the alarm system.

Liam stopped her before she could squeeze the key into the hole.

"Avery."

She turned and found him staring. His eyes were hungry and his body close.

"I'm not going in. I wanted to make sure you made it home safely."

She knew that was coming. This would be the time she'd normally show the guy exactly what he would be missing if he didn't walk through her door.

But she was out of practice and she'd have to see Liam again. If he turned her down, the humiliation wouldn't be something she'd want to revisit every time they sparred in krav.

Avery responded with the only weapon she had. "I don't think I asked you in."

There it was . . . Liam's smirk. The smile in his eyes, the tiny lift of his lips.

He placed their gym bags on the floor and brought his hand up to her chin. "I do, however, think that our first date deserves an exclamation point."

"It wasn't a date."

"We did have dinner." He traced the back of his hand down her arm.

"But no long walks on the beach . . . or hand-holding."

"There was a little hand-holding."

Yeah, there had been.

He gently tugged her phone out of her hand.

"What are you doing?"

A smile was his answer. He pressed in a few numbers, and she heard his phone buzz in his pocket. "In case you want to send a flirty text after midnight."

"We're not dating."

He placed her phone back in her hand.

"You don't want to date me, Liam. I'm a bad bet."

He took a step closer. Lifted both hands to her face and touched her neck with the backs of his fingertips.

She shivered from head to toe.

"I'm not a gambler."

Her mouth went dry, her breath caught in her chest.

"Your mother will hate me."

Her lips parted while she watched him move closer.

"Avery?"

It was getting really hot in the hallway.

"Yes?"

"Stop talking."

His soft lips took hers in the slowest, most exquisite kiss she'd ever had the pleasure of swallowing. There was nothing rushed in Liam's body. Avery felt the door at her back when Liam leaned her into it. His hands on her face moved her where he wanted to deepen this meeting of lips.

Her eyes fluttered closed, and she opened her lips to his, tempting him with the tip of her tongue. He gave in for a few swipes against hers and then held back and continued to kiss her slowly. By the time he pulled away, Avery had clenched his shirt in her hands, and her cell phone and keys had found their way to the floor. She was heated, charged . . . and more than ready to see what else Liam could do with his lips.

"I'm going now," he whispered.

She was pretty sure her face told him he didn't have to.

When his hands left her, she cooled instantly.

He bent down and gathered her keys and her phone. He turned the key in the lock and opened her door.

"Good night, Avery."

She watched as he retreated down the hallway and disappeared into the elevator.

"Good night," she said to the empty corridor.

$\sim$

"Someone is awfully happy out here."

Michelle walked out the back door and onto his deck. Liam turned around and lowered the volume on his speaker. He put aside the drill and dusted off his hands.

"I'm always happy when I'm working with my hands." He didn't do it often enough once he earned his contractor's license and started employing other people.

"Yeah, but you were singing and dancing."

He looked at the sky. "The sun is shining, the music is loud. Good day to break out in song. Life is a musical."

They shared a memory of something their mother always said when they were growing up.

Michelle shook her head. "Uh-huh . . . okay, give it up. Who is she?"

"She who?" Whiskey barked at his feet as if adding her two cents.

"The she who put that grin on your face. The house isn't that big. I heard you come home late last night."

"It wasn't after midnight."

"But still late for you. Nice diversion. Does she have a name?"

Liam picked up the two-by-four he'd predrilled holes into for his screws. "She does, and I'll tell it to you when I'm ready."

"I knew it." She giggled like a schoolgirl. "Are we going to meet her?"

"It's new. I don't know." Yes. He wanted to say yes. Introducing Avery to his sister he could deal with, but not Cassandra. She wouldn't understand if it didn't work out.

"You should bring her to Sunday dinner."

"Michelle!" Her name was a warning.

His sister turned back around to go inside. "You're still okay with watching Cassie tonight?"

Two Saturdays a month, he watched his niece so Michelle could do an all-nighter on the crisis hotline.

"Of course. We have a date planned."

"Please don't stuff her with sugar. She was a pill the last time."

He saluted his sister and revved his drill bit.

"Liam!"

"Don't worry, sis. I got it figured out."

꩜

"That hot fudge sundae is bigger than you."

Liam sat across from his niece in the restaurant portion of the arcade, where they'd finished their cheeseburgers and fries . . . or at least he had polished off the fast food–type meal while Cassandra saved room for desert.

Whipped cream and fudge were stuck to the corners of her mouth.

"Your mom's going to kill me."

His niece giggled.

The kid had him wrapped around her little finger. He didn't know how to say no to her.

"We won't tell her," Cassandra pretended to whisper.

Liam reached over, dipped his clean napkin in her water, and wiped fudge off her pink shirt. "I think she'll figure it out."

He cut her off halfway through the sundae with the lure of games and miniature golf.

Liam found himself receiving the attention of several women in the arcade who were entertaining their children. He was used to the attention whenever he was out with Cassandra alone. When he was with Michelle, he knew people assumed he and Michelle were a thing. Once he got over the yuck factor, he realized it was an easy assumption. But when alone, he was the poor single dad, or maybe the weekend dad . . . the results were the same. Women emerged, flirted.

Assumed.

Like the brunette smiling at him from across the room.

Nope, nope, nope . . . he was into blondes these days.

Liam leaned against the wall next to a row of Skee-Ball stations and tried not to make eye contact. Only the woman had caught his scent and was working her way to his side.

It was his shot with the ball, so he turned his back on her just as she approached. He purposely tossed the ball to the side and scored low.

"No, Uncle Liam. Throw it in the middle," Cassandra instructed.

"Do you need some help with that?"

It was the brunette, and she was standing right behind him.

Cassandra, not catching on to a female on the prowl, shook her head and invited conversation. "He's bad at this game."

Liam saw the woman's eyes light up. "I can show you a few pointers."

"I'm sure you could, but I'm here with my niece tonight."

She smiled at Cassandra for all of one second. "That's sweet. Maybe another time."

Her voice was hopeful, her eyelids fluttered.

Liam didn't add to the conversation with the stranger. Instead he focused on Cassandra. "Show me how you do it again."

The woman walked away and Liam sighed in relief.

At eight o'clock sharp, his phone rang. He answered without looking at the number. "Hello, Michelle. Before you start . . . yes, we're still out, but I'll have Cassandra home by nine . . . maybe nine thirty." His sister always gave him the same rundown every time he had his niece.

"Liam?"

Not Michelle.

The arcade made it difficult to hear.

"Who is this?"

"It's not Michelle. And who is Cassandra? Or do you have a harem you want to add me to?"

Liam closed his eyes. "Avery."

"Glad you could get the name right."

Liam felt panic crawl up his spine. "It's not what you think—"

"It's okay. I get it. One kiss and an exchange of phone numbers . . . I don't need to know who Michelle or Cassandra is. Obviously I've called at a bad time."

She was going to hang up . . . he felt it. "Avery!"

Yup, the line went dead.

Cassandra tugged on his pants and looked up at him. "Who is Avery?"

Chapter Ten

Avery tapped her phone against her chest as the conversation from the previous night ran through her head. Liam had made it sound like he wanted to start something. Something that included predetermined dates and maybe the occasional plus-one event.

For one night and most of the day, Avery actually considered it. It wasn't like she was doing anything else with her love life. Liam seemed harmless enough, even for the size of the man.

And damn, the man could kiss. She didn't think her brain cells started circulating until after he was on the freeway headed home.

Even though her curiosity was piqued and her hormones were leveling up a notch, or ten, she'd picked up the phone tonight not to flirt . . . but to see if Liam could meet her at the Brentwood house and offer some advice. The flirting could continue while on the clock, so to speak.

"What's the point?" she asked the empty room.

Two women's names rolled off his tongue when he wasn't paying attention. When you catch a man off guard, you learn his secrets . . . or at least the things he doesn't want you to know.

Avery knew what she was talking about when she labeled men as players that never fessed up to their lifestyle.

She'd joined the rank of players long before she married Bernie as a temporary bride and took a year and a half off while playing wife. All that pent-up energy exploded once the divorce was final.

Avery looked down at the sweatpants and oversize T-shirt she wore with a frown. It was Saturday night and what was she doing? Standing in the middle of her living room, pining over a man.

"Screw this."

She dropped her phone on her couch and walked into her master suite. She opened the double doors to her walk-in closet and switched on the chandelier.

Shoes first. Four-inch Pradas that laced over her feet like sexy gloves. Black.

Leopard print, low-cut top with shoestring sleeves. No bra needed. Tight black mini.

Perfect.

She spent ten minutes freshening her makeup and five pushing her hair into a messy bun.

One more layer of red on her lips and she made a kissing motion in the mirror before tossing the lipstick into her clutch.

On her way to the door, she picked up her cell phone off the couch. She found a voice mail from Liam. Her finger hovered over the button to hear what he had to say, and she stopped.

It didn't matter what he had to say, she didn't want to hear it.

Tonight was about reminding herself why she had the perfect life. Young, single . . . rich. She could have anyone she wanted.

Leaving her phone behind, she set her alarm, grabbed her keys, and walked out the door.

The Basement was a club where the music was so deafening you couldn't hear yourself think. It was the perfect place to get lost in the crowd, dance with complete strangers, and never have to hold a conversation.

The line outside waiting to get in was halfway around the block. Avery stepped out of the courtesy car her complex offered and headed straight to the bouncer.

"Hello, Freddy." She leaned in and gave the familiar man a kiss on the cheek.

"Avery. I haven't seen you in a while."

"I've been busy."

"Is it just you tonight? Or do I need to add a name to my list?"

"Just me."

He winked and unchained the red rope, letting her pass.

Those standing in the front of the line glared.

Sound blared and the thump of the bass pulsed deep in her chest. She missed this. Why had she stayed away for so long?

The bar was three people deep, but a drink was needed before she joined the grinding on the dance floor. In a tactic she'd used many times in the past, she found what appeared to be a single man sitting in a far corner and wiggled her way between him and the person on his left.

She smiled at him briefly and lifted her hand to get the bartender's attention.

With her chest eye level with the stranger, he'd have to be gay not to notice or appreciate it.

The way his gaze took her in said he didn't play for the other team.

He was older, by a good ten years, and out of place in a room filled with college kids or those who were just turning thirty.

"Hello."

She smiled and leaned in so he could hear her. "Sorry, the bar is crazy over there. I hope you don't mind me barging in."

"Quite all right," he shouted over the music.

Yeah, much older. No one in this crowd would say *quite*.

He said something she couldn't hear, and she simply smiled and ignored the fact that he was staring at her chest. He wasn't unattractive. Just not what she was looking for.

Her bar mate signaled for the bartender by reaching around the people on his right. "The lady would like a drink."

"Vodka martini," she shouted.

The bartender, much more her speed, didn't look twice.

"Nice choice."

She looked at his glass. "What are you drinking?"

He said something she didn't catch. Avery didn't ask that he repeat himself.

"Do you come here often?"

Could there be a worse line?

"I've been here a few times. You?"

"It's a little loud."

She nodded as the bartender slid her glass in front of her. As she reached for her purse, her admirer placed a hand on her arm. "I got it."

With a toss of her chin over her shoulder that she'd learned in college, she smiled and leaned a little closer. "You're too kind."

"I'm Gary."

"Avery."

She took a sip of her drink and felt some of the tension leave her shoulders.

"Did you come here alone?"

"How can anyone be alone in a room full of this many people?" Each time she spoke to him, she leaned in so he could hear. Which kept his eyes glued to her shirt—he was probably hoping that something would pop out.

The DJ changed the song to one she liked.

"I'm an engineer . . . What do you do?"

This was not a conversation she wanted at the club.

"What?" She pretended not to understand him, and he shouted the question again.

Avery looked over the crowd of people and waved across the room like she knew someone.

When Gary turned to follow her gaze, she put more room between the two of them.

"I see a friend. Thanks for the drink." And she was gone, swallowed by the dance floor and everyone on it. She lifted her drink above her head and moved to the other side. If Gary was watching her, he'd lose sight of her before she reached the hall to the bathrooms.

It wasn't long before she downed her drink, left her glass on a side table, and joined the crazy. She circled her hips and let her legs do the talking. It didn't take long to attract someone more her speed. Someone hot, firm, faceless, and young. This guy didn't try to talk, they just danced. On the second song, she felt his hands on her hips. She didn't dust him off but kept some distance to avoid being groped before knowing his name.

Not that she cared.

Four songs in, he tugged her arm toward the bar in the back of the club. "Can I buy you a drink?"

She looked him up and down.

"How about shots?" It would take a few shots.

"Oh, sexy. I like that."

She hated cheap liquor, and after the second shot, she gave up trying to drink. But her buzz was decent enough to keep the night going.

The music grew louder, and the dance floor was a smash of bodies, making it impossible to dance without touching everyone around her.

Shot Man kept a hand on her while they danced, every once in a while dipping down her hip to her thigh. When she felt him dragging his hands under her skirt, she felt a chill.

Do I really want this?

A year ago she'd have already left with this guy. No strings, no names.

She dislodged his hand with a twist.

He took her gesture as a challenge and attempted to come at her from the other side while they danced.

This time she knew it wasn't going to happen.

He was practically panting.

With hands on her shoulders, his lips touched her ear. "Let's get out of here."

"I don't think so."

He stopped dancing, and the smile he'd been flirting with all night disappeared. "Seriously?"

"Yeah."

He looked at her as if she'd grown warts. "Fuckin' tease."

Avery watched him walk away and took the other direction. She reached for her purse to see what the time was and realized she'd left her phone at home.

She made small talk with the women in line for the bathroom and realized it was after one. No wonder she was tired.

This wasn't going to happen.

Picking up a nameless bed toy had lost its charm. Not that she couldn't, she reminded herself. She should just go home and drink good liquor until she dropped.

Back into the crush of dancers, she squeezed through the club, ignoring several one-liners delivered by men standing in groups of other men. One reached out like he had the right and stopped her by holding on to her arm. "Hey, baby."

She froze, looked at his hand and then into his face. "I'd let go if I were you."

"C'mon. Sexy thing like you shouldn't be leaving alone."

His buddies laughed.

College kids. She'd be surprised if this one was even old enough to be in the club.

When he tugged her arm, Avery reacted.

Quick.

Decisive.

Don't hold back.

She pushed in, twisted, found his gut with her elbow, and then brought the same elbow to his chin.

He let go with a curse.

The laughter from his buddies grew.

"Bitch."

Avery squared her shoulders. Those close enough to see what happened gave her a wide path.

On shaky legs, Avery stepped outside and once again realized she didn't have her cell phone to hire an Uber. She could walk home, but at that time of night, and dressed like she was, it wouldn't be surprising if someone stopped her and asked how much.

The line at the door was still there, but the staff had changed.

She crossed the street in an effort to get a taxi headed in the direction of her complex. Two blocks up, she waited on the busy corner.

She shivered.

What was she doing?

Showing Liam. Only he wasn't there to see her standing on the corner, waiting for a cab to drive by.

Someone in a passing car whistled.

Avery rolled her eyes.

At least she felt armed enough to ward off unwelcome hands. In fact, the adrenaline of doubling over the dude who grabbed her was higher than when Shot Man wanted to show her a good time.

Maybe next time she went out she'd skip the high heels and mini.

She wrapped her hands over her bare shoulders and looked around. The streets held a few die-hards returning to their cars or walking in and out of the open bars.

Avery stepped into the street and waved at a lone cab.

The short ride to her complex with a cabbie who obviously smoked, and either didn't bathe or did so in garlic, reminded her never to leave home without her phone again.

She paused outside her complex and looked around.

The hair on her neck prickled.

No one was there.

Except James . . . the doorman.

"Good evening, Ms. Grant. Are you expecting any visitors tonight?"

She shook her head. "Have a nice evening," she told him.

Avery removed her shoes in the elevator. From her front door, she beelined to her alarm panel and stopped the ringing. With a sigh, she flopped on the couch, realized she sat on her phone, and pulled it out from under her butt.

Liam's message called out.

What would he say?

They were old girlfriends? Women who didn't let go? Or maybe he'd be honest and say he had several out there. With his broad shoulders, sexy grin, and capable lips . . .

Avery pressed the button.

Liam's voice was deep and clear even though the background was noisy. "Okay, you're impulsive . . . and jump to conclusions. I get it. But before you delete this message, I want someone to say hi to you. Say hi, Cassandra."

Avery was about to toss her phone against the wall. No way he was going to have a woman come to bat for him on a phone message.

"Hi."

Avery's heart jolted. A child. Liam was a dad?

"Tell Miss Avery who I am." It sounded like he had the phone on speaker.

"Who is Miss Avery?"

"A friend. Who am I?"

The girl laughed, and Avery found herself smiling. "Uncle Liam."

Oh, shit.

"And who is Michelle?"

"My mommy. Can we play more Skee-Ball now? I was winning."

"Sure can."

Avery rested her head in her hands. *What an idiot.*

"There you go, Miss Avery. Michelle is my sister and Cassandra is my niece. My Saturday night is being spent in a kids' arcade, eating ice cream and french fries while I'm babysitting."

"I'm not a baby, I'm five."

"Call me" were Liam's last words before he hung up.

Chapter Eleven

Liam woke to a text. It had come in at two in the morning.

I owe you an apology was all Avery said.

Yes, she did. He'd stayed up until after one, seriously contemplating calling her multiple times or dragging Cassandra out of bed and driving to Avery's complex. He remembered the guy at the door and realized he wouldn't be able to just waltz in. What if he did manage to make his way to her condo and she wasn't alone?

That would suck.

It was Sunday, and Michelle was sleeping in. Cassandra was on the couch with the Disney Channel on low. It looked like Michelle had managed to pour a bowl of cereal before climbing back in bed. Whiskey sat next to Cassandra on the couch, hoping the girl would drop a Froot Loop or two.

"Good morning, Sweetpea."

Messy hair, eyes glued to the TV. "Good morning."

Straight to the kitchen, he worked his way around the coffeepot and opened the back door.

Whiskey shot around the corner and out to the yard.

The fog in his head started to lift with the first sip of coffee. Liam sat on the deck and watched the dog sniffing for the perfect place to pee.

He was contemplating how to respond to Avery's two a.m. text when the woman he was thinking of called.

It was seven thirty in the morning.

"You're up early for someone who was up so late."

"I'm awake, not up." Her voice was husky, like she was still lying in bed. The image that came to his mind was her head on a dozen pillows, with down comforters swallowing her whole. She wore silk in his fantasy. White silk to go with the pristine white sheets . . . a zillion thread count. Her barely there nightgown had strings for sleeves, and one was falling off her shoulder.

"Are you still there?" she asked.

"I am." He brought his coffee cup to his lips and waited.

She paused.

He kept waiting.

"I'm sorry."

He grinned. "Did that hurt?"

"Yes. It did."

He sipped his coffee again.

"I shouldn't have jumped to conclusions. I have no right to jump. Even if it were true, my reaction was juvenile and stupid." She took a breath. "I am impulsive and juvenile, and I'm not the sharpest pencil in the box. I told you I was a bad bet and I—"

"Avery," he interrupted.

"I'm on a roll, Liam. I've apologized maybe five times my whole life and actually meant it. Once was when I hit my neighbor's cat when I was seventeen. Stupid thing ran out in front of my car. Still, the cat meant everything to my neighbor. Then to my college girlfriend when I caught her boyfriend cheating on her and I was the one that delivered the news. I kinda had to eat crow when I misread my girlfriend Trina's fiancé. Although that wasn't an apology, per se."

Liam's amusement caught in his throat. "Avery."

"I'm sorry," she said one last time.

"Apology accepted."

She sighed into the phone. "Really?"

"Yeah."

"That's it?"

"Yeah. Next time give me a chance to explain."

"Really? You're not going to drill me about it? Make me eat my words?"

Whiskey had unearthed a ball and now stood in front of Liam, slobbering all over his knees.

"You forced your own words down your throat. You don't need me to add to them. But if you want to make it up to me . . ."

"There's a catch."

"Only if you want to make it up to me."

His comment was met with silence.

"Okay, what?"

"A plus-one."

"What?"

"Your choice . . . make me your plus-one to whatever you want. Dinner with friends, cocktail party. Work event . . . a distant relative's wedding. I don't care what."

"Seriously?"

He liked the idea as it formed in his head. If he added her to a plus-one event, she would likely be uncomfortable and unhappy. If she added him, it placed the control in her court. Besides, his plus-one would consist of a family dinner, and he knew she didn't want that.

"Anything. Uptown, downtown . . . don't care."

"I should bring you to high tea with my mother. That would take away your desire to be added to a guest list."

"Mothers love me."

"My mother doesn't love anyone but maybe her hairdresser . . . or the doctor injecting Botox."

"So your mother's doing the Botox doctor, huh?"

"I wish. That would take the spike out of her ass."

He laughed. "Dads love me, too."

"My father hardly knows I'm alive, except to parrot my mother's complaints about how I'm wasting my life. Trust me . . . a plus-one with my parents is like watching children's television filled with repeating chants of life lessons I never wanted to learn."

"No parent dinners, then. You choose the event."

"You're not letting this go."

No, he wasn't. "We have a deal?"

"You're pushing me out of my comfort zone," she told him.

"I know." He pulled the ball from his dog's mouth and tossed it across the yard. "Now that we've covered that, was there a reason you were calling yesterday, or did you just miss hearing my voice?"

"You're full of yourself."

"I'm self-assured. As are you."

He liked her laugh.

"I was calling to ask you a favor."

"Yes."

"What?"

"To the favor. The answer is yes."

The dog returned and dropped the ball.

"What if I wanted to seek revenge on an old boyfriend?"

"You don't collect boyfriends. So I think I'm safe."

"Rob a bank?" she asked.

"That's how you make your money, I knew it." He was laughing along with her.

"I wanted your opinion on a house I'm working on in Brentwood."

"Working on how?"

"I help people with estate sales. Mainly with the wealthy and most often after the death of a parent or a spouse."

Liam winced. "Sounds morbid."

"I'm not a director of a funeral home. I deal with stuff. Dead people's stuff, but just things. Most of the time my clients are either living out of the state or the country and need to make sure Grandma's antique watch that's worth a hundred grand isn't being sold at a garage sale on the two-dollar table."

"That happens?"

"All the time. Anyway. My client is selling the house but wants to get a ballpark of what it would cost to bring it into this century. You're probably way too busy for a project like this, but if you could offer your expert opinion, and maybe toss a few phone numbers my way of contractors that would be interested in the job, that would be great."

"The answer is still yes."

"Two weeks."

Safe to say Trina was excited about tying the knot . . . again.

Avery set her phone on speaker and continued to talk while she did her morning stretches. "Yes, I know. I have my countdown list, and it does say you're collecting a ball and chain in two weeks."

"He's a very sexy ball."

"You're killing me."

"Diane and Andrea are definitely coming to the bachelorette party, so we need to add two to the guest list."

Avery made a mental note. "Got it. You sure you don't want to take that party to Vegas?"

"Nothing good happens in Vegas at a strip club."

Avery could tell her otherwise. "I'm guessing the club in Houston will be just as hot." And since Avery was the one in charge of said party, she was making damn sure it was a night Trina would remember for the rest of her married life.

"So you're flying in Friday night, right?"

"Yes." She made another mental note to tell Brenda that she was going to miss Friday . . . actually, two Fridays in a row.

"Are you sure you can't just stay until the wedding?"

Avery shifted her legs and bent into a stretch over her right knee. "I'm a working woman these days. The old Avery would happily blow off her new client. The adulting Avery has to show up on Monday. But don't worry, I'll be on the charter on Wednesday with Lori, Reed, and Shannon."

"I'm getting nervous."

"Nerves are good. Second thoughts, not so much."

"Not a chance. I'm not letting Wade get away."

"I didn't think so. Just enjoy the whole thing. When you're back from your honeymoon and need some air, we'll book a girls' trip to Paris. I could use some new shoes."

"Speaking of shoes . . . who is Liam?"

Avery stopped her stretch. "What do shoes and Liam have in common?"

"Nothing, but I couldn't think of a smoother way to ask about the guy in your life."

"He's not *the* guy in my life," she said.

"Lori said she met him. That he's a stalker and she's worried about you."

Avery gave up on her stretches, grabbed her phone off the floor, and moved to sit on her bed. "He's not a stalker. I think I'd know it if he were. He's just a guy I met. No big deal."

Trina paused. "Just a guy?"

"Yeah. You know I collect them."

"How's the sex?"

"We haven't gone there."

"Whoa, back up the truck. You're saying he is *just a guy* and *no big deal*. And you haven't slept with him?"

Avery deserved that.

"I don't sleep with every guy I'm attracted to."

"Since when?"

"Jesus, Trina, I'm not a slut."

"Calm down. I'm not calling you anything and you know it. But Avery Grant prides herself on her prowess. You telling me he is part of the collection and yet you haven't gotten naked with him tells me he is more than a number."

"*Yet.* I haven't slept with him *yet.* I'm sure we'll get there sooner rather than later."

"Uh-huh."

"Don't analyze this, Trina. I don't date. You know that."

"Have you had dinner with him?"

"Once," Avery admitted.

"That's a date."

"No, it wasn't."

"Were you with a group of people or just the two of you?"

Trina was backing her into a verbal corner.

"There were other people there."

"In the restaurant or at the table?"

Avery shook her head. "This is a ridiculous conversation."

Trina wasn't fooled. "I wanna meet him."

"No." Avery stood from the bed and started to pace the room.

"Bring him to the wedding."

"Absolutely not. Your wedding is about you, not me flirting with a guy." The conversation was making her angry.

There was silence on the line.

"You're my best friend, Avery. You know that, right?"

She smiled through her annoyance. "Yes. I love you, too."

"Remember when I was in Venice last year and you told me you were worried about me?"

"Yeah." Trina had been in Italy, escaping the anniversary of her first husband's death and trying to power through on her own.

"Well, it's my turn to tell you I'm worried about you."

"Why? I'm actually working and self-sufficient for the first time in my life. I'm more capable of taking care of myself now than ever before." When you added the krav she'd been studying, it made her even more adept at dealing with whatever life threw at her.

"Because you've closed yourself off. You don't laugh as much or joke as often. Now there is a guy who, from what Lori says, worked hard to get you to go out with him. Maybe he isn't the one, but how will you know if you never give a guy a chance?"

Avery closed her eyes. "Can you accept the fact that you're in a heightened state of *I do* and *happily ever after* and not everyone wants that in their life? I love you, Trina, but you're wrong on this one. If my lack of joking or laughing is bothering you, then try and understand that I'm trying really hard to grow up here. I spent the first twenty-eight years of my life being a spoiled brat with crappy parents, the next three playing pretend wife and new divorcée with a shit ton of money. It's only been since New York that I'm finding me . . . the real me. Admittedly, I'm picking up the pieces of my personal mess, but I'm doing it. And that doesn't include me finding a man to break my stride. I'm finally doing well on my own and want to keep it that way."

"Oh, Avery. I'm sorry." Trina sounded teary.

"It's okay. You're excited and emotional and want everyone as happy as you are. Please know that I am. Just in a different way."

"Okay . . . I'll let it go. Please talk to me. Anytime."

"I know you're there, Trina. I have to get in the shower. I'm meeting a contractor at my new client's house and want to be there on time." Omitting Liam's name wasn't an accident.

"I miss you."

Avery smiled. "I'll see you in a few days."

Chapter Twelve

Liam was fifteen minutes early. Wearing a pullover shirt that hugged his chest like a glove and denim that made Avery's palms itch, he looked even better than the last time she saw him.

He walked through the open front door while Avery stood alongside Felicia, the art expert from a local auction house.

Avery removed her reading glasses and excused herself from Felicia to greet Liam.

"Good afternoon," he said. His eyes took her in, looking at her face, her head.

With an unconscious hand, Avery smoothed over her hair and ponytail. Work mode meant she hadn't paid too much attention to what she was wearing. Today was about digging in closets and unearthing treasures. Skirts and fancy shoes didn't hold up in those circumstances.

"You found the place okay?"

"Sat nav is an amazing thing."

There was a moment of awkward silence when Liam stared at her and smiled.

Avery shifted from foot to foot, willing her pulse to slow.

"Thank you again for coming by," she said, breaking the quiet.

Liam finally looked away and glanced at the foyer. "This is definitely in need of an update."

"The question is how deep."

Liam turned his gaze back to her. "Deep?"

"Yeah, beyond the cosmetic stuff. My client has no idea how new or old the plumbing is, the insulation. It was built in the late thirties originally, and then massively updated in the fifties. There were a few changes on record in the eighties, but I'm not sure the extent. The home is three generations old. Which is a lot of years for homes in the LA area."

"Seems a shame to sell."

Avery agreed, but who was she to judge? She'd sell her parents' estate in a heartbeat. "C'mon, let me show you around." She pulled him out of the hall. "If you need me, Felicia . . ."

"I have it, Ms. Grant."

She walked him through the family room and around the crates that were already set up to accept the artwork on the walls. "There are four fireplaces. None of them look like they've had a fire in them for several years."

Liam walked over to the hearth and knelt down. "This one is massive." He knocked on the plain facade. "Bet this is covering up something."

Avery shrugged and pulled her eyes away from his butt as he stood.

They walked through a den, or as Sheldon called it, his father's smoking room. The massive dining room was off a spacious kitchen that needed a total gut, in her opinion.

Liam wrote a few things on a notepad as she continued the tour.

Outside, she pointed to the patio living area. "It's been maintained out here. I think because the wife liked her garden."

"Greenhouse?" he asked, pointing to the far side of the property.

CATHERINE BYBEE

"Yup. The groundskeepers use it now, but Sheldon said his mother once grew orchids."

Back inside, she took him up the stairway to the upper floor. A maze of smaller bedrooms, a second laundry room, and a his and hers master suite. The rooms were separated by a sitting room like you'd see in the Windsor House in Westminster.

"Parents didn't like each other?" Liam asked with a smirk.

"Maybe he snored."

He traced his hands on the bedpost. "Do you?"

"Do I what?"

"Snore?"

Caught off guard, Avery stuttered. "Is that . . . is that a professional question from a contractor to a client?"

"Nope. It's one hundred percent personal." He was smiling.

Avery paused. "Like a trucker. All night. I'm told it's miserable."

He laughed. "I sleep like the dead." Liam moved away from the bed and opened a door. "A nursery."

"Yeah, strange that it still looks like that. Their son is thirty-five years old."

"Maybe they were hoping for grandchildren." The room was a mausoleum, complete with scary dolls and black-and-white photos. And dust. Lots of dust.

"Sheldon's single. But who knows."

"Avery?" Felicia called her name from the hall.

Avery pointed toward the door. "Let me see what she needs."

"Take your time. I need to poke around, get a few things from my truck, and look under the sinks, check the electrical panels."

Damn, he was easy to look at. Tall enough, but not towering. Thick in all the right places . . . well, as much as she could tell without seeing him naked. *Does he have any tattoos?*

"Avery?" Felicia yelled again.

She jumped. "Right. Coming!"

Liam's laughter followed her out of the room.

Avery jogged down the main staircase to the foyer and found the back of the Uber food delivery guy. "Perfect timing."

He turned around and Avery almost tripped.

The *dance all night, buy me drinks, but I'm not going home with you* dude from the Basement.

Yeah, no name came to mind. Then again, she didn't think they'd exchanged names.

"You," he said, staring.

"Yeah . . ." Avery glanced up the stairs.

"Avery?" he asked, looking at his slip.

This wasn't good.

She pointed a finger at the bags of food in his hands. "That's for me."

"Hundred and thirty dollars' worth of sandwiches and salads . . . I'm guessing a chick like you can afford her own drinks at a bar."

"Right." She took the bags from him slowly. "About that. I'll be sure and tip you well."

He dragged his gaze over her frame. "You do that."

"Hey, Avery?"

Oh, geez, what now?

Liam had turned the corner on the stairs.

"Yeah, just a minute." She practically pushed what's-his-name out the door. "Thanks for bringing the food."

"I see what's going on." They had made it to the front porch, and Avery half closed the door behind them.

"I'm sorry," she whispered. "Saturday was a weird night."

"Uh-huh. Right."

"I *will* tip you."

"You be sure and do that, *Avery*."

"I will . . ." What the hell was his name?

Nothing.

She had nothing.

It took him forever to get off the steps and into his car. He drove a Prius.

He buzzed around the driveway, coming way too close to her Aston for her taste, and disappeared.

With a sigh, she pushed back into the house and painted on a smile.

"I ordered lunch. I hope you're hungry."

∾⟨∾

Liam wandered the eight-thousand-square-foot home and the grounds for two hours. Every time he told himself to hurry up, that he had other jobs pulling at him, he ignored the voice in his head. This was a favor for Avery, and he didn't want to lead her wrong.

His work phone buzzed. "Hey, Carlos."

"When are you getting back here? The developer is poking around and asking for answers I don't have for him."

Carlos was his first in charge when Liam wasn't on-site.

"I wasn't expecting him today."

"That doesn't mean he isn't here."

"I'll call him." Liam checked his watch. "Give me forty-five minutes."

He hung up the phone and searched for Avery.

He found her in a study, or a home office, although there wasn't a computer on the desk or any sign of the normal equipment one would find in a functioning office space.

For a moment, he stood in the doorway and watched her.

Sitting behind the substantial wooden desk with her elbows firmly planted on the top, she rolled a thick pen between her fingers and stared beyond the object in her hands. Her eyelids twitched and her lips were in a thin, expressionless line. Liam couldn't tell if she was deep in thought or upset . . . or what?

He cleared his throat and jarred her out of her trance.

"Am I disturbing you?"

Avery closed her eyes briefly and painted on a smile. "I'm fine . . . I mean, you're fine." She took a few quick breaths and dropped the pen on the desk. "Did you finish up?"

Her voice sounded strangled.

"Are you okay?"

"Fine." Again she grinned and shook her head. "Of course."

"I need to get back to my job site. I think I have everything I need here."

She stood from behind the desk and walked toward him. "Let me walk you out."

The closer she came, the better he could see the lack of color on her face. He glanced back at the desk. "What was that you were looking at?"

Avery looked over her shoulder. "Nothing, really. A pen." She walked beside him down the hallway and around the crates that now lined the foyer walls.

Liam placed a hand on her elbow to have her walk in front of him through the door.

Her skin was cold to the touch.

Outside he let go and she rubbed her bare arms.

"You sure you're all right?"

"I'm fine. Long day." She stopped at the bottom of the steps. "So what do you think?"

"I need to crunch some numbers before I give you a realistic bottom line."

"Sounds reasonable."

"We can go over them Friday after krav."

She looked away. "Actually, I need to skip Friday for the next two weeks."

The air swished out of his sails.

"My best friend is getting married. We have a bachelorette party this weekend and the wedding next."

"Do you have time on Thursday?"

"I'll be here all day."

"After work, then. I'll call you." He didn't give her an opportunity to say no. He opened the door to his truck and stood beside it.

"Thanks again for doing this."

"You're welcome."

The heat outside seemed to transform her fake smile into something he could believe in. "Have you thought about that plus-one?"

The teasing grin was even better.

"No, I haven't." She blushed.

"You're not a good liar."

"I'm busy."

"We all are." He thought about her excuse for missing their sparring match. "Weddings are perfect plus-one events."

Her eyes narrowed. "No. I already told Trina that wasn't going to happen. I'm the maid of honor. I have duties."

"Who's Trina?"

She looked at him as if he were missing a few cards in his deck. "The bride."

It was his turn to find a shit-eating grin and use it. "You told your best friend about my plus-one date suggestion?"

"No!" She shuffled her feet. "Yes."

It was entertaining to watch a woman get caught in her own lies. "Trina suggested her wedding?"

"Not going to happen, Liam. I don't know you well enough. It's Trina's day. Nope, nope, and nope."

He put one foot in his truck. "Whatever you say, Princess. You figure it out and I'll be there."

She tossed her hands in the air and turned back toward the stairs.

"Avery?" He called her attention back as he climbed into his truck.

"What?" She was flustered.

He liked her that way.

"You're beautiful."

She opened her mouth like a guppy gasping for air, twice, and then jogged up to the house.

Chapter Thirteen

"I'm not bringing him!" Avery exclaimed.

"I don't see what the big deal is. Any man in your life is going to have to meet us eventually." Trina sat in the back of the limousine, wearing a white cowgirl hat, white boots, white skirt . . . white everything. They were starting their night with a decent meal, and then on to the strip club, the dance hall, and whatever bad decisions they could find before the night was over.

"He isn't the *man in my life*. We've already gone over this."

"You were on the phone with him before we left the ranch," Lori pointed out.

"I was talking about work. He's helping me with a project." Thursday didn't pan out, so she had to call him.

Lori, Shannon, and Trina all exchanged glances.

"You guys are hopeless," Avery told them.

"I think Trina's wedding is the perfect place to flesh out a new man," Shannon told her. "Think about it. Men and weddings . . . they are either into the idea or completely turned off by them. By the end of the weekend you'll know if he is even marriage material."

"I don't want to get married," Avery reminded them. Not that her friends were listening.

"Not to mention that your status in life is going to be an issue," Lori offered.

"My status?"

"Your wealth. The lifestyle you like to live. I don't have to tell any of you how a woman having her own money emasculates many egotistical, chauvinistic men."

Shannon nodded. "Even if the guy isn't a chauvinist, they still have a hard time dealing."

Avery thought about their one meal out and how Liam refused to let her pay for her half of the meal. It was strangely satisfying to have him take the check. Outside of getting men to buy her drinks in bars, where she looked like just another girl in a miniskirt instead of a woman who drove up in a quarter-of-a-million-dollar car and returned to her two-million-dollar condo, Avery always found herself pulling out her wallet.

"The decision is up to you," Trina told her. "But I think it would cut a lot of BS if he could handle a weekend wedding with all of us around. You'll know if you're wasting your time."

"Thank you for your endorsement and parental guidance, now can we get on with the party?" Avery leaned over and turned on the stereo, filling the limo with music that had them singing along. Lori opened the champagne, and by the time they reached their first stop, they were laughing and out of breath.

༄

"Hey, Michelle?" Liam captured his sister's attention from the textbook she currently studied.

"Hey, what?"

"Have you ever been to a bachelorette party?"

"A couple. Why?"

He shrugged. How bad could they be? He thought of the hired strippers and the clubs he'd gone to in his years of playing partygoer when his friends bit the marital bullet. "Nothing."

She lifted her gaze.

"Nothing, huh?"

"They can't be as crazy as a bachelor party."

Michelle smirked. "You go ahead and believe that if you want."

"What's that supposed to mean?"

"Does this have anything to do with Miss Avery?"

Cassandra had let the Avery cat out of the bag the morning after Liam had had his niece record the message.

"No." He shook his head and then slowly started to nod.

"I think the party intensity has a direct coordination to the closeness of the friends that are going."

"Explain, please."

Michelle leaned back in her chair. "Well, if the bride has a handful of really close friends and, let's say, a strip club is involved . . . well, those parties are often forever remembered and only talked about by those that were there."

"What happens in Vegas?"

"Right. Now, if there is a large party, a dozen or more, things tend to be a little more politically correct. No one wants rumors to get started right before a wedding. Truth is the bride almost never does anything crazy . . . but the single girls, or those that have been married forever, those women tend to go nuts. Like a bachelorette party is a permission slip for impropriety. I bet the women have a better time than the guys do. Men get drunk and watch a woman dancing on a pole. Women get tipsy and pay for lap dances for their friends."

"Sounds dangerous."

"Sounds fun. I haven't been out on a night like that in years." Michelle drifted off in her own thoughts.

The images pixelating in Liam's head started to come into focus. He could see Avery being the life of the party. He also envisioned her putting a guy in his place if he went too far.

Unless she wanted him to go far . . .

He had no hold on her. So why was he thinking about what she was doing and whom she was doing it with?

"Do you know where the party is?"

He shook his head. "Somewhere in Texas."

"Texas?"

"Yeah, her friend lives in Texas."

Michelle scooted her textbook closer. "I can't help you with Texas. I would imagine there'll be men dressed in boots and hats and little else." She sighed. "I like that idea."

Liam moaned.

Michelle kept her eyes on the pages in front of her while she spoke. "You know the best way to make sure a woman isn't surfing for a date other than you?"

"What's that?"

"Text her, call her . . . tell her to have a good time and that you're thinking about her."

"Sounds too easy."

"If she's at all thinking about you as much as you're obviously thinking of her, and you reach out . . . chances are she'll avoid the private lap dances."

"Private?"

"Yeah, the kind where they ask if you want to go to a private room."

Liam stopped smiling. "They do that?"

Michelle looked up long enough to roll her eyes. "Where have you been?"

Liam reached for the phone in his back pocket and stepped out into the backyard.

Currently onstage, the Cowboy Connection was living up to his name. Avery had to appreciate a man wearing chaps with a thong underneath.

"That man can move," Andrea, one of Trina's aunts-in-law from her first marriage, was well on her way to being sloshed. She and her sister, Diane, were screaming the loudest and tipping the most. It was hysterical to watch. For once Avery wasn't kicking back drink after drink. While she wouldn't currently get behind the wheel of a car, she wasn't drunk. Even Shannon seemed to be a few more ahead of her than normal.

Their waiters, all wearing next to nothing, kept coming by their party to pour their drinks and flirt. Now that they'd been in the woman-filled room for an hour, and the crowd had grown considerably, the noise level was close to deafening. Avery decided it was time for some bride attention.

Once Mr. Cowboy finished his set and his chaps had found their way to the side of the stage, Avery flagged over their concierge. At that moment, two of the best dancers flanked Trina and took her to the stage.

"Oh, no."

"Oh, yes!"

Trina didn't put up much of a fight. Blushing and more than a little tipsy, Trina sat center stage.

"Welcome Trina to the stage."

Their party cheered the loudest.

"You're looking a little nervous, darlin'."

Trina couldn't talk. She was too busy smiling.

"When is the big day?" Stud Number Two asked.

"Next Saturday," she said into the microphone.

"That gives us plenty of time," Stud Number One said.

The music started, and the men turned on like a switch had been thrown.

Like something out of *Magic Mike*, there was flesh, and push-ups . . . and taking Trina out of the chair and laying her on a bench. She would reach out when encouraged, and laughed with the fun of it all.

Somewhere in the middle of Trina's wedding dance, Avery felt her phone buzz in her pocket.

Flushed and slightly embarrassed, Trina left the stage and dropped into her chair. "I'm going to make that up to you," she told Avery.

"I look forward to it."

"Where were you guys when I was getting married?" Andrea said.

"In elementary school?" Lori teased.

Avery moved back to the man in charge of their party and pulled out her wallet. With lap dances ordered for them, the married women offered weak protests and then gave in.

Lost in watching, Avery felt her phone buzz again.

She checked the number and smiled. "Hold on," she told Liam after she picked up. Avery moved to a balcony, where some women congregated to smoke or just escape the noise for a few minutes. "Hey," she said once she could hear him.

"Sounds like quite the party."

"We're having a night to remember."

"Really? I've never been to a bachelorette party."

"That's because you're not a stripper." She peeked through the glass.

"I thought only men went to strip clubs."

"You'd be wrong."

"My sister corrected me."

Avery smiled at the thought of him asking his sister about the shenanigans of women at a prewedding party.

"So why are you calling, Liam?"

"Uhm . . . well," he stuttered. "To say I was . . ."

"Checking on me?" He was totally checking on her.

"Of course not."

"I don't believe you." Avery leaned against the wall, her back to the door.

He paused. "I'm thinking about you."

Avery fell silent, her heart skipped a beat. "You knew I was out with the girls."

"Yeah. I won't keep you. I was thinking about you and wanted to let you know."

Did she tell him she had thought about him multiple times during the night? Like when one of the bigger strippers had managed a back-flip on the stage while taking off his Velcro shorts. The image of Liam bending over backward had her grinning.

"There you are." Trina's voice penetrated Avery's brain. In a few steps, she was beside Avery, hands on hips. "Who are you talking to?"

"I've got to go," Avery told Liam.

"That's him, is-isn't it?" Trina slurred her last words.

When Avery didn't comment, Trina reached for her phone.

Avery attempted to grab it back and gave up when Trina put the phone to her ear. "Is this Liam?"

Trina grinned like a kid. "Uh-huh . . ." She pulled the phone away from her ear. "He sounds cute."

Avery tried to grab her phone again, failed. "What are we, thirteen?"

With her ear back to the phone, Trina went on. "I'm not drunk. Okay, maybe a little. Oh, don't worry. My fiancé's bodyguard is right outside." She pulled the phone away from her face again. "He's worried about me. Isn't that sweet?"

"Give me the phone." Avery placed her palm out.

Trina lifted a finger in the air. "You're coming to the wedding, right?"

Avery's jaw dropped.

"Well, consider yourself invited. I can't wait to meet you."

Avery mouthed the words *I'm going to kill you.*

"Oh, good," Trina said. "Okay, I'm going to give the phone back to Avery and hide. Nice chatting with you."

Avery yanked the phone from Trina's hands.

"You're welcome," Trina said before disappearing behind the door and into the club.

"She's drunk," Avery told Liam.

"I like your friend."

"Good thing I do, too, or I'd kill her."

"Is there really a bodyguard there?"

Avery thought about Jeb. "Yes."

"I feel better."

"Because I can't take care of myself?"

"Someone is jumping to conclusions again. No . . . I of all people know you can fend for yourself. But a gaggle of drinking females always gathers the attention of drinking males. And since I'm a couple of states away, it's nice to know someone has your back."

"Oh." He really was sweet.

Someone knocked on the glass, jerking her attention back to the party.

Lori waved her back inside.

"I have to go. I'm in charge and need to order more lap dances."

"Lap dances, huh?"

"Yes. Where almost naked men strut and women scream."

"You're torturing me."

"I am? I'm sorry."

"No, you're not."

Avery opened the door to the club, and the thump of the bass strangled their conversation.

"You're right. I'm not. I'll text you later and let you know if we need bail money." She hung up.

"Avery! Get your blonde butt over here and say hi to my friend," Lori yelled.

It was Avery's turn for the dancing cowboy in a leather Speedo.

Chapter Fourteen

It took twenty-four hours to sober Trina up enough to send her off with her fiancé and for Avery to fly back to LA. Avery scrambled to cram a full work week into three days and agreed to meet with Liam for a sparring match during her Tuesday krav session. He'd checked in with her twice since the strip club: once after she'd sent him a text with the local sheriff's department's phone number as a hoax, saying he could find her there for the next seventy-two hours, and the other time after she'd gotten off her flight back into LA on Sunday night. Now she was racing from her condo to the studio, determined to be on time.

She was five minutes late.

"You're making a habit of this, Grant," Brenda snarled at the door.

Liam caught her attention with his smile.

Was it her, or had his shoulders grown in the week they'd not seen each other?

"How was your date?" Avery asked Brenda in an effort to change the subject.

"Your warm-up is on the board."

Already dressed in spandex, Avery dropped her gym bag at the door and lifted her arms over her head to stretch as she walked farther into the room. "Hey."

"Hey back. You look surprisingly vertical, considering the weekend."

Avery glanced at the warm-up. *Fifty burpees . . . again?*

She sat on the mat, put her legs out in front of her, and reached for her toes. "I wasn't the one who was toasted. That was Trina. And Lori, surprisingly."

"Lori the lawyer?"

"Yup. She almost never lets loose that way." Finished with her stretches, Avery stood to start her routine. "Are you finished with the burpees?"

"Haven't started."

"Waiting for me?"

He lowered his voice. "If I finished before you got here, I'd be forced to watch you do yours." His eyes traveled the length of her. "That's distracting."

Heat traveled up her neck.

"Less talking. More doing!" Brenda yelled from her office.

Avery jumped in the air and then shot to the ground for a push-up. "I'm going to buy that woman a T-shirt that says that."

Liam followed her burpee lead.

An hour and a half later they were at Pug's, settled in a back booth.

"I think your client would be an idiot not to remodel that house and get as much as he can for it."

Liam had given her an estimate with a lot of zeros.

"That's what I came up with. The real estate agent I spoke with is already encouraging the owner to fix the place up."

"Does he have the capital to do the work?"

Avery thought the question was comical. "There's enough wealth inside the house to renovate it three times over. If he didn't have money in the bank, and I'm sure he does, he could wait for the auctions to close to fund the job. I don't think it's about money as much as it is painful memories in the house."

"That's too bad. It looks like it could have been a great place to grow up."

"Looks can be deceiving."

"You say that like you know the feeling."

"I do. If something happened to my parents tomorrow, I'd hire someone like me to do the work and get rid of that house as soon as I could."

"That bad?"

"I never measured up to my parents. I didn't follow the rules as a teenager, bucked the private schools they shoved me into. The therapist they made me see said I was looking for their positive attention. Which as an adult I can completely agree with, but it didn't work. Eventually all I seemed to do was hurt myself instead of them."

Liam reached a hand out and covered hers. "I'm sorry."

"Not your fault."

"I can't imagine not having parents who adore their children and shower them with affection."

"One lunch with my parents and you'll know what that looks like."

Liam ran the pad of his thumb over the inside of her palm. "I look forward to it."

"That wasn't an invitation."

He rubbed a little harder. "Sounded like it to me."

It was distracting . . . this thumb rubbing, hand-holding thing he was doing.

"I already told you I'm not the kind of woman you date."

He stopped rubbing until she met his eyes.

"And why is that, Avery? Are you afraid the affection you seek won't be reciprocated, like from your parents?"

His words were uncomfortably accurate.

She pulled her hand out from under his.

Liam's smile faded. "I shouldn't have said that."

One vertebra at a time, Avery's spine sat taller and her defiant chin came up. "That would have hurt more if there wasn't a sprinkling of truth."

"Still wasn't my place to say it. I'm sorry."

He looked it.

It was time to make damn sure Liam knew who he was trying to date.

"I was married."

He kept his eyes focused. "Are you now?"

"No."

"Then I don't care."

"Even my ex-husband will tell you I married him for his money."

Liam kept silent, eyes straight.

"When we split, I was given five million dollars and my condo."

"Did your ex end up on the street?"

She smiled, not helping herself. The thought of Bernie on the street, wearing Armani and holding a cardboard sign, made her laugh. "Not hardly."

"Everyone has a past."

"I snore." Which was once true, but after the nose job, not so much.

"Like a trucker. You told me." Liam sat forward and placed both hands over hers and held them tight. "Now let's talk about this friend's wedding."

～⌒～

It was Liam's turn to scramble. "You sure you have Cassandra covered for your shift on Saturday?"

Michelle stood in the doorway of his bedroom, watching as he packed for the weekend.

"We're good."

Liam zipped up a garment bag carrying a suit. He owned two, one for the occasional wedding or funeral, and the other he used when meeting with the city or client functions required more than a shirt and jeans.

"Is it an outdoor wedding?"

"I have no idea."

"Do you know the bride or groom?"

"Nope. Friends of Avery's."

Michelle crossed her arms over her chest. "How did you end up getting a ticket on the same flight?"

Liam closed the suitcase and zipped it up. "Avery said there were extra seats. I'm guessing that means they'd booked them for people that can't come."

"Sounds fancy."

It did. But he wasn't backing out now. Not when he'd finally managed to have Avery add him as her plus-one.

He looked at the time and pulled out his phone to order an Uber to the airport.

"I can drive you."

"This is fine. You'll get stuck in traffic coming back."

He gathered his luggage and kissed his sister's cheek. Out in the living room, Cassandra jumped off the couch to hug his leg. "Bring me back some cake."

He kissed the top of her head. "I'll see what I can do."

Without any more fanfare, his niece peeled herself off his leg and returned to the dolls she was playing with.

"Have fun," Michelle said as he walked out the door.

"I will." Or at least he hoped he would.

Thirty minutes later, the driver dropped him off in front of terminal three. Even with the huge sunglasses covering her eyes, he recognized Avery standing outside the doors, watching for him. She wore a short, peach colored dress and white boots that went up to her knees. The outfit was like nothing he'd seen her in before.

The woman had many sides, each of them just as fascinating as the last.

Outside the car, he rolled his suitcase to her side and stopped. "Love the outfit."

She hiked her sunglasses up to look him in the eye. "The short skirt or the tall boots?"

"Both."

She tilted her glasses back onto her nose. "You sure you're ready for this?" she asked him.

Liam ignored the people whizzing past. "The question is, are you?"

"No." She shook her head. "But my friends wouldn't shut up and you weren't helping."

"I like your friends." They seemed to be on his side already.

Avery shook her head and turned toward the doors. "I don't think you're ready for this, but here goes nothing."

He grasped her arm before she could take a step.

"Second thoughts?" she asked.

He moved his hand up to the back of her neck and pulled her in. "None."

Liam kissed her doubting lips long enough for her to sigh and kiss him back. Only then did he let her go.

He pulled his luggage behind him and held her hand as they walked into the terminal.

Avery led them past the ticket gates and toward what looked like an exclusive lounge. "Are your friends here?"

"They're already on the plane."

"They're what?" He must have got that wrong.

Liam couldn't say he'd ever had the need for a private airport lounge, so this was a first. They walked through the double sliding doors to be greeted by a smiling hostess. "Hello, Ms. Grant. You must be Mr. Holt."

Definitely a first. "I am."

"TSA is ready for you. Do you have any more luggage?"

He shook his head. "No. This is it."

"I'll show him the way," Avery told the woman.

Liam walked further down the rabbit hole.

They waltzed through the lounge and down a nearly empty hall. At the end was a metal detector and a conveyer belt for his luggage. The TSA officer stood by the metal detector with a smile. "ID?"

"Right." Liam removed his wallet and presented his driver's license while Avery walked through the metal detector.

He started to toe off his shoes.

"That isn't necessary, Mr. Holt. Just put your phone through and any keys in your pockets."

Less than twenty seconds later, Avery and Liam were being escorted out of the terminal and into a waiting car.

"Are we driving to Texas?"

Avery smirked. "You can back out anytime."

Everything came into focus when the car stopped next to a private jet and Avery stepped out.

Holy shit.

The driver from the car took Liam's luggage before he could grab it.

He stood looking up at the plane like it was a new invention.

"You're serious."

Avery took two steps up the stairs and turned toward him. "You coming?"

෬

Avery took the final step into the private jet and wanted to glare at her friends, who had choreographed Liam's being there. She noticed Shannon's eyes light up when Liam stepped through the door and exhaled.

"You've met Lori and Reed."

Reed stepped forward and shook Liam's hand. "Nice to see you again."

"I'm glad to be here."

Lori smiled and shook his hand. "I'm still unsure if you're a stalker."

"Hopefully I'll squelch that thought by the end of the weekend."

Avery stood back. "And this is Shannon."

Liam held a look of confusion. "Do I know you?"

"Shannon Wentworth. Former first lady of California, now making a name for herself in the world of photography." Avery's introduction made Shannon blush.

"I'm not sure about that world thing, but the rest of it is accurate."

"A pleasure," Liam said.

"Oh, the pleasure is all ours. Avery hasn't invited a male friend into the fold, ever."

Avery crossed to the bar and poured a glass of champagne. "Like I had a choice. First Trina drunkenly snags my phone and extends the invite, and then this one doesn't let it go." She pointed to Liam, who appeared pleased with himself.

"Avery frazzled is a good look," Lori said.

"I am not . . ." Yes, she was. "Whatever. I hope you and Reed get along," she said directly to Liam. "This weekend is about Trina."

"You've warned me," Liam said.

Reed patted Liam on the back. "Well, now that we got that little tantrum out of the way, how about a drink before we take off?"

"Beer is fine."

Liam did a complete turn and took in the space.

It wasn't the largest private jet Avery had been on, nor the smallest. There were half a dozen executive chairs that reclined into a comfortable sleeping position, a sofa, a TV, a bar, and of course, a bathroom.

"Do you guys always travel like this?"

"Every weekend," Avery exaggerated.

Shannon sat back down. "Don't listen to her. No. We don't. Trina insisted."

"The bride."

"Yes."

"This is pretty spectacular. Who is she marrying?"

The cabin went silent. All eyes traveled to Avery.

"Did you tell him anything?"

"I told him what time to be here."

Reed chuckled and handed Liam a beer. "Do you listen to country music?"

Chapter Fifteen

Liam really thought that Avery's strong protest of him not knowing what he was getting into had been nothing but smoke.

He was wrong.

Private planes and rubbing elbows with political wives . . . okay, ex-wife. Still, he didn't think he had more room for new experiences until Reed informed him that he'd be attending the Texas wedding of the century. That might be an exaggeration, but Wade Thomas? His face, and that of his bride, had been pasted all over the tabloids at the checkout stands for weeks.

For once he was bummed he hadn't picked up the magazine his sister had sitting on the end table in his living room to check it out. He might have put a few dots together if he had. Trina wasn't a common name, and a wedding in Texas . . . Who was he kidding? He wouldn't have figured it out.

It became painfully clear that this was not the first time this gaggle of friends had been on a private jet. Not every time, Shannon had said. But oftentimes. It appeared that Avery had been known to pay for the things. Who did that?

Who was she really? He started to wonder if his blowing off her telling him she'd married for money was a mistake.

If money made her tick, then why was she wasting her time with him? He did okay, moderately better than okay, but he hadn't so much as sprung for a first-class ticket, let alone a private jet.

When the jet landed and they were picked up by a stretch limo and carted off the tarmac like the president, Liam ditched all hope of paying his way for any of this.

They arrived at Wade Thomas's ranch, where the roads leading to it were lined with media and photographers wanting pictures of the bride and groom.

Their party was escorted beyond the gates and down the tree-lined road.

"Incredible, isn't it?" Reed offered.

"I've never seen anything like it."

"Today is about immediate family and friends. The rehearsal and the dinner . . . and then we're taking Trina into one of the guesthouses for the night," Avery reminded him.

"Down-to-earth people with money. Don't let it get to you," Reed told him.

Too late.

As he thought the words, Avery, who was sitting next to him in the limo, reached out and placed her hand over his.

His world, which had started to tilt off-kilter, began to settle.

He turned his eyes to hers, squeezed her hand, and smiled.

They pulled up to the main house and climbed out one at a time. "Holy wow." He'd have to be blind not to be impressed. Massive beams spanned a front porch that you could put his entire home under.

"Don't let me drool," he whispered to Avery.

He loved hearing her laugh.

"You're here!" A woman's voice echoed through the open front doors.

"Did you think we would miss it?" Shannon asked.

Liam stood back while Trina hugged and giggled and smiled more than any woman he'd ever seen. When her attention landed on him, she pulled in a quick breath. "Oh my God, you're Liam."

"I am." He put his hand out, which she ignored, pulling him into a hug. "I can't believe she let you come."

"Me either," he confessed.

"Oh, good Lord," Avery sighed. "I'm not that bad."

A chorus of "Yes, you are" ensued.

Trina walked them into the foyer, and once again Liam was lost in the architecture.

"Sounds like the wedding party has arrived."

Liam turned to find a living, breathing celebrity walking down the stairs to greet them.

Play it cool.

Wade shook Reed's hand and hugged the women before offering a smile to Liam.

"Look who Avery brought," Trina told her fiancé. "Liam, this is Wade."

"I can't believe the blonde pit bull caved," he said, grinning as he shook Liam's hand. The handshake said a lot.

"Blonde pit bull?" Liam questioned.

"Long story," Avery offered.

"Not that long. She hated me," Wade told him. "Said I wasn't good enough for Trina. Which might be true, but that didn't stop me."

"He exaggerates."

Wade lifted a hand in the air. "Can I have a witness?"

Shannon, Lori, and Trina joined the hand waving.

"Good thing I like you now, Cowboy."

Wade dropped a hand over Avery's shoulders and pulled them into the great room.

Avery had to admit, even to herself, that she was a little unnerved by how well Liam adapted to the group. They'd been placed in different parts of the house, mainly because Trina, Shannon, Lori, and Avery had already planned on spending the two days leading up to the wedding doing all the girl things that needed one more round before Trina took the plunge . . . again.

Within an hour of arriving, the four of them were whisked off for some spa time.

While sitting in crisp white spa robes with their feet soaking, they sipped wine and gossiped.

"Is Vicki behaving?" Avery asked Trina about her soon to be mother-in-law.

"She's been quiet."

"Is that good?" Shannon asked.

Trina shrugged. "I'm tired of trying to figure that woman out. One minute I think things are fine, and the next I swear she's powdering my sugar cookies with arsenic."

"Let it go. She'll come around when she realizes there isn't any going back," Lori advised.

"So, Sunday?"

They all laughed.

Avery pulled her foot out of the pulsating water so the woman doing her pedicure could make her toes shine.

"Liam seems like a really nice guy," Trina told Avery.

"Which begs the question what he wants with me."

"Where did all this negativity come from?" Lori asked. "What happened to the self-assured woman who marched into my office before Bernie and said, and I quote, 'He's lucky to have me. Let's do this.'?"

"That was different."

"How?"

"It had an end date," Avery said without thinking.

"And Liam doesn't?" Shannon prompted.

"Of course he does. I just don't know when that is." She switched feet for the technician. "Saturday night dates end on Sunday . . . weekend dates end Monday morning. Liam isn't shaking."

"That's a good thing," Trina said.

"It's because we haven't had sex."

"What?" Lori asked.

Avery glanced at the three sets of eyes on her. "I know, right? He's kissed me three times, and that's it. It's not like I haven't encouraged it."

"He's into you." The technician, who Avery didn't think was listening, added her two cents.

"I think she's right."

"Or he's gay. Could go either way."

"He's not gay," Avery told the virtual stranger.

"I don't think that's the case," Shannon said. "The way he looks at you is anything but platonic."

"You've known him for what, five hours?"

"Which is the normal time span of your dates, Avery. Maybe you should try and stop worrying about when it will end and enjoy what you have going on now."

Avery glared at Lori. "He's here, isn't he?"

"Bridesmaids always get lucky. I bet he doesn't bolt after."

Avery didn't offer a comment.

"I didn't get lucky at Lori's wedding," Shannon said.

"Let's try and fix that this weekend." Avery leaned back to enjoy her foot massage.

"This I want to see," Lori added.

Chapter Sixteen

Avery said he wouldn't see her . . . and she wasn't kidding.

Liam found his time filled with Reed, Wade, and two of the guys from Wade's band. There were plenty of marital tips offered, a lot of beer, and food. So much food. Liam wondered how the men in Texas stayed in their Levi's.

The ranch was a massive venue setting up for a colossal wedding.

On Friday, during the rehearsal, Liam stood back and watched as the wedding coordinator directed Avery and the others in their duties.

Wade made time with his future wife when they pretended that the minister had announced them husband and wife.

Trina's father gave Wade a hard time, entertaining the small crowd.

When Avery walked back down the aisle, this time on the arm of Wade's best man, a stab of jealousy smacked Liam's brain.

He reminded himself that the other guy was married.

That didn't stop Liam from swooping in as soon as the opportunity presented itself.

"Looks like everything is set for tomorrow."

"I don't think they forgot anything."

They took a seat in the back row of the chairs set up for the next day. "Let me know if there is anything I can do."

She blinked as she looked at him. "Are you having a good time?"

"Weddings are always an adventure."

"Adventure sounds like drama."

He shook his head. "None of that from what I can see."

She turned back to look at the bride and groom, who were talking with the minister. "Let's hope it stays that way. Trina deserves her day."

Liam had heard through some of the conversation around him that Trina's first husband had died. No one had elaborated on the details, and he didn't feel at liberty to ask.

"At my sister's wedding, my brother-in-law got hammered."

"You're kidding."

"Fall down, pour him into the car drunk. Michelle told me it took him two days to sober up."

"What an ass," Avery said.

"Yeah. They're divorced now. Took her some time to get over him."

"Trina cared for her late husband, but it wasn't anything like her love for Wade. Which is a blessing, all things considered."

Liam took the opening to learn a little more. "Reed implied that he died."

Avery kept her eyes glued in front of her. "Killed by his own dad. Doesn't get more dramatic than that."

Chills ran up his arms. "You're kidding."

"Nope. It was all over the papers last year." She nodded toward the mother of the groom, who stood to the side of where the ceremony was going to take place the next day. "Vicki didn't heed the threats of Trina's former father-in-law and ended up kidnapped. I think that's why she's so butt hurt about Trina. Not that any of it was Trina's fault."

"Kidnapping and murder?"

"Money does crazy things to people."

He sighed. "Makes me happy I don't have much."

Avery grinned. "You didn't like the private jet?"

"I didn't say that. But not at the risk of someone killing someone I loved for it."

"Those are the risks when dating someone who has a big bank account."

Liam rested his arm around Avery's shoulders. "Trying to scare me off again?"

"Stating facts."

"I've been warned."

She turned to him then, eyes stoic. "You're really okay with all of this?"

"The wedding?" he asked, confused.

"Not just the wedding. The jets, the private cars, celebrities?"

"The question isn't if I'm okay with it so much as are you? I can't compete with any of this, so there's no use trying. Doesn't mean I can't buy a meal or a round or two."

She offered a soft smile.

"I've been crushing on you long before I realized this was in your back pocket."

That smile grew. "Crushing?"

"What's the matter, hasn't anyone ever crushed on you before?"

"Maybe in junior high."

He envisioned short skirts and attitude. "I bet you had all the boys wrapped."

"What do you mean, *had*?"

Liam leaned his head back and laughed.

༄

Saturday was a blur. Twice Avery flushed out Liam to check on him, even though she told him she wouldn't. Between bridesmaid duties and the chaos of getting ready for such a big event, Avery had a hard time breathing.

When the hour finally came and Shannon, Lori, and Avery surrounded Trina right before walking down the aisle, there were misty eyes all around.

Trina wore her dark, long hair down and draped to the side. Her slim-fitted dress was a bright contrast to her dark complexion. The off the shoulder neckline matched that of her bridal party's dresses.

Avery and the girls wore dusty gray three-quarter-length gowns by Ralph Lauren, with shoes that would be a part of Avery's collection for years. They'd made a pact when Lori had married that the bridesmaids' dresses would probably be mothballed in six months, but the shoes had to last. So far, Avery was pleased with her collection.

Even though the venue was closed to the public, that didn't stop security from being everywhere.

A massive canopy had been lifted above the outside seating for the ceremony to discourage media helicopters from flying overhead. Not that it completely stopped the paparazzi from trying.

Avery poked her head around the corner of the courtyard and took in the guests. "That's a lot of people," she said to the girls.

The wedding coordinator slipped around the corner. "You ladies ready?"

Avery turned to Trina and her father.

Trina offered a thumbs-up.

Music quieted the guests, and Wade and his groomsmen made their way to the spotlight.

One at a time, Shannon and Lori slowly preceded Trina to the front of the celebrity packed crowd.

When it was Avery's turn, she painted on a smile and concentrated on walking slowly. She spotted Liam next to Reed and a few of their friends. Even through the mass of people, she read Liam's lips as he mouthed the word *beautiful*.

Her cheeks grew hot and her eyes lowered to the ground as she walked past him.

No matter how good she might look, nothing would upstage what came next.

The second Trina rounded the corner, Avery heard Wade's heartfelt swish of air escape from his lungs. She turned to look at the groom and saw tears in his eyes. For the first time in well over a year, Avery felt moisture sting the backs of hers. The love Wade had for her friend was palpable. In that moment, she knew this was a marriage that would last.

Thirty-eight minutes later, after Trina and Wade had delivered their own vows to each other and the minister had given his blessing, and all the *I do*s and *kiss the bride* were over, Avery sighed as if she had been the one getting married.

She had two minutes to breathe while she signed as a witness on their marriage certificate and kissed the bride and groom. Then they were whisked off for pictures.

Liam stood to the side and brought her a glass of champagne.

"You took my breath away," he told her.

She touched his tie. "You clean up pretty well yourself." Most men in suits did nothing for her. Her father had worn one every day to work, and Bernie never went anywhere without one. She couldn't remember if Bernie owned a T-shirt. Probably not. Liam, on the other hand, filled his out perfectly. Avery wondered what he would look like in a suit tailored only for him.

"Avery?"

She handed Liam her wine and moved beside the wedding party and smiled for the camera.

Trina had opted for an oversize round table to accommodate their wedding party and significant others. Considering Avery hadn't seen much of Liam the entire weekend, it was nice to have him sitting next to her instead of across the tent next to some Kardashian wannabe.

Food rolled out in courses, and she knew from experience that if they didn't eat quickly, the guests would descend and make it hard to chew.

"Did you help with the guest list?" Liam asked close to her ear.

"I did."

He glanced over his shoulder. "Is that Steven Tyler?"

Avery lifted a fork to her lips. "Yup."

"Doesn't that make you a little giddy?"

She looked again. "Sure does."

"I'd love to know the story of how Wade and him met."

Without missing a beat, Avery lifted her voice. "Hey, Wade . . . how did you meet Steven Tyler?"

Liam nudged her under the table.

"The Grammys. Three years ago. Had a complete fan moment backstage, and we've been friends ever since."

"What does a Wade Thomas fan moment look like?" Reed asked.

"There was stuttering involved. It wasn't pretty."

"Good to know you're not unaffected," Liam told him.

"This guy was a complete dork for years once we went big," Gus, Wade's best man, said.

"I'm much better at playing it cool now."

During their limited dinner conversation, Avery sensed Liam start to relax.

Once the dinner plates left the table and settings were in place for cake later in the evening, Avery and Liam mingled around the room and were introduced to dozens of people. Reed stood by a tall, olive skinned woman she'd never met before. He motioned them over when he caught her staring.

"I don't think you've met Sasha."

The woman wore Versace. The black dress stuck to her like a glove. The angle and cut crossed over the front of her body in an asymmetrical way that only a woman as lean and fit as this one could pull off. Avery had instant arm envy. The woman didn't appear to have an ounce of fat on her.

"I have not. I'm Avery." They shook hands.

"I know." Her exotic voice matched her dress. "You must be Liam Holt."

"I am." He seemed as surprised to hear his name coming from her lips as Avery was.

"Sasha is Trina's late husband's half sister," Avery explained to Liam. She'd leave the rest of the woman's significance in Trina's life for a later conversation.

Sasha had played an intricate role in stopping Ruslan Petrov from hiring any more killers to cover up his crimes. *Intricate* meant being nearly killed by the man's hands while the authorities rushed in at the last minute and put a bullet in him. If it wasn't for her, he would have fled and still been alive to cause misery and pain to Trina and everyone she held dear. Including Avery.

"I feel the need to thank you," Avery said.

"That isn't necessary."

"Sasha is occasionally helping with our security team, so hopefully we can convince her to join us outside of work."

"That would be great, and you can tell me where you got that dress. Versace, right?"

"Paris." A woman of one-word answers.

"It's stunning."

"Thank you. If you'll excuse me." And she was gone.

Reed moved closer once she walked away. "I'm surprised she came."

"She's intense" was Liam's take on the woman.

"I don't remember putting her down on the table assignments," Avery said.

"She refused. Said she would witness the wedding, blend in at the reception, and drill security to make sure they were doing their job while everyone ate." Reed glanced around the room.

"And is security doing a good job?" Liam asked.

Reed looked down his nose at him. "Our team never fails."

Liam patted Reed's back. "I feel safer."

"Good to know. Now let me find my wife. I wanna dance."

Later, after Avery delivered a toast alongside Gus, and the obligatory wedding party dance after Trina and Wade took the stage, Liam claimed her as his for the rest of the night.

He lost his tie, ditched the jacket, and swung her around the dance floor.

There wasn't any of the bumping and grinding that went along with the club scene here. Just good moves with dips and turns for the rock and roll, and plenty of line dancing and two-stepping when the country hits were sung.

Flushed and breathless, Avery pleaded to step away from the crowd.

Liam tugged her hand toward the back of the covered dance floor and out into the night.

"You're crazy out there."

He did a little shuffle. "Love to dance."

"I can tell."

Liam slid a hand around her waist and swung her in a circle when some of the other guests walked by.

Avery glanced at them and laughed.

"I think that was Faith and Tim."

Liam wasn't listening. He wrapped his arms around her waist and walked behind her until they were on the edge of the manicured outdoor space, overlooking the moonlit valley below.

"Beautiful, isn't it?" Avery said once they stopped walking.

"Peaceful. I managed to take a walk before everything started today. Wade has quite the spread."

"Texas has grown on me a little," Avery admitted. "But I wouldn't want to live here."

"City girl?"

"I like where I live. But I don't think I'll be there forever."

She felt Liam's breath against her ear.

"Where else would you go?"

"Somewhere, anywhere. What about you? Ever wanted to live somewhere different?"

"I haven't really thought about it. My family is close by, my business is in LA."

She held his arms, which wrapped around her shoulders, keeping the cool evening air away from her bare skin. "I guess that's the difference between a close family and what I have."

"Is it really that bad?"

Avery thought about the measures she'd gone through, marrying Bernie for a short, contracted time for a massive payoff to get out from under her parents' financial thumbs. "It's not good."

"My sister and I are eleven months apart. For a long time people thought we were twins. You'll love her, and Cassandra . . . that kid has my number."

"How often do you see them?"

Liam laughed. "They live with me."

Avery leaned back to look at him. "Really?"

"Michelle's ex left without financial support. She was out of choices. Not that she needed to ask. I offered."

"What about your parents? Couldn't she move in with them?"

Liam's smile faded. "My mother has Alzheimer's."

"I'm so sorry."

He kissed the top of her head. "It's okay. Right after Cassandra was born, she was diagnosed. It's been a slow, steady decline. My dad kept up with her care for a while, but last year we had to hire help during the day so he could work. He encouraged my sister to move in with him, but the stress of a five-year-old is too much day in and day out."

"I can't imagine."

He tilted his head. "My parents love us unconditionally and with every ounce of their being. I can't imagine that you've lived a life without that anchor."

"Don't feel sorry for me. It no longer rules me. Do I wish it was different? Yes. But it isn't. Now I take my parents in small doses and leave when it's unbearable."

Liam turned her around and rested his hands around her waist. "They're missing out. You're a special lady."

"You hardly know me."

"That's changing rapidly. Besides, if I wasn't figuring that out on my own, your friends have all told me."

"They're biased."

He brushed his hand along her chin and watched his fingers as he traced them down her neck and shoulder. The touch was more intimate than if they were naked and skin to skin.

Avery shivered.

"Are you cold?"

"No."

His eyes smiled, and he leaned closer and touched his lips to hers.

Avery closed her eyes and melted. Like every time he kissed her, there wasn't a rush or any urgency. Only the movement of his mouth on hers, the slow request for her to open and let him inside. Her body quivered and her mind went blank.

What was it about this man that was so different from any other? Was it the fact that he wasn't rushing? Or maybe it was the way he slowly ran his hands over her back, as if he were memorizing her. Maybe the difference was how much she knew about him. Since before Bernie, she hadn't bothered to know more than a first name and a short sexual history. Family history and desires for the future only shortened the time she spent with the previous men in her life.

This one was different.

Liam was different.

Following his leisurely pace, Avery stroked his back and squeezed his shoulders when he nipped at her bottom lip. He heated every cell that begged for his attention.

His fingers squeezed her hips but didn't move lower. As the bases went, he hadn't rounded second, and she wanted a home run in the worst way.

Avery pressed closer and knew without any doubt Liam had all the working parts fired up and ready.

Unlike the man holding her, she let her hands drop lower on his hips until his firm ass filled her palms.

Liam stalled, his mouth open over hers, eyes closed. "Careful, Princess."

The huskiness of his voice empowered her. "Why?"

He gripped her hips and brought her as close as two standing bodies, fully clothed, could get. "My control is painfully close to snapping."

"Have you considered that I might want that?"

Liam opened his smoky eyes. "I didn't force my hand at you bringing me here for this."

She lifted her hand from his butt to his hip. "I know that, Liam."

There was something he wasn't saying; she could see it in his gaze.

Noise from the reception cut in through the night. "Now isn't the time," he told her.

She wanted to argue but knew he was right. Avery swallowed and shifted her weight.

His grip stopped her. "Never think, for one second, that I don't want you. That I haven't dreamt of peeling each layer of your clothing off your skin and kissing every bare spot until you can't take the torture any longer."

Her chest lifted with every short breath she took.

He pressed his lips to hers, eyes wide open.

"You're not like any man I've ever met," she whispered when he released her lips.

Liam smiled as if she'd just given him a gift. "Good."

⁓

Monday was met with a gallon of coffee and a hard-on.

"You mean to tell me you were at Wade Thomas's ranch the whole weekend?" Michelle stared at him across the table at six in the morning.

"I was."

"Holy cow. Who is this woman you're dating?"

Are we dating?

"Avery Grant." He wondered if that was her maiden name or her ex's.

"Do you have a picture of her?"

Liam fired up his phone and pulled up a text from Shannon. She'd added him to a group text where she'd sent a dozen pictures taken over the weekend.

He pulled up a shot from during the rehearsal dinner and twisted his phone toward his sister.

Michelle squealed. "Oh my God! That *is* Wade Thomas."

Sipping his coffee, he said, "Avery is the blonde standing next to me."

His sister expanded the picture on the phone and glanced at him. "She's gorgeous."

"I noticed that."

"Her skin is flawless. What is she, twenty-fourish?"

Liam thought about that for a second, did a little math based on the timeline of her past. "I think she's in her early thirties."

"Kids?"

"No."

"Ever married?"

"Once."

134

Michelle zoomed out and flipped through the pictures on the thread. "That's good."

"Is it?"

"Yeah. A woman previously married isn't rushing to put a ring back on and makes a better decision the second time around."

Liam opened his mouth to comment and Michelle cut him off.

"But thirty . . . her clock is ticking."

Liam thought about Avery's lifestyle. "I don't think so."

Michelle looked at him like he was missing a few brain cells.

He avoided the argument and stood to refill his coffee. He had a long weekend's worth of pushed aside work to get to.

"Who is this?"

He glanced at his phone. "Shannon."

"She looks like a movie star. Is she?"

"Ex-wife of Paul Wentworth."

Michelle did a double take. "The governor?"

"Yup."

"What an idiot."

Yeah, that's what Liam thought.

Michelle grinned and hiked a brow. "Looks like someone wants to say good morning to you."

Liam snatched his phone from his sister and opened his messages. It was Avery.

I hope you slept well.

He considered lying.

Tossed and turned all night. You?

He sipped his coffee and waited for her reply.

Like a baby.

He shook his head.

Liar.

Good thing I like you, Holt.

The use of his last name made him laugh.
Michelle cleared her throat.
"What?" he asked.
She crossed the kitchen and kissed his cheek. "She's a lucky woman."
No . . . he was the lucky one.

Chapter Seventeen

Sheldon walked alongside Avery as she described his childhood home in the way Liam had described it. Once all the walls were stripped of art and knickknacks collected over a lifetime, the lack of upkeep became strikingly clear.

"Any real estate agent worth their salt will tell you to paint all the walls and replace old and worn carpet at the bare minimum. But in the case of this house, I would seriously consider a heavy renovation. The kitchen and bathrooms will cost the most but make the biggest impact when finding a turnkey buyer who will pay top dollar." Liam's exact words.

"What did your contractor estimate?"

She told him Liam's numbers and added that he should expect to spend 20 percent more. Better to come in under budget than over.

Sheldon whistled.

"Consider this. While you might not have had a lot of love for the paintings on the walls, they were done by artists that catch a decent paycheck. The floral pieces in your mother's sitting room were painted at the turn of the century. The receipt of purchase was found in her files."

"How much?"

"She spent half a million dollars each, forty years ago. One can only imagine what they will go for now. There is your renovation budget, which will give you a much bigger return on the house." She paused while standing at the French doors leading to the backyard. "Of course, that means you'll have to hold on to this place a little longer."

"How long?"

"I don't have that answer. My guy said four to six months isn't unheard of on a renovation this size. But we are in California without weather mucking up construction schedules."

"How long before your work is done?"

"I need two more weeks to clear the house of everything worth sending to auction and then arrange the estate sale."

"So I have three weeks to decide."

"Have you picked a real estate agent yet?"

He shook his head.

"They're going to tell you to keep some of the furnishings in the main rooms if you're going to sell as is. If you're renovating, then it's best to purge everything and bring in a professional stager to sell."

"Is your contractor able to do the work?"

She hesitated. "I asked him a favor to give an estimate, I didn't imply that he'd get a job."

Sheldon rocked back on his heels and tore his gaze away from the yard. "If you recommend him, it's good by me."

Avery tried not to think of the ethics behind her suggesting Liam for the work. "I'd recommend you get a couple of estimates before picking a team."

He stared at her.

"I didn't need two when I hired you."

She couldn't argue that.

"Let me see if he is available. If he is, I'll put you two together."

"Sounds good."

Avery followed him out of the room and down the main hall.

"I found some items in your father's study that you might want to look at."

For a second, Sheldon stared, stone-faced. Once again his cold eyes had her taking a slight step back.

"Nothing, Avery. I want nothing from this house."

"I won't ask again."

And just like that, he was smiling again. "You know how it is . . . self-centered parents who considered you only in passing."

"Right."

He nodded toward the door. "Walk me out."

What she really wanted to do was get back to work and distance herself from this man.

Outside, the Santa Ana winds were kicking up dust and blowing leaves from the trees. She closed the door behind them to avoid it crashing against the wall inside.

He took the first step and turned. "Avery."

"Yes?"

His lips pulled into a grin. "I'd like to take you out."

His words didn't register at first. She thought maybe he was suggesting a work-related meal . . . but they'd never done that, and there wasn't a need.

"On a date. Dinner," he clarified.

"Oh, ah . . ." *Think, Avery . . . hell no.* "I'm flattered." In a creeper kind of way.

His smile tilted.

"I'm seeing someone." *Oh, Liam, don't fail me now.*

"Exclusively?"

She bobbed her head like one of those dolls. "Yup."

His eyes narrowed.

"I thought you said after your divorce you poured yourself into your work and that nothing got in the way of your getting the job done."

This was going from bad to worse. Not to mention *get a hint, dude.* "It's new. Besides, I'm working for you, and that wouldn't feel right even if I was available."

He smiled again. "So if things don't work out with you and . . ."

Avery didn't offer a name.

"You'd say yes? After the work is done, of course."

No! She couldn't say that.

Her skin itched. "You're a very nice man."

Not the right words. She could tell by the expression on his face.

"Well, then. We'll revisit this conversation when the job is over."

Before she could suggest he not ask again, he bounced off the stairs and ducked behind the steering wheel of his Volvo.

Avery scurried inside and leaned against the closed door.

With a shudder, she rested her head in her hand. She didn't see that coming. How the hell was she going to handle him?

∽

"I'm blowing off krav on Tuesday," Avery told Liam over the phone later that night.

"Brenda's going to make you work harder on Friday."

"I know. But I can't help it. I have a late appointment with an art dealer and a whole house filled with old furniture. I have no idea how long it will take. I want this job done as soon as possible."

"Late hours and stress. You sound like me."

Avery kicked her feet up on her coffee table and drank from her bottled water. "Who would have guessed?" She considered telling him about Sheldon but decided to hold off. She'd been keyed up about the man all day and needed time to sort out how to handle him.

"I have back-to-back inspections all week, and my second crew is starting a job in Santa Monica."

"More work than you can handle?"

"No. I probably need to hire a couple more guys and tell my secretary to increase the payroll."

Avery watched her feet as she spoke on the phone. "You have a secretary?"

"Yup. My sister."

"So it's a family business."

"No. She's in school for a psychology degree and helping me while she lives here. I told her she didn't have to, but she insisted."

"Sounds like a winning combination for everyone."

"She wants to meet you."

Avery froze. "Ah . . ."

"Let me rephrase that. I'd like you to come over for dinner and meet my family."

She didn't mean to hesitate, but the words took a while to form in her mouth. "I just got used to talking to you on the phone . . . and texting."

"Am I pushing you outside your comfort zone?"

"Yes."

He chuckled.

"Liam."

"No pressure," he told her. "We have Sunday dinners almost every week. The invitation is open. This weekend, next weekend."

She pushed off her sofa and walked into her open kitchen and grabbed a bottle of wine. "Meeting your family implies . . ."

"Implies what?"

"I don't know, but it implies something. I'm pretty sure I'm not ready for that something."

He was laughing now. "You think about it."

She rummaged through a drawer, looking for a wine opener.

"I will." She should just say no.

"I have to go over some invoices and bury myself in paperwork for a couple hours."

"Aha!" She found it.

"Excuse me?"

"Nothing. Fine. Go. I have some busy work to do myself." Like opening the bottle of wine.

"Avery?"

"Yeah?" She pulled the foil off the bottle and tossed it aside.

"I miss you already."

Her fingers stopped playing with the bottle as she sank into his words. "I saw you yesterday."

"That doesn't stop me from missing you today."

Had anyone ever told her they missed her? Other than her girlfriends? Sure, the occasional guy on rotation would offer a *Miss ya, babe. Need ya, babe.* But what they missed was the horizontal time. Not one of them suggested they stick around once she called it off.

She poked the wine opener into the cork. "You haven't been gone long enough for me to miss you," she told him.

"Uh-huh."

"And don't call me a liar. That's rude." He'd been implying she was a liar since they first met. Today she wanted to cut him off before he had a chance. Even if most of the time he'd been right about the white lies that had passed her lips.

"I didn't say a thing."

The cork gave way. "Good." The wine went in the glass and she lifted it to her lips. "I'll see you on Friday, right?"

"I'll be there."

She sipped the wine, welcomed the flavor on her tongue. "Good."

"Good night, Avery."

"Good night."

For several seconds she looked at the dark screen on her phone. What the hell was happening in her life? She dropped her phone on the counter, grabbed the bottle by the neck, and walked over to her couch. After switching on her TV, she vowed to stay awake long enough, or drink half the bottle, so she wouldn't toss and turn, thinking about him.

Chapter Eighteen

Avery arrived at Brenda's studio early, determined to get some extra time on the mat. All the time off made her feel weak and rusty.

She dropped her bag by the door and started to call out to Brenda when Avery realized she was talking on the phone.

"I told you I have a client on Friday night. We have to meet after nine."

Avery's footsteps stopped. Even as she listened in, she scorned herself for eavesdropping.

"I think about you, too," Brenda said.

It had to be Brenda's mystery guy. Not only was the woman saying romantic words Avery didn't think Brenda could piece together, but she spoke them in a softer, gentler way.

"It's only a few hours."

Avery turned her head and forced herself not to listen.

Was that Brenda giggling?

Did Brenda giggle?

Avery paused again.

Stop listening.

Her shoes squeaked on the mat. The sound shot through the silent room.

"I've got to go."

Oh, shit. Busted.

"Hey, Brenda." Avery recovered quickly. "I'm early."

Brenda poked her head out of her office. "Nice of you to join me."

"I called."

"Yes, you did. But did you work out while you were on vacation?"

Avery didn't think drinking champagne and eating wedding cake constituted a workout.

"That's what I thought. Fifty burpees, twenty-five squats, and three minutes of plank."

At Avery's thumbs-up, Brenda turned back into her office.

"Phew." Danger averted.

Twenty-five burpees in, Liam waltzed into the room.

Same broad shoulders, slim hips, and sexy smile. So why did he look different?

"Hello, Avery."

Just her name from his lips made her blush. Damn, what was she, sixteen?

"Hello, Liam."

His sexy smile grew bigger.

Brenda cleared her throat.

"Hello, Brenda," Liam said with a laugh.

"Three minutes of plank, and then I want one hundred push-ups from you. I need your arms tired for today's lesson."

Liam saluted the open door.

Avery went back to her burpees, counting them down. By the time she was on her squats, Liam had finished his plank and started the push-ups.

He really should do those without the shirt. Women everywhere would applaud, and what red-blooded American man didn't want that?

"Are you staring?" he asked without looking up.

"I most certainly am."

"Do you like the view?"

"Are you searching for a compliment?"

"No, no."

Twenty-seven. Twenty-eight. "Liar." It was sweet turning the tables on the man.

She struggled through the last minute of plank while he eased down the final count of push-ups.

"You two are awfully quiet today," Brenda said as she left her office.

"That's because I'm dying here." And had nothing to do with the fact that if she said anything to Liam, it would be to demand he take off his shirt so she could at least see what he was denying her. Dreams of him had plagued her all week. If the man didn't give in to her lust soon, she wasn't going to make it.

"Speak for yourself," Liam teased.

"Oh, don't be cocky. I saw you slowing down on the last ten."

"I have another twenty in me."

"Let's see them," Brenda told him.

Avery pointed his way. "Backfired," she said, laughing.

Liam didn't pause. He pushed right into position and started counting backward from twenty. When he got to ten, Avery decided to make it harder. Without asking, she planted her butt on his back and crossed her legs.

"Playing dirty."

"That's how I roll, Holt."

Even Brenda smirked. "Let's see what you got," she said.

Avery toppled a couple of times and then grabbed hold of his shoulder with one hand and his ass cheek with the other.

He kept going.

When he reached ten, she wasn't sure who was more worked up.

She patted his butt, like she had the right, and jumped off his back.

"That was entertaining," Brenda said. "Let's get to work."

Enough, enough, enough.

Their relationship had changed, somehow become intimate without intimacy. Liam wasn't sure that was possible, but that was his explanation when his concentration went to zilch.

Brenda had Avery practicing getting out of bear hugs, knife to the throat, attacks from behind. Only Liam wasn't feeling it. All he could sense was the way Avery's skin felt against his, how her breathing made her chest rise and fall against his arm as he held her. He wasn't completely geared up in protective padding as he had been in the past. So she stopped short of actually striking him but had to use her weight, strength, and speed to untangle from any hold he had on her. All her wiggling, kicking, and twisting had him sweating and his body rock hard.

Avery noticed.

Oh, she noticed and let her gaze drift down to his pelvis several times.

Her smirk only made it worse. Or better if they were alone and naked.

Only they weren't.

"One more drill and we're done for the day. Avery, I want you on your back."

Like a puppet, she rolled onto the mat and smiled up at Liam.

"Liam, you've met at a bar, taken her home. Plan on going at it . . . but what she doesn't know is your kink is strangling women."

Liam looked at Brenda like she was nuts. "I don't like this game."

"It's not a game. Avery tends to freeze when she's on her back."

Liam had noticed but never pointed it out.

Brenda knelt down. "I want you to sense the second his body language changes, get out of his hold and up on your feet. And you." She pointed to him. "A blow to the groin will make you recoil but not disable you. You've been doing drugs, you naughty man. So you come back and try and take her down."

She stood and took a few steps back. "Drills, Avery. Don't hurt the man."

A month ago, Liam would have laughed at the thought that she could. Now he knew better.

Avery crooked her finger in Liam's direction and shifted her knees, giving him room to settle between her thighs.

Oh, yeah . . . that wasn't helping his erection, which had subsided slightly during Brenda's instructions.

"What's the matter, Holt?"

He narrowed his eyes at her. "You're enjoying this a little too much."

Avery wiggled her hips. "You know it."

Brenda huffed. "Stop playing. I don't have all night."

He wiped his palms on his sweatpants and lowered himself to the mat. He crawled toward her until the feel of her thighs warmed his hips.

"Lean over like you like me," Avery prompted.

He was blushing, he knew it.

He bent at the hips and rested on his elbows on the mat until their chests were touching.

Avery rested one hand on his waist. "Comfortable?"

He moaned. The last thing he wanted to do was pretend like he was going to hurt her. Not in this position.

"You're okay with this?" he asked close to her ear.

Her fingers flexed and then caressed his side. "Uh-huh."

Liam placed a hand on the side of her face, took a breath, and clamped on.

She bucked her hips, hard, nearly removing him. Then her hand came from nowhere, her leg wrapped around and tossed him to his side. She stopped short of kneeing him in the groin, and he hesitated.

Avery was halfway on the balls of her feet, and Liam rushed her. She pivoted on the floor and sent a kick. "Shin," she yelled out without taking him to the floor.

"Missed," Brenda yelled.

Liam moved forward, on his feet now.

Avery kept her angle to where her legs were always between the two of them. She kicked a second time. "Shin."

When Brenda didn't say she missed, Liam stopped and dropped to the mat. Something that would happen if her kick had landed its mark.

Like a cat, Avery was on the balls of her feet, and Liam sat.

"Perfect," Brenda called out. "Now do it again."

Avery smiled as if she'd just won the lottery, and pumped both fists in the air.

Two more mock going at it strangling assaults and they were being shuffled out of the gym before they could shower.

Avery teased Brenda without mercy. "Someone has a date tonight."

Only Brenda had a pretty accurate comeback. "I'm not the only one."

Outside the gym, Liam took Avery's bag from her hand and swung it over his shoulder along with his. "Pug's?" he asked. "We're sweaty, but I don't think anyone there will notice."

Avery took his hand in hers and pulled him down the street. "I have a better idea."

He followed.

"That was epic tonight. I didn't freeze, not once."

"Not once."

"God, I feel good." She was practically jumping up and down.

This side of Avery didn't come out often. He loved it. Carefree, no filter. To be fair, she never seemed to have a filter except when clamping down on her emotions. Which was another habit of hers, he'd noticed.

She'd marched them straight to her complex and through the doors.

"Hello, James."

"Good evening, Ms. Grant."

In the elevator, Liam could see some of the adrenaline seep out of her pores.

"Drinks at my place don't require a shower."

He watched the numbers light up as they moved. "True."

"I won't jump you," she told him.

That was unfortunate.

"Wait, I can't promise that."

He was smiling.

The door dinged, and Avery dug into her bag for her key. She led him into her place and switched on the lights.

"Wow." The view of the city at night was nothing short of spectacular. "I see why you like it." He dumped their bags by the door and moved deeper inside. The lofty space was a massive open room with a state-of-the-art kitchen that didn't look like it had been cooked in.

Avery kicked off her shoes and jumped up to sit on her kitchen island.

She spread her knees apart, just a fraction, and leaned back on her hands.

Liam forgot about the view, or the grandeur of her home, and only saw her.

Without invitation, he wiggled between her legs and clamped his hands over hers.

Staring down her pert nose, she grinned.

"See. I'm not jumping you."

That made one of them.

Holding her hands so she couldn't get away, which he knew was an absolute joke, Liam lowered his mouth to hers.

The heat between them was instant. Or maybe it had never cooled off. From the moment she jumped on his back during his push-ups to the tiny slaps on his ass during their workout, he hadn't had a single minute to let his brain catch up with his groin.

He opened his mouth to hers. The taste of her drove him high, but the feel of her . . . it wasn't expected. There had been women he kissed before that he thought he cared for. Knew he did on some level. And then there was Avery. He'd been cautioning himself every step of the way with her. Letting her lead . . . or maybe he had cut her off.

Not now.

Not this time.

She inched closer to the end of the counter and stroked the back of his leg with her foot. A simple touch, and the slow burn that he'd kept on low flipped to high.

He let loose her hands, pressed his palms onto her hips, and pulled her flush.

Avery wrapped her arms around him and fanned her fingers through his hair while her legs clamped on and she pressed her core against his erection.

He saw stars. Serious specks of light as all the blood rushed below his belt.

Liam kissed her harder, cautioned himself to not leave a bruise.

For a woman with her strength and agility, she felt small in his arms. He traced the edge of her spandex pants and ran his hands up the back of her shirt. She was soft against his worn hands.

Avery broke from his kiss and moved her lips to his neck. "Please don't tell me you're going to stop," she said.

He traced the sides of her breasts with his thumbs. "Not unless you tell me to."

Avery shook her head. "Not a chance."

He chuckled. "Shower first?" he asked. "Finish what we've started, then shower?"

Her hands ran over his ass.

Making it to the shower might not be an option.

Avery leaned back, pulled her shirt over her head, and tossed it to the floor.

A sports bra couldn't diminish her beauty.

"This. Here. Now." She smiled. "Shower later and then repeat."

He tugged his shirt over his head to follow hers. She never unwrapped her legs from his hips. "What if I'm too tired for a second round?"

"Then I'll do all the work." She traced her hands over his shoulders and down his chest. "This looks even better than I imagined."

He dropped his lips to the top of her breast and tasted the salt on her skin. "So good." With a quick movement, he unclasped her bra and let it fall from her shoulders.

"You've had practice."

He gathered the firm mounds of her breasts between his fingers and lifted them, one at a time, to his tongue. "I work with my hands," he told her.

Her head fell back. "And your mouth."

Yes to the left, and yes to the right. She was perfect. All of her.

The control he'd felt as he turned her into putty fell away when she traced the outside of his cock through his pants. Resting his forehead on her shoulder, he pushed into her touch.

"I want this inside of me, Liam." Her husky voice drove through the fog in his head. "I want *you* inside of me."

He pulled his wallet from his back pocket and tossed it on the counter.

Avery reached beneath the elastic of his pants and wrapped her delicate fingers around him.

"Good God, woman."

She offered a deep laugh. "Feels like God was good to you."

He dragged her off the counter long enough for her to peel her spandex off while he kicked his sweats and briefs to the side. The desire to stare and study and taste was overpowered by the need to feel.

"Here?" he questioned one more time.

With a grin, Avery wiggled back up onto the countertop. "Here, there . . . against the window where someone below might see us. I've pictured you everywhere, and now I want to make that happen."

With hands on her thighs, he smiled into their kiss. "You have quite the imagination."

"It isn't as good as the real thing."

From his wallet, he retrieved a condom and tore it free of the wrapper. "Next time we go slower," he promised.

Avery opened for him and looked between them as he positioned himself.

Her breathing matched the quick staccato of his. "Please, Liam. I've waited long enough."

With a sigh, he pressed into her warm folds and paused.

Avery's long release of a breath tightened her body around his.

He shook his head, already fighting for control.

"Liam?" she questioned.

"Shhh." He pulled away and slowly moved back in. "I got you."

And he did. Standing as he made love to her made it a little easier to hold off while she warmed to the feeling. Her kiss was a barometer of where she was at and how close she was to the edge. Slow and easy at first, then a little faster, until she wasn't kissing him at all. With her lips hovering over his, he felt her start to go. As she did, he lifted her from the counter and moved deeper until she called his name.

The feel of her insides squeezing took him over the cliff. He set her back down and rode the last waves of his release until his legs felt like blobs of Jell-O.

They breathed hard into each other's necks while his heart rate returned to normal.

Avery pounded a fist to his back. "Don't ever make me wait that long again."

Liam kissed her shoulder. "Yes, ma'am."

Chapter Nineteen

They made it to the shower, and that was when Avery digested every ounce of him.

The tattoo on his right shoulder was a geometric design he told her didn't have a meaning. He'd been on spring break his second year of college, drunk with his friends . . . yeah, she could identify with that. She wasn't sure how much of her college years she'd actually spent sober.

There weren't many times in Avery's sexual life that she'd showered with a man. Early on, when she wanted to try everything once. But in her most recent past, she never wanted a man to look at her the way Liam did. Every gentle swipe of his soap-filled hand told her she was beautiful . . . said he was lucky.

The moisture dripping off her hair as she stepped from the shower matched the volume of the ice that had been around her heart. Even as the thought entered her head, she tried to pull it back.

It's just sex.

Even alone with her thoughts, she couldn't convince herself that was true.

Liam was different. What that meant she couldn't name. Refused to name. Men bounced once they slept with her. They always did.

With a towel wrapped around her and another one in her hands as she dried her hair, she watched Liam come up to stand behind her. Their reflection in the mirror brought a smile to her face.

"What has you so quiet?"

"Nothing."

He rested his chin on her shoulder and stared at her in the mirror.

Before he could call her a liar, she squeezed out the only words she could find. "I really like you."

He bit his lip as if he was trying not to smile.

"You just figured that out?"

Avery rolled her eyes and dropped her gaze. "Men never stick around. And you're kinda growing on me."

"I'm not like any other man in your life."

"Yeah, I know. It's scary."

He laughed.

"Stop. I'm serious." She shivered, looked at him. "Ever since we met, I've felt like there's a wool coat on my bare skin, but I'm fine with it because feeling the coarse fiber is better than feeling nothing at all."

His laughter faded. "I want to be the silk against your skin. But I'll take the wool coat for now."

He took the towel from her hands, set it aside, and grabbed a brush. With slow strokes, he brushed her hair without so much as a tug.

"You're good at this."

"I have a niece who doesn't sit still unless I'm brushing her hair."

"You're too much."

He nodded without shame. "I am."

"Humble, too."

Moving her hair to the side, he kissed the back of her neck. "Tell me something."

Avery tilted her head to the side and encouraged him to kiss her again. "Yes."

"Do you ever let men spend the night?" Lips on her neck, a tiny lick.

She shivered.

"No. I kick you all out once I'm done."

He untucked her towel and ran the bristles of the brush gently over her back.

Her sex fluttered.

"What side of the bed do I get?"

Avery stretched like a cat waking up in the sunlight streaming through a window. Her eyes blinked open and the previous night rushed in. She closed them again and smiled. They'd made love until she cried uncle and then proceeded to curl into a ball at Liam's side and fall fast asleep.

With one hand, she patted the space beside her, searching him out.

Not there.

Damn it.

On her way to rolling over and pounding the pillow beside her, she heard whistling coming from her kitchen. And coffee. She smelled coffee.

She left her bed naked and searched out a robe. When she couldn't find it, she pulled on an oversize T-shirt she often wore as a nightgown.

In the kitchen, with his back to her, Liam sported her white, fluffy bathrobe. She swam in it. On Liam, it came up short on his arms and just hit his knees.

He looked ridiculous.

"Perfect fit," she teased.

Without looking her way, he lifted a hand in the air to ward her off. "Desperate times deserve desperate measures. Don't judge."

He stopped chopping whatever he was cutting up, turned, and crossed to her side.

After dropping a kiss, he said, "Good morning."

"Morning."

His gaze lowered. "I'd offer you your robe, but then I'd be naked and you'd be dressed. And I like this ensemble you have going. The only thing that would make it better is if that were my shirt."

Liam turned back to what he was doing.

"Are you cooking?"

"I am. But first thing, you don't snore. And the second thing . . . there is nothing but rabbit food in here."

"Organic rabbit food."

He traversed her kitchen and poured her a cup of coffee. "What do you take in it?"

"Raw sugar. It's in the—"

"Got it." He had the lid off her sugar container before she could finish her sentence.

"Are you always this awake first thing in the morning?"

He paused, looked at her, then turned to the clock on the wall. It was almost nine thirty.

"Oh."

"I am. After last night, I could take on the world." He handed her the cup and kissed her forehead. "I hope you like omelets."

"I can't believe you're cooking."

"We need to eat. Don't you cook?"

"Not if I can avoid it."

He put oil in a hot pan and added the egg mixture. The man looked like he knew what he was doing.

"I don't mind it. Most days I don't have time."

She sat at the kitchen counter and watched him channel his best impression of a short order cook. It was hot, even while he was wearing her bathrobe.

A few minutes later Liam placed a plate full of food in front of her.

"This looks amazing."

"Taste it and tell me if it needs anything so I get mine right." He winked.

There were onions, feta, spinach, and a spice she didn't recognize. "Heaven."

Before she could butter her toast, he had managed a second omelet for himself and was taking a place beside her.

"This is really good, Liam. Thank you."

He took a bite, nodded. "A little bacon would round it off perfectly."

"Love bacon, just hate cooking it."

"Bake it in the oven. No mess."

"Really?"

"Yup. The way my mom always did."

"I'll have to try that."

Avery sipped her coffee and watched him finish.

He glanced over. "You're done?"

She wasn't about to tell him her normal breakfast was java alone. "I'm stuffed."

He pulled her plate over and dug into the last few bites. "You drained me."

She leaned back and placed her foot in his lap. "Worth it?"

"Just need to fuel up so we can do it again."

"First you won't, now you don't want to stop."

He wiped his mouth with his napkin and sat back. "Need to make up for lost time."

Avery laughed.

"What is on your agenda today?" he asked.

"I was going to stop by the Lankford property for a couple hours."

"Working on Saturday?"

"Don't look at me like that. I've heard your phone buzzing constantly."

"True, but most of the time construction stops on the weekends." He started absentmindedly rubbing her foot that rested in his lap.

"I want this job done. Especially after Sheldon asked me out."

Liam's hands stopped. "He what?"

"Don't stop." She wiggled her foot before placing the second one in his lap for attention. "Yeah. Out of the blue. I'm thinking no. And *hell no*. I work for him. Even if I didn't . . . no."

"So you don't want to date the man. Got it." Liam smiled.

"I told him I was seeing someone."

Liam pointed a finger to his chest and mouthed the word *me*.

Avery rolled her eyes. "No, James, the doorman."

"I knew he had a thing for you."

"You would think *I'm seeing someone* would end the discussion. Not with Sheldon, he practically quizzed me. Said if it was new, then he would check back with me later. The whole thing struck me as weird. Uncomfortable."

"Like wool on bare skin?"

She took a hasty drink of her coffee. "No, like bile coming up your throat. I'm overreacting, but I didn't like the whole exchange. Especially on the heels of him asking you to take the job."

Liam rubbed her feet a little harder. "Asking me to what?"

"Okay, so right before the awkward date request, he asked that I inquire with you about taking the remodeling job."

"He wants to do it?"

"Yes, but I didn't think it was very ethical of me to suggest someone I'm seeing do the job. Like insider trading."

Liam's slow smile went full force.

"What?"

"You just admitted, twice, that we're a thing."

She slid her feet off his lap. "I did not."

Liam reached down and pulled her feet back up. "You did, too. But you're right. Unless Sheldon knew we were dating and wasn't going to use our relationship against us, I would have to pass."

Avery ignored the fact he said *dating* and *relationship* in the same sentence. "I'm glad you agree. Do you know anyone else who can do the work?"

"Tell you what, I'll get ahold of this Sheldon guy and take this off your plate. I have a couple companies that do similar work I can refer."

She started to relax. "Okay, but you can't tell him about us."

There his smile went again.

This time she swung her feet off his lap and stood.

"I'll tell him I'm unavailable for the job, unless you want to tell him we're a thing."

She picked up her dish with his and kissed him briefly. "Thanks, and thanks for breakfast."

"What are you doing next Sunday?"

"I don't know, why?" She turned the faucet on to rinse the dishes before placing them in the washer.

"I want you to meet my family."

The plate slid out of her hands and crashed in the sink. The racket made them both jump.

Liam was at her side and peering down to assess the damage. Nothing broken.

"Too soon?" he asked.

"Yes. Maybe. I don't know." And she didn't.

He took her hands in his and kissed her fingertips. "It's okay. We have all the time in the world."

⚬

"Normally I would plague Trina with this, but since she's AWOL—"

"On her honeymoon," Shannon corrected.

"Honeymoon, AWOL, whatever. He's calling us a thing, Shannon. Asking me to dinner with his family. He spent the night. The whole night. I don't do that. I never do that. Even if I accidentally fall asleep, I certainly don't wake up the next morning, eat the breakfast he cooked—and yes, Liam cooks. I don't get up and continue to spend almost the whole weekend with him." It was Monday morning, and Avery hovered over her Starbucks, talking on the phone and sliding into her car. She'd waited until eight o'clock to call, and now she was going to be late to the Lankford estate. But a girl did need to sleep. After Liam left, she was sexually limp and exhausted.

"What has you more upset, the fact he is into you or you're into him?"

Avery turned over the engine and made sure her Bluetooth was working before tossing her phone in her purse. Careful with her coffee, she pulled out of the parking space to join the droves of cars clogging up the roads.

"I don't think it's that simple."

"I don't think it's more complicated. You don't do long-term. We all get that. I will let your future therapist discover why. In the meantime, stop and ask yourself this: Does Liam make you happy?"

"Yes." She turned onto the road. "And frustrated, and anxious . . . nervous. He makes me nervous."

"Like you're afraid he is going to hurt you nervous?"

"No, nothing like that. He wouldn't raise a hand to me."

"That isn't what I mean," Shannon said. "Emotionally. Are you fearing he will damage something inside of you?"

Avery stopped at the light and paused her thoughts. If any of them knew the deep pain of love unrequited, it was Shannon.

"Maybe. Yes . . . I don't know. This is all new for me, and I don't know how to walk on this road."

"One step at a time. That's how you do this. If there is something in the road that is going to hurt, walk around it, or over it. Or through it. If it stops feeling good, end it. If it only gets better—"

Avery cut her off with a moan.

"There is the crux of this issue. You're afraid it will get better."

"I will do something to fuck it up."

"I'm not sure where that is coming from."

She crawled onto the freeway. "Why is this so hard?"

"Relationships aren't always perfect."

"It's not a relationship."

Shannon filled the line with laughter.

Chapter Twenty

Avery was systematically closing up one room at a time in the Lankford estate. The ones that took the most time, and were often the most lucrative in terms of lost treasures, were offices and attics. She had every intention of lowering the ladder to the top floor of the house after one last run through the home office.

She'd boxed the trinkets she'd suggested Sheldon look over after he denied the need. The paperwork that might come into play was in temporary file folders and boxed for storage until everything in the estate was sold and gone. Then it could all be tossed in an incinerator.

Avery started on one end of the room, looking for the unconventional, but almost always there, hidden spaces. The built-in bookcases didn't look suspect, but she tapped on them anyway. She climbed on a ladder to look above the dust and see if there was something that might be concealed.

When she didn't see anything, she stepped out of the office and looked at the span of walls between one room and the other.

Nope. No hidden room.

She pulled cushions off the sofa and dragged it away from the wall. Only dust.

The unused chair behind the desk was pushed out of the way, and Avery dropped to her knees.

She chilled.

This she'd done before. For Trina. The idea had come to Avery because she'd found a hidden drawer in her father's desk as a child. She'd been hiding in his office, a place she wasn't welcome to play, and stumbled upon it. Her father kept papers in his hidden space, papers that at the time, Avery couldn't read. By the time she was old enough to see what was so important that they were hidden where no one else could find them, she'd forgotten they were there.

Until the Hamptons.

Until the weekend Trina had gone off to meet her now husband for a weekend trip and Avery was rummaging around Trina's late husband's space.

She hadn't found treasures.

She'd found blood.

And that's when everything started to fall apart.

Avery pushed away the painful memories, straightened her shoulders, and closed her eyes. She ran her fingers along the edges of the desk to feel for any abnormality. It would be something you couldn't see but could only feel. Like a ripple in the fabric of the wood. Kinda like . . . she pressed the ripple, and her hand was knocked back.

"Kinda like that." Her eyes sprang open. Using her cell phone light, she guided a small drawer free of the underside of the desk. In the light, she gently blew the dust off the contents.

Pictures.

She turned them over one by one to see them.

Just pictures.

Avery froze.

"Why, Mr. Lankford . . . who is this charming young woman who isn't your wife on your arm?" She flipped through a half dozen pictures, faded and yellow at the edges. "And who is this?"

~⌾

"Okay, who is she?"

Liam had been attempting to find the perfect bouquet of flowers to send to Avery for the past thirty minutes. How hard could it be? Roses were a staple for any man's romancing toolbox, but how many men had sent her roses in the past? Tons, he'd bet.

There were spring arrangements and tropical sprays, live plants . . . maybe he needed to call his sister for advice.

"Hello?" Carlos tapped his hand on the desk that separated them. The two of them were supposed to be researching companies that specialized in modern art mosaics, which the owner of the loft space wanted. Only somehow Liam became sidetracked.

"Sorry. What?"

"You've been somewhere else for weeks. Now you're looking up . . ." Carlos stood and glanced at the screen on Liam's phone. "Flowers. Since you're smiling, I'm guessing it isn't for a funeral or someone in the hospital. Who is she?"

"Her name is Avery."

"Is Avery the reason you were gone for a long weekend?"

"Yup."

Carlos added a nod while Liam scowled through the next page of floral arrangements.

"So what's the flower occasion?"

"No occasion."

Carlos put down the pen in his hand and cocked his head to the side. "There is always an occasion. You fight, you buy flowers. It's a birthday, you buy flowers. Anniversary."

"Yeah, none of those things. I just want her to know I'm thinking of her."

"Ahh . . . *I'm thinking about the great sex* flowers."

Was he that obvious?

"Roses are too tricky. Red means you love her. White is too pure. Yellow says thank you—"

"There's a meaning behind roses?"

Carlos looked at him like he was dense. "I've been married for five years. Women put meaning into everything."

Liam had lived with his sister and niece long enough to know that truth.

"I already ruled out roses. Overdone." He tossed his phone to the side. "Everything looks overused and under-thought-out."

"Is this Avery a jeans and T-shirt girl or dress and fancy shoes?"

Liam blinked. "Yes."

Carlos laughed. "Both. That's good. Simple or exotic?"

"I think she tries to be simple, but she's really exotic." Hadn't she mentioned something about a trip to Paris to go shoe shopping?

Carlos tossed a hand in the air with a flip of his head. "Well, then. Orchids. But not cut. Buy a plant. They last forever. Since you're buying 'awesome sex flowers,' she will see them all the time and ask you around more often."

Liam liked the idea, snatched his phone off the desk. "It's a little scary that you know so much about the subject."

"What my sisters didn't teach me, my wife has. Besides, if I didn't move you along with this, I'd be looking at the top of your head for the next two hours, getting nothing done."

༄

Avery answered the knock on her door without looking through the peephole. Why her condo even had a peephole had always boggled her mind. No one could get through the staff downstairs without their name being on a list or the concierge calling her to see if she was expecting visitors . . . but still. Peephole.

She swung the door wide. "Hey, Lori. Thanks for coming up."

Lori's condo was a few floors down from hers. No name needed on a list, and no call from downstairs.

"I brought wine." She lifted a bottle.

Avery turned her back to her friend and crossed to her kitchen. "How did you know I needed wine?"

Lori paused, her mouth dropped open. "Are those from Liam?"

Avery took in the flower shop that now lived in her home. Six orchid plants were awaiting her when she arrived from work.

"Yes."

Lori absently handed the bottle to Avery and stood in front of the flowers. "Why so many? It's lovely, don't get me wrong . . . but six?"

Avery handed Lori the card that came with the field of flowers.

"'I'm thinking about you and wasn't sure the meaning behind the colors of orchids. So here are the six the florist had. I'm sure whatever the colors mean, I'm feeling it for you.'" Lori dropped her hand holding the card and stared blankly. "There's meaning behind the color of orchids?"

"Apparently."

Lori pulled out a kitchen stool and had to push one of the plants away to look at her. "I take it you and Liam finally went all the way."

Avery had to laugh. The night before Trina's wedding, the topic of discussion was how long it was taking for Liam to go there. Somewhere between eleven and one, the four of them had reverted to high school and used the term *all the way*.

"Yes, he did, and twice on Sunday." Avery paused. "Actually it was three times on Friday, twice on Saturday, and once on Sunday before I let him go home."

"So you spent the whole weekend in bed?"

Avery poured them both generous portions of wine and motioned toward her sofa.

She shrugged. "There was the kitchen counter, the shower . . . and yeah, a bed was involved."

Lori laughed as she kicked her shoes off and tucked her feet under her butt. "That's fabulous. Good for you."

She looked over at the flowers and sighed.

"Is that why you wanted me to come up?"

"Partly. He's freaking me out, Lori. I'm not sure what to do with him."

"I think you have that covered."

"I'm not talking about sex. Yes, I know what to do there. Now that he's finally putting out, he's complicating me even more."

Lori chuckled.

"He's falling for you."

Avery shook her head.

"It's obvious to everyone but you."

"It's all moving too fast."

Lori sipped her wine. "Two weeks ago you were whining because he wasn't stripping you. Now he's too fast?"

"He wants me to have dinner with his family. There are flowers with notes that make me giddy."

They sat in silence, drank their wine.

"Have you ever been in love?" Lori asked.

"No." Avery's answer was immediate.

"Not even close?"

"What's close?"

Lori looked at the ceiling. "Close would be the man sneaking into your thoughts off and on. Wondering what he was doing at odd hours. Worrying about him when he doesn't text back . . . and not an *Is he into me?* worry, but an *Is he hurt? Did something happen to him?*"

"The only people I worry about something happening to are you and the girls."

"Not Liam?"

Avery considered the thought. "He hasn't really left me alone long enough for me to worry. There is a lot of texting. Even if it's just a wave or a silly emoji. We've spent a lot of time together in the past few weeks. He's my first real *relationship*."

Lori grinned. "That's a big word, coming from you."

"Yeah, well . . . Shannon wouldn't shut up about it this morning. So . . ." She released a long-resigned sigh. "I'm in a *relationship*."

"It's not a jail sentence."

"Whatever."

"Why are you so opposed to a relationship?"

"Relationships don't fit my life," she said as if on autopilot. "It's easier to flutter around and come home alone than end up like my parents." As the words left her lips, she was reminded of her dedication to stay single.

"Not everyone is like your parents," Lori told her.

"I know that. But my gene pool says I'm destined to be as miserable in their roles as they are."

"Something tells me Liam is making you consider that might not be the case."

Avery scoffed and changed the subject. "I didn't ask you up here to bend your ear all night about Liam."

Lori glanced over her shoulder. "That's too bad. I want to know more about the kitchen counter. You washed it, right?"

Avery chuckled. "Yes." *No*, actually, Liam had. After pointing out what he said looked like an impression of her bare butt. Which wasn't there. But telling Lori that would keep the topic going, and Avery really needed a night or two to think about the whole Liam thing.

"So what else is on your mind?"

Avery set her glass on the coffee table as the amusement of all things Liam left her brain. "This falls under Lori Lawyer category. As in no one can hear about this."

"Not even Shannon and Trina?"

"It probably wouldn't be an issue with them, but I thought it would be best to run it past you."

Lori's smile faded as she sat poised for the conversation.

"It's about my client, Sheldon Lankford."

"The Brentwood estate."

She nodded. "First off, I'm paid to snoop. Right? I'm hired to find the big and little stuff that's worth money for my clients."

"Oh, no," Lori said. "You found something stolen."

Avery shook her head. "No. Stolen I could deal with. I think." Could she? What would happen if she did find something like that? "Nothing like that."

"Criminal?"

"You'll have to tell me."

Lori blinked. "You might need to elaborate."

Avery flexed her sweaty palms. "I found pictures in Mr. Stewart Lankford's desk. Hidden. Secret drawer stuff."

"I hide a gun in my secret drawer."

"You do?"

Lori nodded. "Reed insisted. Sorry. Go on."

Avery unfurled herself from the couch and brought her folder over for Lori to see.

Lori set her glass to the side and opened it. "What am I looking at?"

Avery sat close and pointed. "That is Mr. Lankford Senior. Only that isn't Mrs. Lankford."

"He had an affair."

"That's what it looked like to me."

Lori skimmed over the pictures. "I can't imagine it's uncommon for these things to come to light after someone dies. Does your client know?"

"I haven't told him yet. The picture that concerns me is this one." Avery removed the picture of Mr. Lankford, his mistress . . . and a young boy around the age of seven. "That isn't Sheldon, my client."

"Oh . . . you think this might be Lankford's kid."

"He kinda looks like he could be, don't you think?"

"Hard to say. But yeah. Could be."

"Sheldon told me his parents were old when they adopted him and didn't have the energy to chase him around as a child. He was thrown from nanny to nanny, then boarding school. Hell, that's the way my parents are, and I'm not adopted, and they weren't old when they had me."

Lori closed the file and put it aside. "Let's for argument's sake say that Mr. Lankford is this child's father and Sheldon knows nothing about it. Showing him these pictures does what?"

Avery shrugged. "I don't know. He's the sole beneficiary to the estate. Does this kid, probably a man by now, have any right to it?"

"I'd have to see the family trust. Probably not. Not that an illegitimate child can't claim differently to a court."

"That would put a halt to everything we're doing. Am I legally obligated to say anything? To question the estate and who has the right to sell it off? Sheldon hired me, but it isn't like I have ever needed to see a will to prove my clients own what they say they own. That's between the bank and them, right?"

"Yeah. You're in the clear. Maybe you should just show them to Sheldon and let him deal with it."

Avery shivered.

"You don't like that idea," Lori said as she peered closer. "Why?"

"I want to avoid any personal conversations with him. Asking him if he knew his dad was sleeping with someone else and possibly fathered a child is entirely too personal. What if Sheldon's father treated him differently than he did this child, assuming it is his? Showing him these pictures might open a door that, while painful, at least has answers. What if he knew, or assumed? Not knowing and questioning yourself can haunt you. Trust me on that. Even though I don't really like the guy, I don't think this kind of secret should be kept."

"Why don't you like the guy?"

Avery gripped her glass. "He has a strange affect. Like he watches and studies people. Then there is the fact that he asked me out."

"You refused."

"Of course I refused. I'm seeing Liam. Even if I wasn't, the guy just gives me a weird vibe."

Lori lifted a hand in the air and started clicking off facts one finger at a time. "So the guy likes you, asked you out, you turned him down, and then you show him these pictures. That does exactly what for your business relationship?"

Avery cringed. "Makes it even more uncomfortable. It forces intimate conversations about his family that I really want nothing to do with."

"Right." Lori dropped her hand and pulled her wine back to her lips. "This is a rock and a hard place. You want my advice?"

"God, yes."

"You don't tell anyone about the pictures. Finish the job. Once you're off the payroll, you can give them to him. These kinds of things can be embarrassing even if the affair is decades old. It isn't up to you to investigate the rightful heirs to Mr. and Mrs. Lankford's estate."

There was some relief in that route. "So do nothing."

"For now."

Avery sighed. "Thanks, Lori. I knew you'd have the answers."

"Not all of them. I work with divorce, not this."

The two of them sipped their wine in silence for a few seconds.

"Are you going to tell me about this haunting thing?"

Avery snapped her head toward her. "What?"

"You said the *not knowing* haunts you."

Avery needed more wine for this. "You know it's almost been a year." She crossed to the kitchen, grabbed the bottle, and moved back to the living room.

"You're thinking about what happened in New York. I'm guessing that's normal."

She refilled her glass, set the bottle down. "I haven't stopped thinking about it. I'll go down on the mat in krav and freeze. I think I see his face, something. Then it's gone."

"We'll circle back to the krav thing in a minute. Although that does explain a few things. Why haven't you told any of us this?"

Avery looked over her glass. "You were getting married. Trina was engaged and on cloud gazillion . . . and Shannon has her own demons to chase."

"So we only get to be there for you when things are good? That's not how friendship works."

"If you haven't noticed, I don't foster too many friends. I suck at relationships. All of them."

"That's where you're wrong. As Wade pointed out, you're the blonde pit bull. You're fiercely protective with your friends but won't allow us inside to be there for you."

Lori was right, but Avery didn't want to admit it. "You guys know me better than anyone."

That seemed to satisfy Lori. "I know. Don't be afraid of talking to us. It's why we formed the club to begin with."

"We formed the First Wives to deal with dating after divorce. Somehow that has turned into a murdered husband, assaults, spies, and all kinds of soap opera drama."

Lori refilled her glass. "Krav. Seriously, you've been taking krav?"

Avery found her smile. "Yeah. That gym I said I met Liam in . . . krav studio."

"Why the secret?"

"Didn't want anyone to worry about me."

Lori narrowed her eyes, lips flat.

"Okay. Got it. I'll try."

"You do that."

Chapter Twenty-One

For the first time in six months, Avery's haunts woke her in the middle of the night.

Cold sweat, racing heart. She shot straight up in bed, screaming. Her hands went to her face, and she expected them to fall away soaked in blood.

The vividness of the recurring dream was palpable. She could smell the stench of cigarettes and asphalt. And blood. Her blood. She tasted the salt in the back of her throat and gagged.

The clock by her bedside flashed 2:20 a.m. She swung her legs off the bed and padded into her bathroom. She switched on the glaring light and turned the water on hot. When she looked in the mirror, she briefly saw the image of her face the first time she was allowed to look at it after the attack. The bandages covered nearly everything, her eye swollen shut, the other just a slit. No wonder she needed to use reading glasses a decade sooner than normal age would have suggested.

She peered closer to the mirror. Almost forgetting what her nose had looked like before the surgery to correct the break and stop the bleeding. Nothing had been wrong with her other nose. This one was smaller. The scar underneath was a little bigger than most since the bastard that had kicked it in shredded it with his boot. Razor sharp tread, like they were new. Work boots. She closed her eyes to capture the image. Pants. Not jeans. Tan pants, frayed at the bottom. Dirty with her blood splattered on the leg.

The vision vanished.

She opened her eyes. Her pale image stared back at her, hands gripping the sink as the water flowed down and steam filled the mirror. "Holy shit." She remembered something.

Avery ran to her kitchen and yanked open her junk drawer to find a pen. She found a notepad and frantically scratched down her thoughts and images. What she'd smelled. Anything.

When done, she stared at the piece of paper in front of her. She conjured up the face of the man the police said did the deed. "Why can't I see you?"

He was already dead, killed by the man who hired him.

But Avery couldn't see him.

She pulled a bottle of water from her refrigerator and her telephone rang.

She jumped, nearly dropping the bottle.

"Who the hell? Hello?"

"Avery?" It was Lori.

"Is everything okay?"

"I was going to ask you the same thing."

"It's two thirty in the morning, Lori."

"I know. Alliance security called Reed. They heard a scream and then logged in on the cameras. Are you okay?"

"Jesus, I forgot about the cameras. I thought they'd been turned off."

"Off, but not disconnected. Are you okay? You sound okay."

"I had a bad dream. I'm fine. The phone ringing scared the crap out of me."

"She says she's fine," Lori said, away from the phone.

"Hey, Lori?"

"Yeah?"

"What security company takes ten minutes to ask if I'm okay?"

Lori sighed. "You're wearing a red T-shirt and standing in your kitchen. Reed said you were fine. But after tonight's conversation—"

Avery looked across the room to where she knew the camera had been placed the year before. She stared right at it. "I'm fine. Now turn off the damn camera or I'm ripping it off the wall."

"I can't do that," Lori said.

Avery turned her attention back to the phone. "I was talking to the guy watching the camera. I'm okay. Go back to bed."

"Okay. Good night."

"Good night, Mother Hen."

This was why she didn't tell her friends what was going on in her head. The security guys would have heard her scream, clicked on the camera, seen she was fine, and then turned it all off. Over-the-top for a security system, but when the guy who hired the man to kill her last year was still alive, it had been necessary. Now, not so much.

Avery twisted until her gaze landed on the kitchen counter. The memory of Liam as he . . .

Oh, yeah. The cameras had to go.

⤳

Avery's ass dragged the next day. She was 100 percent sure her emotional barometer was not ready to tackle the attic, but she was doing it anyway.

The Santa Ana winds were in full effect, with red flag warnings everywhere. The lack of rain and dry heat were a disaster waiting to happen. Days like this always made her happy she lived in a high-rise. Not much chance of a brush fire attacking her home.

The lack of cars in the driveway was a blessing. Her occasional helper wasn't coming in today, and it didn't look like Sheldon was there checking on the progress. In fact, she hadn't seen him since he'd asked her out. Maybe it would stay that way. She had two more weeks on the job but was pushing to get out of the house in one. It would still take time to sell everything, between auctions and estate home garage-type sales. But her day in and day out would be over. Avery looked forward to it.

The air snapped when she walked into the house. Or maybe it was just the vibe coursing through her skin. Knowing the skeletons that were hiding in the Lankford closets wasn't a comfortable feeling.

She glanced into the study where she'd found the hidden drawer in the desk. At first, she had every intention of selling the thing to an antique dealer. It wasn't auction worthy, but it was old. But if there was any question from Sheldon about where she'd found the photos, having the desk, and the drawer, would make it easier for her to show him. Since he'd given her permission to determine where the best dollar would be found, she'd lie about the desk and keep it there until the last possible day. After she gave him the photographs.

She set her empty coffee cup on a hall table and walked upstairs to the attic access. The stairs had been pulled down the day before, but Avery hadn't sucked up the nerve to climb them.

In addition to the concern that she'd find more shit she didn't want to see, Avery had a deep respect for spiders. Respect defined as *you stay on your side of the room and I'll stay on mine*. Again, a plus for high-rise living. The little shits had a harder time finding her than they would if she lived in a normal house with the foundation sitting on dirt, where those eight-legged, fast crawling creatures lived. Then again, maybe the guy she hired to spray for the things every year was doing his job.

She stared at the space above her head for several seconds. "Stop being such a girl."

Avery forced a fast pace up the steps and hauled herself up at the top. Two dormers on the east and west sides of the house let natural light into the space, but it wasn't enough. There looked to be old hanging lights, with chain cords to turn the things on, spread out every twenty feet or so.

She brushed away a cobweb and told herself it was probably decades old and the spider that made it was long gone. "Nope. Spiders need food to survive. None of that up here."

Yeah, except the few flies she'd already swatted away from her face. Maybe opening the stairwell the night before hadn't been a good idea.

She turned on the first light and took in the space around her. It was huge, spanning nearly the entire frame of the house. Most of it had plywood covering the floor space, except closer to the dormers. The musty smell of insulation and maybe the decay of a mouse or two rounded out the joys hitting her brand-new nose. Attics in larger, older homes all held the usual suspects. Old furniture people weren't ready to part with, some of it worth something, most of it sentimental to the dead, so in other words, worthless.

Boxes of holiday decorations sat closest to the stairs. Which made perfect sense. Those things were brought down year after year, while the other stuff morphed into the dingy space.

Avery moved deeper, turning on lights as she went. Old lamps, one that had a Tiffany thing going for it. Was it Tiffany? Rare? She had no idea.

She wiped dust off an old chest and clicked the stiff locks until they sprang free. "Quilts?" The Lankfords didn't seem like quilt people, but clearly someone had been at one time. The homemade blankets were stacked on top of each other without any other protection than the box they were in. Again, Avery knew nothing about these kinds of handmade items except that they didn't tend to fetch any money. The chest itself was 1920s modern. The deeper in the attic she went, the fewer furnishings she found. Old toys. Some that looked much too old for something that Sheldon would have played with.

She turned a corner and found a desk that looked a lot like the one in the father's study. Her hand hesitated before opening the drawers. A few old coins, a pen, and a paper clip. She once again looked under the desk but had no intention of searching for a secret drawer. Her quick visual made her jump.

"Hello, Charlotte." It was big, it was black, and it was definitely alive. "You just stay right there." She backed up on the balls of her feet, lost her balance, and fell on her ass.

She bounced up. "Okay, I'm done in here." She'd hire a crew to bring everything into the light, and keep an eye out for the things she thought held value. But right now, she wanted out. The stale air was stealing her oxygen.

Avery dodged at least four spiderwebs before reaching the stairs. She backed her way down and brushed at her arms and legs with her bare palms, muttering, "Yuck, yuck. Yuck!" A mirror and a bathroom, that's what she needed.

She turned around and nearly toppled over Sheldon.

She screamed for the second time that day and lunged back.

He lifted his hands. "Didn't mean to startle you."

Avery clenched a hand to her chest. "Son of a . . ."

"Sorry."

"I didn't see you."

"I called your name downstairs."

Her heart was still in her throat. "I didn't hear you."

She brushed at her arms again, certain a sticky web was taking root.

"It's pretty dirty up there."

"Yeah."

She dared to look him in the eye and found him looking at the top of her head.

Avery froze. "What is it?"

"I think you have a hitchhiker."

Her squealing girl meter ramped into overdrive. She didn't care who he was or how much he creeped her out—a spider in her hair ushered her toward him. "Get it off! Get it off!"

She suddenly felt like she did when she watched *Raiders of the Lost Ark*. Things were crawling on her, she could feel them.

Sheldon calmly lifted a hand to her head and brushed at her hair.

She held perfectly still, eyes closed. "Did you get it?"

He backed away. "I got it."

She finally had the nerve to swipe at her hair as she opened her eyes.

What she saw then made her head explode in pain.

Sheldon was letting the long legged, hairy spider crawl on his arm.

"What's the matter? It isn't going to hurt you."

Only it was.

A spider on the inside of his arm. A tattoo.

She was going to pass out.

Avery stumbled away from him and the insect, or small animal, whatever you wanted to call it. "I've got to go."

"I think you should sit down. You don't look too good."

She backed away from Sheldon, keeping him and the spider in sight until she found the top of the stairs. "I can't. I have to go."

"I'll take it outside."

She ran down the steps, finding air in gulps as she went.

"Avery?"

She snatched her purse and ran to her car.

For two seconds, she gripped the steering wheel, closed her eyes, and slowed her breathing.

Then she tore out of the driveway as if hell's hounds were biting at her ankles.

Nine hours later she was stepping off a plane at JFK.

By the time she reached her hotel it was after eleven New York time.

She dropped her bag on the bed and opened the blinds wide. There would be no sleeping in tomorrow.

Her phone buzzed in her purse.

It was Liam.

She forced a smile she knew would help her sound normal and answered, "Hey."

"Hey back. Are you still at the studio?"

Avery cringed. She'd forgotten to call Brenda.

"No, uhm, I had to fly to Seattle." Even as she told the lie, she looked out over the dark vastness of Central Park and the skyline surrounding it. "An unexpected problem with my client up here."

"Oh, okay. I was going to see if you wanted to grab a bite. I know how hungry you get after krav."

"I'm going to have to take a rain check."

"When do you think you'll be back?"

New York was a big ass city. Lots of places to hide. "I don't know. A couple of days, I think."

"Must be a big problem."

"Nothing I can't handle."

He paused. "Are you okay? You sound tired."

"I *am* tired. Not a lot of sleep this weekend, or last. Now I have to be here. I think I need to go to bed early."

"Sounds like a good idea. We wouldn't want you getting sick."

"Not that, please."

"What hotel are you in? I'll send flowers since you had to leave the ones at your place."

"You're too much, Liam." No point in telling him a hotel. That would be the fastest way for all of them to know she wasn't there. "Orchids last forever. They'll be alive when I get home."

"Okay, then. I won't keep you."

"We'll talk soon," she told him.

"Good night."

"Night."

Avery tossed her phone on the bed, opened the notebook she'd been drawing in since she made it to the airport, and continued to sketch.

∾

"Detective Armstrong." Avery stared at the uniformed officer. "Or Gray. Either one will do."

"You are?"

"Avery Grant."

"Are they expecting you?"

"No."

"I'll see if they're available."

"It's important."

It was coffee-and-donut early, so Avery banked on them being in.

The officer lifted the phone to her ear and dialed. "Yes. An Avery Grant is here to see you."

Good, they were in.

"Grant?" the officer asked Avery.

She nodded.

"Yes," the officer said back into the receiver.

She hung up the phone. "He'll be out in a minute. If you'll take a seat."

Avery moved away from the desk but didn't sit.

She recognized Detective Armstrong when he pushed out the doors leading to the back of the police station. "Ms. Grant."

He reached out a hand.

"Detective."

"You look much better than the last time I saw you."

"That wouldn't have taken much." She'd been black, blue, purple, and green for six weeks.

"What can I do for you?"

"I need to see the pictures of the man who attacked me again."

"The case has been closed."

She lifted her chin. "I think you need to reopen it."

Armstrong shifted back on his heels, his eyes blank. "Okay, then. Come with me."

He walked her behind the reception desk and through the doors he'd emerged from. The noise behind the wall was ten times what it was in the lobby. It might be first thing in the morning on a Wednesday, but apparently that didn't matter when it came to cops and their work. She walked around several old desks, all of them piled with papers. There was a wild-eyed young man sitting with his hands behind his back, telling an officer he "wasn't there." The exhausted officer talking to him wasn't buying it.

They rounded the corner to a slightly less populated part of the space and into a semiprivate office.

"You remember Detective Gray."

"Vaguely. I was pretty drugged up when I saw you both last." They shook hands.

"Sit."

She took the edge of the chair and waited for them to follow.

"I've started remembering things. Details of that day."

"What kind of details?" Gray asked as he picked up a pad of paper and held a pen at the ready.

Avery held her notebook in her hand but closed her eyes in an effort to bring the image back up. "Boots. The work kind. I think they were new, because I remember a spiky edge to the tread coming at me." She looked beyond the boots in her mind and described the man's tan pants to them. "New boots and old pants you'd see on a homeless man, the contrast is clear in my head." She opened her eyes to see the men watching her.

"The man who attacked you is dead, Ms. Grant."

She narrowed her eyes. "No. The man in my memory is not the man in the morgue."

The detectives looked at each other.

"Anything else?" Armstrong asked.

She nodded and placed her notebook on the desk.

Opening it to her amateur artwork, she turned the page around and pointed. "He had a tattoo on the inside of his right arm. I saw it when he dragged me around the car. This spider. It covered his skin and was so lifelike . . ." She shivered. "There were bones and hair. The eyes had color. Red." No wonder she had blacked the image out.

Avery shifted her gaze between the two detectives and placed both hands on the desk. "I don't remember this from the pictures you showed me. All I've seen in my nightmares is the mug shot of the guy you said did it. All the while I've kept thinking it wasn't right."

"Do you remember a face?"

She shook her head. "No. But I'm remembering details every time I close my eyes. The doctors said the day of the attack might flood back in, and it is. So it's only a matter of time. I need to see the evidence you have. I need to know if this guy"—she pointed at her drawing—"is still out there."

Armstrong sat back in his chair. "We need to pull your files and bring you back in. Where are you staying?"

"Manhattan."

Once again the officers exchanged glances. Their precinct was in Suffolk County, a good hour and fifty minutes outside the city. While her assault case had originated in Manhattan, it had merged with the murder case of Trina's late husband, who lived in the Hamptons. Officers

Armstrong and Gray had the cases combined. Left alone, Avery's assault case would have gone to the bottom of the page in terms of priority. A murder case of a wealthy man, on the other hand . . .

Avery turned several pages over in her notebook, took a pen from the desk, and scribbled down her cell phone number. "How long will it take to retrieve the file?"

"Later today, maybe tomorrow."

She tore the paper out and placed it on the desk as she stood. "I remember you saying that you had a video of the man you believe responsible leaving the garage."

"I think that's right," Gray said.

"Was there any other evidence linking this scar-faced man to me?"

"Physical evidence? No. Not that I recall. But one of Petrov's men turned state's evidence on the other in the suspicious deaths of your suspect and the housekeeper," Armstrong told her.

No evidence. None? "What was the state's evidence?"

"That Ruslan Petrov had put a hit out on you. His man hired Scarface, as you call him."

"What was the name of the scum that you assumed altered my face forever?"

"Mason, I think." Armstrong looked at Gray.

"Ken Mason. Went by Krueger on the street," Gray added.

"As in Freddy?" Avery asked.

"That's what his rap sheet told us. A known hit man."

"Did this Krueger have spider ink?"

They were silent.

"I'd have to look at the photos again," Armstrong eventually said.

Avery felt her blood pressure rise. "I will bet my next paycheck he didn't. The picture of Krueger that you showed me was a man with acne scars and haunting eyes. No ink on his neck from the mug shot. And while I don't remember the whole conversation, I do think you said something about him liking ink, but he kept it off his neck and arms. Since this Krueger made his living killing people for money, that would make sense. If he had two brain cells to rub together, he would keep any defining marks like this one"—she slapped her hand on her open notebook—"hidden."

Armstrong raised both palms in the air. "I understand your frustration. But at the time this was happening, you remembered nothing, and all we had to go on was the evidence we did find and the testimony of those in Petrov's circle. Now that you've remembered something distinctive, we can look into the case again. If Krueger didn't have this tattoo, we will reopen it."

She really wanted to scream. "By reopening it, what does that mean? Put out an APB on a tattoo?"

"Let's cross that bridge when we have to." Gray stood, along with Armstrong. "We need to do our job and get back to you."

She felt a brush-off coming.

"If you remember anything else, call us." Armstrong handed her a business card.

Avery started toward the door.

"Ms. Grant, don't forget your purse."

Avery glanced at the chair she'd just vacated. "I didn't bring one." No, she had the rental car key in her front pocket, a pocket wallet on her right hip, and her cell phone on her left.

"Let me walk you out," Armstrong said.

They zigzagged through the station and out into the lobby. From there he walked her to the front door and matched her pace down the steps. "Where are all of those bodyguard friends of yours, Ms. Grant? The last time we saw you, you were surrounded by an army."

Avery stopped in front of the rental car she didn't bother locking and opened the door. "You only need an army when you can't defend yourself."

He hiked a brow.

"Have a nice day, Detective." Avery slid behind the wheel, started the car, and reversed out of the space.

Armstrong stood, hands on hips, in her rearview mirror until she drove out of sight.

They had the wrong guy. She'd seen the looks on their faces, expressions that shadowed doubt on what they remembered about the case.

They had the wrong fucking guy.

Chapter Twenty-Two

Derrick Armstrong walked back into the station and straight to the office he shared with Gray. His partner was busy clicking behind the computer monitor. "Did you find it yet?"

"I'm not that fast."

They did have to dig a little deeper for archived files. But unlike the days when everything was paper and physical photographs that were stored in remote locations, they didn't have to leave the station to find what they were looking for.

Armstrong looked at the chair Ms. Grant had sat in. "A woman without a purse?"

"Less likely to get mugged," Gray said.

"More prepared to fight if she were."

Gray glanced up. "She doesn't look like a fighter."

"Looks aren't always what they seem."

"She sure as hell didn't fight the last time." Gray went back to the computer.

"No guarantee she wouldn't now." In fact, he would bet his next paycheck she would.

Thirty minutes later they were both staring at the postmortem pictures of Ken "Krueger" Mason.

"Well, shit."

The man had lots of ink but nothing that looked like a haunting spider crawling on an arm.

"What about the video we have on him leaving the garage?"

Gray pulled up the file and they watched the only footage they had of Krueger leaving the scene.

"Jeans. He's wearing denim, not tan pants," Armstrong pointed out.

"He looks like he's wearing boots."

"Yeah, but that's the only thing that matches Grant's description. She said tan pants and a spider tattoo. This guy might have been the one hired to take her out, but he isn't the one who did it." Armstrong turned from the desk. "Damn it."

"I'm not sure what you think we're going to do."

"We reopen the case."

Gray paused. "Okay, fine." He was the older of the two of them and tended to be more pragmatic about their cases. "But this guy, the one hired to murder Ms. Grant, is dead. And the man who hired him is also dead. Which leaves whoever beat up our victim only guilty of third-degree assault."

"Second-degree," Armstrong corrected. "Broken bones, ICU."

"Good luck making that stick. No weapon was used, she's not a public servant. And there were no long-lasting effects of the attack."

Armstrong doubted that.

"Any wet behind the ears public defender will get the charge dropped to a misdemeanor, and Spider Man will be back on the streets in a few hours." Gray pushed back from the computer and grabbed his cup of coffee.

"Unless he has priors."

Gray rolled his eyes. "A few days, then. C'mon, man. It's a low priority."

"Not for her."

"I understand that. Let's give her a day and then let her know we're reopening the case."

"Opening and then ignoring." Armstrong looked at the pile on his desk. They didn't have a choice.

"We can find all the ink in the world, but unless there is something else to go with it . . ."

"I know." Armstrong released a sigh and went back to his desk.

∞

Avery shed the rental car as soon as she entered the city. She didn't fool herself for a minute that she'd find her assailant by looking at arms throughout the streets. Besides, it was fall, and the nip in the air had everyone in long sleeves and sweaters. Then there was the pesky fact that there were one point six million residents in Manhattan. Even if you cut it down by race, that left 56 percent of that one point six falling into the Caucasian category. The arm bearing the spider tattoo had been white. Cut that in half for gender and take out the percentage of children in the mix . . . yeah, Avery had done the math. She was searching for one man in a sea of four hundred thousand. Omit the old, the ones that didn't have tattoos . . . she'd hated math in school, and she hated it even more now.

But nothing was going to stop her from looking. Spider, which was the name she used in her head for the guy who attacked her, was out there. He'd haunted her dreams, altered her appearance, and changed her life. She deserved to face him.

Avery stuffed a few hundred-dollar bills into her wallet and put it into the inside zippered pocket of the parka she wore. No subway pickpocket was getting the drop on her. One of the many things she'd learned from Brenda. The woman was practical to the core and assumed everyone was out to get her. It suited her teachings of krav well.

Avery left the luxury hotel just after two and started toward the West Village. Once there, she searched out the local college and then a coffee shop. Her stomach reminded her that she'd skipped breakfast and was working her way toward dinner without so much as a piece of toast. After grabbing a coffee and a bagel, Avery sat at the far end of the small café and waited.

College art students started pouring in and scouting out tables. Avery nibbled on her bagel and watched. Some of the kids sat absorbed in their phones, while others hovered over their textbooks with earbuds blaring music into their brains.

Avery abandoned her seat and meandered through the room. Two guys and a girl sat closest to the window. On their table were unopened artist sketchbooks and coffee.

"Which one of you is the budding artist?" Avery asked as she pretended to walk by.

The three of them stopped talking and looked her way.

"We all are," the girl said. She was white, average height, sporting coal black short hair with a streak of red on her bangs.

"Any of you good?"

They glanced at each other and smiled. "Lady, we wouldn't have gotten into the institute if we sucked." This from the Asian guy.

"Sorry, didn't mean to offend you. I was looking for someone who might want to make a little cash for a quick sketch."

College kids and cash.

Bait and hook.

"What kind of sketch?"

"Can I sit down?"

The Asian guy stood and offered his chair while snaking one from another table.

Avery thanked him and removed the picture from her pocket. "I'm Avery, by the way."

Their names were Hiraku, Monique, and Emmett.

"I want someone to do a better job at sketching this." Avery showed them her paltry scratches.

"Spiders. Cool," Emmett said.

"Is this supposed to be an arm?" Hiraku asked.

"Yeah. I'm thinking of a tattoo here." She patted the underside of her right arm.

Monique leaned back. "That's all you guys."

"Oh?" Avery questioned.

"I'm all about the face. Hiraku is anatomy and Emmett is still life."

Avery looked between the two of them. "Think you can sketch something if I can describe it to you?"

"What's in it for us?" Hiraku was the businessman.

Avery liked that.

She removed three one-hundred-dollar bills from her wallet and set them on the table.

Monique snatched up the money.

The guys looked at her.

"What? The rental agreement is in my name. Consider it an advance."

The kids shrugged as Hiraku tugged his sketch pad closer. He pulled out some kind of fancy case and removed a few pencils and got to work.

Avery would guide him once in a while. "More muscular. The veins protruded more. Hairy." With each instruction, the sketch came to life.

When Hiraku was done, he sent the page over to Emmett, who had been studying the image she drew.

"What's the scale on the arm?"

"Three-quarters, with the bulk of the body here and the legs spanning around."

Hiraku pulled another pad out and started drawing a posterior forearm.

Avery concentrated on what Emmett was sketching.

"It was long legged but hairy. You can see the joints. Almost like you're looking at it through a microscope."

"Wicked," Monique commented.

"More pointy on the legs," Avery encouraged.

Around them, the coffee shop buzzed with movement in and out. As the image in her head slowly came into view on the page, chills ran a path down her spine. But unlike before, this time the chill was laced with excitement. Like she was discovering something for the first time.

"Like this?" Emmett turned the sketch around for her to see.

"Yeah, only more lifelike. Dimensional."

Emmett shrugged like she had requested ice in her water. He twisted the page around several times, making slash marks on one side of the spider until it looked like it was crawling off the page.

"That's it." She stared at the paper like it was fine art that cost a fortune. Avery didn't doubt she would see this image in her head for years to come. But right now it was a blessing after months of darkness. This was the hand that hurt her.

Emmett took the paper back from her and drew over Hiraku's posterior arm.

Seeing the tips of the spider legs come to life on the other side of the arm was alarming. Almost like someone was grasping her with sharp nails that she couldn't krav her way out of.

"Dude, that's seriously good," Monique praised her friend.

"Spiders are cool. They get such a bad rap," Emmett said while he continued to add the dimension needed to match the other side of the arm.

"They run too fast," Avery said under her breath.

"You would, too, if you had eight legs and an exoskeleton," Hiraku said.

Emmett handed her the other page. Together they were matched perfectly.

"You guys are really good."

"Damn straight." Monique had attitude.

Avery loved it.

Avery stood with the papers in her hand.

"Here." Hiraku handed her a plastic sheath to put the sketches in.

Avery set them back on the table. "You should sign them. Since you're going to be famous one day."

Even though they laughed, they totally scratched their signatures on the bottoms of the pages.

"Thank you, guys." She dug back into her pocket and placed several hundred-dollar bills on the table. "Dinner's on me."

Stunned silence.

"Ah, anytime you need any other help. We're here all the time."

Avery winked. "I'll take you up on that."

Chapter Twenty-Three

She was busy. That's what Avery told him in her morning text.

But then nothing.

Liam tossed the ball for Whiskey in the backyard while drinking a beer. The days were getting shorter, but there was no lack of heat in the air.

The back door opened and his sister stepped out. "Dinner will be ready in fifteen."

"Thanks."

Michelle walked all the way outside. "Okay, what's wrong?"

"Nothing." He set his drink down and attempted to wrestle the ball out of his dog's mouth.

"I know that face and it's not okay."

"I'm fine."

Now Michelle just laughed. "It's about Avery?"

Much like his dog, Michelle didn't give up when she was onto something that had anything to do with emotions.

"She's out of town. Working. Not a lot of time to chat."

"In other words, you miss her."

He missed her, worried about her, and thought about her all the time. The dreams were as vivid as the memories. "Yup."

"Sounds pretty normal."

"Yup. Like I said, nothing wrong." Except that before their explosively sexual weekend she would drop a text in the middle of the day with something completely random. An emoji or a picture of a jacked up truck with a comment like *Where is the ladder to get up in this thing?* While it might not have been all that personal, the texts told him she was thinking about him, and he'd grown used to that instant smile.

"Call her. Tell her you miss her."

"You're such a girl."

"So is she." Michelle ducked back into the house the way she'd walked out.

Liam tossed the ball to the back of the fence.

He snagged his phone out of his back pocket and stared at the damn thing. Now who was acting like a girl?

He pressed Avery's number and put the phone to his ear.

The line went to voice mail on the fourth ring. "You've reached Avery Grant. Leave a message, and I'll call you back as soon as possible."

"Hey, Princess." Oh, damn . . . what should he say now? *Miss you* sounded needy. *Thinking of you* was obvious. He should have sent a text. "Do you like dogs?" Where the hell had that come from? "I mean. Never mind. I hope everything is going well in Seattle. Call me when you have a second."

He hung up.

"Do you like dogs?" He might as well have asked if she liked suburbia and white picket fences.

Liam grabbed his beer and jogged down into his yard.

⌒⊙

Her cell phone startled her awake.

Avery plopped a hand on the bedside table to answer the rattle. "Hello?"

"Ms. Grant?"

"Yes."

"It's Detective Armstrong."

She woke up quickly, hearing his name. "Hold on." She tossed back the covers and swung her legs over the side of the bed. She glanced at the clock. Nine in the morning. She rubbed the sleep from her eyes. "Okay. I'm back."

"Did I catch you at a bad time?"

"I overslept. What did you find, Detective?"

"We looked over the pictures of our suspect."

She knew what was coming even before he said the words. "And?"

"He didn't have any tattoo of a spider on his body."

Avery crossed to the windows and pulled the light-blocking blinds open. She winced. "So what do we do now?"

"We're reopening the case."

There was some satisfaction in that.

"I need to caution you . . ."

"Caution me about what?"

"Tattoos are circumstantial at best. Unless there is something else to identify your attacker, the chances of being able to arrest, let alone prosecute, anyone we find with that mark is minimal."

"What does that mean? You're not going to look?"

"We'll look. But . . ."

"But what?" It was too early for her to be this upset.

"Ms. Grant . . . we want men that do the things this guy did to you off the street just as much as you do."

"I doubt you want it more than me."

"Okay. Maybe in this case that's true. Most of us got into this profession because we want to protect and serve. This case is almost a year old, and without a physical description outside of a tattoo, he is going to be impossible to find with the resources we have."

Resources . . . that was what this was all about. "You mean it's not a priority."

"I mean we need more than a spider tattoo. An image that can be repeated on any arm, every arm, from here to Jersey."

She started to pace. "What if I do remember this guy's face and I give you a description?"

"Now we have something to work with. We give our friends in Manhattan the description. We search the prison database. If he is here, we'll eventually find him. Then we can bring you back here to identify him."

The tone in Armstrong's voice told her there was something he wasn't saying.

"And then?"

"We give the case to the DA and hold him as long as we can."

"What does that mean?" She was starting to raise her voice.

"Ms. Grant—"

She was getting tired of hearing her name. "Avery."

"Avery, this guy assaulted you. People are mugged and assaulted every day in Manhattan."

She closed her eyes, her breath coming fast. "I was in the ICU for a week."

"Which will weigh on the case. You have a lawyer friend, right?"

Lori. "Yes."

"Ask her what the chances are of this particular perpetrator doing any serious time for your attack. There are always exceptions, but my guess is your friend will break this down to a few months, maybe a year or two."

"So I'm just supposed to turn my back on him? He fucked me up, Armstrong. I'm not the same person I was before he stomped my head into the pavement." She was seething.

"I'm going to look for him, Avery. Give me a description. Let us do our job."

"Why don't I believe you?"

"Give me his face, and if he is still here, we will bring him in. But finding him is not going to give you the satisfaction you seek."

"How do you know that?"

"Because I watch the face of victim after victim when we have to let their assailants back on the street. We go from hero to asshole in one day in cases like this."

Where was the fairness in any of this?

Since when did she think life was fair?

"I'm sorry, Avery. I really am."

"This is hard to accept." She refused to.

"I know. How long are you in the city?"

Until I find him. "I don't know. I have some work here," she lied.

"If you remember more while you're here, give me a call. I'll come to the city, and we'll sit down with a police artist and get his face in every station. But don't put your life on hold. We can do this remotely."

Out of sight, out of mind.

She wasn't going anywhere.

∽

Avery jumped on the subway and made her way downtown to where the majority of tattoo shops were in Manhattan. After a night of research, she'd learned a few things about the industry and its history.

Sometime in the 1960s, tattooing a person had been banned. The prohibition had lasted over thirty years and was legalized in the late nineties. Like any prohibition, the law wasn't followed, but the places that offered tattoos weren't advertised. Which meant that there weren't as many tattoo parlors in the city as she thought. Of course, there was no guarantee Spider had gotten his artwork done in Manhattan. Still, it was a start. Avery felt better looking for this guy than letting him haunt her dreams any longer.

She walked into the first tattoo parlor just before noon. The walls were filled with examples of what could be permanently placed on your body for a price.

"Good morning," the clerk greeted her.

Avery approached the desk with a smile. "Good morning."

"Looking to get some work done?"

"No, uhm . . . I'm looking for some information."

The guy's smile dimmed.

Avery pulled her sketches out of her folder. "I'm looking for someone who has this on his arm."

The heavyset man rubbed his beard and glanced at her. "You a cop?"

"No." She was taken aback. "I'm . . ." *I have a vendetta against this asshole* probably wouldn't get her anywhere if, in fact, he was a paying customer at this establishment. "I'm interested in the artist who did this."

The man took a breath and pushed her picture back over the counter. "Yeah, right. Never seen it before."

Even if he had, he wouldn't tell her.

"Okay, thanks for your help." *Asshole.*

The next parlor, she took a different approach.

This time a woman was behind the desk, said her name was Zelda. Which fit. Zelda was full of ink from her neck to her fingertips and wearing a spaghetti strap shirt to show it all off.

"I need a little information about your services."

"Thinking of getting some work done?" Was this a standard question?

"Not for me. My boyfriend." Avery presented the pictures. "He likes spiders and was talking about adding to his arms."

"We can definitely do it."

"Do you have an artist here that has done work like this before?"

"Yeah, we all have."

"With this much detail?"

Zelda smiled. "We can show you examples of our work to assure you it can be done." She twisted the image around, looked at the back. "Who sketched this for you?"

Avery smiled. "A friend. How long would it take to do something like this?"

"A couple sessions, about four hours each, minimum."

"So a long time."

"Not really."

Avery leaned forward as if contemplating a true decision about giving a tattoo as a gift. "How much would this run?"

Zelda told her.

"Oh. I didn't realize it cost that much."

Zelda wasn't amused. "You get what you pay for. Any guy who has that on his arm isn't paying a set price but by the hour. By all means, check out more than one parlor. Be careful of anyone who says it will cost less or you'll end up with him." Zelda pointed to a cartoon character in the shape of a spider.

"We wouldn't want that. Have you ever seen a tattoo like this on anyone? I wouldn't want to suggest something that everyone else has."

Zelda shrugged. "I haven't. Not on a forearm."

Avery felt she was on a roll. "Is there anyone in the city that specializes in spiders?"

"Are you asking for the name of my competition?"

Avery took the picture back and put it in her folder. "I guess that wouldn't be a smart business practice. I don't want to make a mistake in the establishment I pick. Things are going really well with my guy, ya know? I would have to pull extra shifts for this kind of money."

Zelda sighed. "Listen, there is a guy in the Meatpacking District. But he is always six months out in his appointments, and his prices reflect that. He specializes in things like spiders and anything that crawls. But I'm telling you. We can do this." Zelda pulled her card out and wrote a name on the back. "If you want this for a fair price, you'll be back."

Avery tapped the card against her palm. "Thank you. You've been so helpful."

An hour later she was in the Meatpacking District, in front of yet another walking piece of art, asking questions.

"Yeah, Van can do that."

"Can I talk to him? It's a big decision . . ." Yadda, yadda. My boyfriend. Avery repeated all the lies she'd used to get her there.

"You can make an appointment. I have room in April."

"I'd like to talk to him first."

"Yeah, well, he isn't here. There's a big expo in Chicago this weekend."

The euphoria of an hour before quickly faded. "Well, can you tell me if he's done anything like this before?"

The clerk glanced at the walls with testimonials everywhere showing spider art. "It's what he does."

"Exactly this. Has he done this tattoo before?"

Did he just roll his eyes?

"Every tattoo is going to be unique due to the canvas you're putting it on."

Avery shoved the paper in front of him. "This?"

He shook his head as if done with the entire conversation. "Yes. Maybe. It looks a little familiar, but that doesn't mean it's common. I see spiders in my sleep after working here."

Not a confirmation, but not a denial. "How much will this cost?"

Zelda was right. This Van Lynch guy wanted triple.

Avery smiled and gathered her papers. "You get what you pay for, right?"

"Right. So do you want the appointment in April?"

"I need to check with my boyfriend."

The clerk seemed annoyed that she'd wasted his time.

Once again it was after two and she hadn't eaten. Avery made her way uptown and walked through Central Park while eating a hot dog. Food on the go. That's what she needed, nothing fancy, and certainly no liquor to accompany anything.

Sitting on a park bench, she watched as people walked by, normal people doing normal things while Spider was out there. Avery judged every woman. Could they handle themselves if Spider attacked them? Would they freeze and cower on the ground while a boot flew into their face?

Her phone buzzed in her pocket. It had been doing that a lot.

She pulled it out. Four messages.

The first was Brenda. *"You missed your appointment. Don't think I won't charge you. We'll work harder on Friday."*

Then there was Liam. *"Hey, Princess."* He paused. *"Do you like dogs? I mean. Never mind. I hope everything is going well in Seattle. Call me when you have a second."*

She squeezed her eyes shut when she heard his voice. He didn't deserve her lies.

The next two messages were from Sheldon. *"Hey, Avery. I hired an exterminator. Take care of that little issue upstairs."* Thoughtful. She was actually a little impressed. Only his next message wiped all that away. *"Two days and you're not here. Are you planning on coming back?"* His voice was angry. *"Call me."*

She'd take care of Brenda later.

There was no way she was going to talk to Liam. She chickened out of a phone call and sent a text. **Super busy. Up early, back late. Damn phone battery isn't holding a charge. Sorry.** She hit send and stared at her message. Lame and lies. She wanted to add that she'd call him. But she wouldn't. Not yet.

Sheldon picked up on the second ring. She was really hoping for a voice mail.

"I'm sorry," she said after they said hello.

"I'm not sure how you're going to get the job done on time if you're not here."

"I understand. The spider thing freaked me out. Took a whole day to stop shaking." She faked a flirty laugh. "I'm a girl sometimes."

Sheldon's voice softened. "I can understand that."

Avery kicked herself for using her breathy voice. "Then something really important came up. It's not avoidable."

"How long will you be gone?"

"It's my aunt. She's sick. I'm in Seattle helping her out." And the lies kept coming.

"I'm sorry to hear that. I guess there isn't a huge hurry if I'm reno- vating. Did you talk to your contractor?"

Avery tossed a silent fist in the air and winced. *Jesus.* "Yes. I gave him your number. But he's busy, Sheldon. I'm not sure if he can help you out, but he might be able to recommend someone who can."

"Do you have his number on you? I can call him."

She bit her lip. "Nope. Left that back in LA. I'm sure he'll call soon. He's reliable." *Unlike me.*

"Okay. Let me know when you're back so I know when to expect people around."

"I will absolutely do that." The only nonlie that left her mouth. "Thank you for understanding."

She hung up the phone and damn near tossed it across the park. "'Oh, what a tangled web we weave.'" *How poetic.*

Chapter Twenty-Four

"Sorry?" From the woman who said she'd said she was sorry five times in her whole life and actually meant it. He understood work, completely got being so busy you don't stop. Her phone not holding a charge was what stumped him. Something about that didn't feel right. Yeah, it happened . . . but what did it take to send a quick *hello, I miss you?*

Had he scared her off so completely that she was running away? *I don't do relationships. I don't date.* Her mantra since they met had been broken through over the last two weeks, yet now she was pulling away. The thought made his chest ache.

"She's just busy working," he told himself.

Yet the other voice, his inside voice, said he was fooling himself. There was more to it.

Avery started back toward her hotel and walked past Bergdorf Goodman. She stopped and tilted her head to take in the high-rise department store. It was one of her favorite stomping grounds when she was in New York. The last time she'd been there was the day of the attack.

Someone bumped into her while walking by, snapping her out of her thoughts.

"Sorry," the guy said, walking away.

"No problem . . ." Her words trailed off when her eyes landed on the parking garage she was attacked in.

Without thought, she followed the rush of people crossing on the not quite green light until she stood where she had been nearly a year before.

She walked in and down the ramp, ignoring the fact that her heart sped up and her palms started to sweat. There had been no anxiety when she'd walked in before. She had finished her first real day of work, and the mom bag she'd used to carry all of Trina's late husband's treasures had been empty. Having several hundred thousand dollars of watches and pens had made her feel like a target. The irony wasn't lost on her now.

Fluorescent lights hummed above her head and attempted to stay lit. The flickering sparked a memory. She glanced up. Fire sprinkler lines crisscrossed the concrete ceiling, which served as a floor for what sat above. Black stains from smog-producing engines stained the dingy white walls. Well, they were once white, though now they sported a dirty gray patina that couldn't be duplicated with a can of paint. You would think a garage on Fifth Avenue would be better maintained. Then again, the garage would always be full, and the people leaving their cars there would pay a premium regardless of how pretty it was or wasn't.

The low ceiling started to weigh on her as she walked deeper. Anyone watching would probably think she was staking out a car. Normally she looked like she belonged there. Fancy shoes, nice skirt, sunglasses that cost what those college kids made in a month. Today she wore black leggings, a comfortable flat boot, a T-shirt, and a short-waist jacket. No makeup and not one accessory. She hadn't even packed a pair of earrings for her trip.

After a year, Avery wouldn't have remembered the space where she'd parked. The injury and trauma had caused some memory loss. But now things were starting to come back to her. And the police report she'd read over and over had spelled it out. Space 16B was currently occupied by a compact Toyota. Not the car she'd been driving.

She'd been digging through her purse when something hit her. She closed her eyes and willed her mind to let the image in. A deep breath through her nose repeated the smell of asphalt. Only it wasn't asphalt, but oil and grime. She moved to the front of the car. There was a little more space in front of 16B than the others in the garage since a support pillar shared the space with the wall. Enough room to dump a woman left for dead where she would not immediately be seen.

Avery ran her hand along the wall and knelt closer to the ground. The smell of tires and oil . . . that's where she'd gotten *asphalt*.

Lights flickered above her head.

She looked up, flinched, and fell back on her butt, which had been only a few inches off the ground.

"Don't look at me. Jesus, don't look at me."

He wore a worn-out sweatshirt with a hood. Most of it covering his face. But not all.

With shaky hands, Avery removed her cell phone from her zippered pocket and opened a voice recording app.

"White. Not too tall, average. Stubble. Lack of shave. Strong chin. Tired eyes." She closed hers. "What color?" Nothing came.

She rewound the tape in her head.

I'm walking through the garage with my head in my purse. How fucking stupid could I be? She shook away her stupidity. Avery wasn't that girl any longer.

He hits me, like a body slam to the ground. I see the boot coming and close my eyes. I open them briefly and see brown pants. Big and loose and too short. Avery lifted her phone to her lips. "His pants don't fit him. They're too loose and too short. Like you'd see on a homeless guy. Only he's fast. And fidgeting. He kicks me a lot. I keep my eyes closed until he starts to drag me." She looked at the ground in front of the car. "I feel my head hit the concrete car stop. He dropped me and that's when I see him. He's cussing and telling me not to look at him. He kicks my face again. His boots are brand-new. There's a plastic tag on the bottom that hasn't worn off yet." Avery went on describing everything she remembered about her assailant until there was nothing left to tell.

Footsteps broke her blank stare and prompted her to her feet.

Twenty feet away, a security guard had a hand on his flashlight. "Whatcha doin' over there?" His accent was pure Jersey.

Avery brushed at her butt. "I was here last week. I lost an earring. Thought maybe it fell out when I was taking my jacket off." She pretended to look around the cars.

"Expensive?"

She shrugged. "Sentimental." A few more passes around the car and she lifted her arms in the air. "Guess I'm outta luck."

The guard relaxed. "You can give me ya number. I'll call if I find somethin'."

"It's okay. Chances are if it is here, it's unusable now." She turned and walked away. "Thanks anyway."

"No problem."

He was definitely watching her ass as she left the garage.

Avery grabbed a taxi and returned to the West Village.

She walked into the coffee shop and sat down. "I need another drawing."

"She's avoiding me. I pushed things and she's bowing out. I can feel it."

"You don't know that. She's working. You zone out for days at a time when you're knee-deep in a new project." Michelle huddled over coffee with him first thing Friday morning.

"Things were going so well. Her friends like me. Getting your friends on the same page with a new relationship is gold, right?"

Michelle nodded.

"For all I know she's back in town and hasn't bothered to call."

"Go to her place."

"I'm not going to stalk her."

"Yeah, but you're not ready to walk away. Maybe she has some emotional baggage she's dealing with. She's divorced, right?"

"Yeah."

"Did she talk about her ex?"

Liam shrugged. "Not much." Only to say she married him for his money. Which Liam still had a hard time believing.

"You're supposed to see her tonight, right?"

It was krav night. "Yeah. But she could blow that off."

"But she can't blow off work. Maybe drop by this house she's working on. If she's there, you know she's avoiding you, and you take it from there. I'm a big one for not jumping to conclusions. Talk to her. Ask her point-blank if she's avoiding you. And face-to-face . . . none of those damn phone conversations or, God forbid, texting."

At noon, Liam detoured to Brentwood. He meandered up the established neighborhood, asking himself if just showing up was a good idea. As he turned into the driveway and didn't see her car, he realized all his worry was for nothing. She wasn't there. Unless she turned her Aston in for a Volvo, which he highly doubted.

He stepped out of his truck and looked around.

The door wasn't open like it had been every other time he'd been there. Safe to say if she was there, the place would be "airing out," as she put it.

"Can I help you?"

Liam turned to the male voice.

"I'm looking for Avery."

"Aren't we all? She isn't here." Strange response.

Liam took the guy in and heard Avery's voice in his head. "You must be Sheldon Lankford."

"I am. You are?"

Liam took a few steps toward the man and reached out a hand. "Liam Holt. Avery's contractor."

"Right." The man's handshake wasn't all that firm. He held on the right amount of time, but he looked above Liam's head instead of in his eye. "I was hoping you'd call . . . or stop by, as it seems. I appreciate you taking the time to look over the place and give me your feedback."

"No problem."

Sheldon motioned him inside. "Avery said you're a busy guy and you weren't sure you'd be available to do the job."

"All true." Half-true. But blowing off the man's work right now, with his relationship with Avery tilting off the ledge . . . yeah, he didn't want to do that quite yet.

"When did you want to get started?" Liam asked, as if interested in the job.

"As soon as possible. I realize that might not be reasonable. A good contractor probably isn't sitting around waiting for jobs to fall in their laps."

Liam looked around the space. It didn't look a whole lot different from the last time he'd been there. "I was going to talk to Avery about when she'd be done with her portion."

"Originally she said at the end of next week. But apparently her aunt is sick and she had to fly to Seattle to help her out."

Liam's step faltered. Sick aunt? Did Avery have an aunt?

"Oh?"

"Yeah. I'm sorry about the aunt, but it's better than her abandoning the job."

Liam narrowed his eyes. "Abandoning the job. Why would she do that?" Did the guy in front of him make a pass at her? If so, he'd probably be nursing a bruise.

"I swung by on Monday and found her coming down from the attic. A baby tarantula was in her hair. She freaked after I got it off her, and she ran out."

Liam wanted to shake. He'd be less than okay if a big spider was on his head.

Sheldon looked at him. "Women."

Forging a smile, Liam agreed. "Yeah, women."

Twenty minutes later, Liam was back on the road. So either Avery lied to him about work or to Sheldon about an aunt. A white lie to the person paying you he understood. Calling in sick on a day you wanted to hit the beach was a norm. But a full week?

The rest of the day, Avery slipped into his head anytime his mind was silent.

Damn, he missed her. Hearing her voice. Teasing her about their not-date dates.

But it wasn't until he and Brenda were sitting at the studio, thirty minutes past Avery's appointment time, that Liam was done sitting back.

Blowing off work.

Blowing off Brenda.

And blowing off him.

None of it felt right. Phones were in every pocket, and there certainly would be one at the hotel in Seattle.

Something tasted funny about the whole thing.

He walked into Avery's complex and was greeted by James. "Mr. Holt. Nice to see you again."

"Thank you."

"If you're here to see Ms. Grant, she's not home."

"Yeah, yeah. I know. She told me." That confirmed that. "I was dropping by to see Lori and Reed Barnum."

"Are they expecting you?"

"No."

James walked him over to the desk and picked up the phone.

"Good evening, Mrs. Barnum. Liam Holt would like to come up."

"Of course."

James smiled. "You know where the elevators are."

Liam took two steps. "Wait, what number are they again?"

James told him and he disappeared around the corner.

Lori answered with a smile and a short hug. "This is a surprise. Come on in."

"Thanks for seeing me."

Reed walked over from their dining room table, dropping his napkin on his plate.

"I'm interrupting."

"No, no. We just finished," Reed assured him. "Sit."

Yeah, Liam didn't want to sit.

"Listen. This feels awkward for me." Liam glanced at Lori. "At the risk of sounding like a stalker, I just have to know she's okay."

Lori moved to Reed's side. "Who, Avery?"

Liam nodded. "Yeah. Have you guys heard from her?"

"No. Not since last Monday."

Liam ran a hand through his hair. "She told me she went to Seattle with some kind of urgency for her last job. She's texted me twice, but all distant stuff. Which, hey, if it's me she's avoiding, fine. Not fine, but okay. Then today I learned that she told Sheldon Lankford that she had a sick aunt she was taking care of in Seattle. Blowing me off . . . yeah, I don't want that to happen. But work and appointments?"

He realized when he was done talking that he sounded like a love-sick teenage boy. Which was sadly accurate.

Lori shook her head while she turned to her husband. "I knew there was a problem."

"We don't know that."

"It's been a year. She was having nightmares."

Liam felt some of his insecurities dissipate, rapidly replaced with concern. "A year since what?" All he could think of was her divorce. But he was pretty sure she said that had been a couple of years past.

"Since New York," Lori said as if he should understand.

"What happened in New York?"

Both Reed and Lori turned to him.

"She didn't tell you?" Lori asked.

"Tell me what?"

"Wait, you work out doing krav with her, right?"

"Yeah."

"And she didn't tell you why she picked it up?" Lawyer Lori kept asking questions. Each one made his concern grow.

"No," he said. "When did she finally decide to tell you she was taking krav?"

"Last week."

"Babe, I'm betting she's just working through it," Reed said.

"I'm betting she needs help with that."

Liam lifted both hands in the air. "Can one of you tell me what happened in New York?"

Lori tilted her head to the side. "If she doesn't want you to know . . ."

No way, he wasn't going to let that happen. "Avery told me she didn't want you knowing about krav because all of you would worry. If you think I should know about New York because of krav, then that ties it together. And now I'm scared shitless."

"She was attacked."

"Reed, damn it," Lori yelled at her husband and smacked the side of his arm with the back of her hand.

"Sorry, hon. He's right. If it were you, I'd be ripping things apart to get to the truth."

Lori tossed her hands in the air and walked away.

"Attacked by who?" Liam asked Reed.

It took ten minutes for Reed to spell out what New York stood for. As Liam heard the story of the brutality that drove Avery to learn to defend herself, a much clearer picture of how strong the woman he was falling for became. The only saving grace to the information was that the man who did it was dead.

"So my take is, she's working through the anniversary. Unlike my wife, I think sometimes that's a solo journey. My guess is she'll be back when things are straight in her head."

"She doesn't have to do this alone," Liam told him.

"Yeah, but Avery doesn't open herself up. The girls know her better, obviously, but even they don't really have a handle on what's going on in her head. Since the injury, that got worse." Reed smiled at Liam. "Until lately. Until you came along. She seems a lot happier and more settled with you in her life."

He didn't mind hearing that. "But she doesn't trust me enough to ask for my help."

"Don't take it personally. We didn't know she was out of town, and we know everything."

During their conversation, Lori was standing by the floor to ceiling window, talking on the phone.

"Of course I'm worried. Even more now. No. Don't hurry. I'll find out what's going on and call you. Love you, too."

"Who was that?" Reed asked.

"Trina."

Reed scowled. "Aren't they still on their honeymoon?"

"Yes. And before you scold me . . . I had to call her."

"Why?"

"Because she's the only one who has Avery on Friend Finder. Guess who isn't in Seattle?"

"Avery," Liam said without amusement.

"Exactly."

"So where is she?" Reed asked.

Lori paused, nose flared. "New York."

Chapter Twenty-Five

Avery walked out of the print shop holding a hundred copies of the man she was searching for. Much as she wanted to put a reward sign on him and wait for his friends to turn, she figured that probably wasn't the best idea. Instead, she left the stack in her hotel room after sending a copy to Armstrong.

He called within two minutes of her sending a text.

"This is him?"

"Yup."

"You're sure?"

It was only a profile, but it was all she could remember. Maybe it was all she saw. "I'm sure. So go tell all your cop friends that this is the guy." Not that they would work hard to find him. Still, she had to try.

"Okay. Thank you. You didn't have to hire an artist. Your tax dollars do pay for this kind of thing."

"Great. I'll be sure and tell my new friends you're hiring."

Armstrong actually laughed. "We'll find him, Avery. I'll do everything I can to get him behind bars."

Yeah, well, she wanted a shot at him first. One solid punch to the nose, was that asking for too much? Maybe he would attack her again and she could . . .

She blocked out the consequences of those actions and would deal when they came. It wasn't like she had kids at home, or a husband.

Liam.

Not a husband. Her friends would understand.

Maybe Spider was already behind bars?

"Are you still there?"

"Yeah, sorry." *Not sorry.*

"Are you back in LA?"

"Not yet."

"Why?"

"Trying to get rid of me, Detective?"

There was static on the line.

"Just making sure you don't have any vigilante tendencies."

"Ha."

"You wouldn't be the first," he said.

Avery reached down and unzipped her boots. "Do I look like a fighter to you?"

"I wouldn't use that word."

"What word would you use?"

"The first time I saw you, you were a victim. The next time I saw a survivor."

"And now?"

He paused. "A warrior."

She liked that. "I don't plan on starting any wars."

Armstrong laughed again. "Women have been starting wars since the dawn of time."

She kicked her boots to the side. "I'm an army of one, Detective. I doubt I can do much damage."

He sighed. "Go home, Avery."

"Have a nice evening, Detective. Take the wife out. It's Friday." She hung up.

"God damn it!" Armstrong kicked the side of his tire. Avery's text came through right as he'd left the station for the night. Now he was marching back inside, pissed.

"Is it Monday already?" Judy, the officer at the desk, joked as he walked past.

"Fuck off."

She laughed.

His butt hit his chair and he woke up his computer.

Gray poked his head in. "I thought you left."

"Grant has a sketch."

"Avery Grant?"

"Yeah." He sent a copy of the picture she texted him to his computer and brought it up on his screen.

Gray rounded the desk to look at the image. "Half a face."

"Better than nothing."

"Doesn't look familiar."

"Yeah, but we don't work Manhattan anymore."

Gray stood to his full height. "Need my help?"

"No. Go. I just need to send this out and look up a few things."

Gray pulled his car keys out of his pocket. "This can wait till Monday."

"Yeah, but she won't."

"What does that mean?"

"I think we have a vigilante on our hands."

"That little thing?"

Armstrong pressed send to put the image of their suspect, and the case number, out into the police universe. "Hey, Judy could kick your ass."

"She could try."

What could Avery Grant do? What was her background? Something told him he was going to come up cold, but he had to look. His hunches were seldom wrong.

"You sure you don't need me?"

"No. I got it. Go."

"You don't have to tell me twice." Gray walked out the door but his voice kept coming. "Sally's gonna be pissed."

Shit . . . his wife.

∽

Avery made it into a department store after all. Mainly because she hadn't packed for a weeklong trip, and it didn't look like she'd be leaving Manhattan anytime soon.

Now she stood in her hotel room, staring at the few things she'd needed.

She slid into a miniskirt made of spandex, the kind she could hike up at the first sign of trouble to use her legs. Wearing pants, jeans, or leggings in the clubs she planned on hitting would make her stand out like an angel at a hell convention. The guy in her drawing was young, maybe late twenties at best. The tattoo cost a lot of money if, in fact, this Van guy created the thing. His boots had been new. Not something a street bum would have on. The clothes in her memory stumped her. But she was going with her gut, and that meant checking out the kinds of places young people with money went on Friday nights. She knew her chances of actually finding this guy ran up there with winning the lottery. She had to try.

Maybe a week more and she'd exhaust herself into acceptance.

Maybe finally having some memory of what had happened would settle the turmoil inside of her and she could return to her normal life.

Maybe.

She didn't want regrets. If she didn't look, that's what she'd end up with.

Avery slipped into the new boots she'd bought for the club. Sturdy heel only an inch and a half off the ground. Club-worthy and *I can still kick the shit out of you* practical.

She skipped the braless look and opted for a skintight halter and short-waist jacket. Inside pockets a must.

Her cell phone now had a wallet case with everything she needed inside.

She puffed her hair in the mirror, added some spray, and dabbed bright red on her lips. Guys talked to pretty girls. Especially blonde ones. The more blonde she acted, the more information she'd get. A fact of life Avery learned her junior year of high school.

Avery left the hotel armed with nothing more than attitude and determination.

She had four clubs on her list. All upscale, all uptown, all hot and new.

Chin high, she winked her way through the door of the first club without paying a cover charge. Women ruled the club scene. Without the girls there, the guys didn't spend money on drinks. And that's where clubs made their money. This fact Avery had learned in college. If she ever had a daughter, there would be a tutorial before her sixteenth birthday. Right along with a lifetime membership at a krav studio.

What had her thinking about a kid of her own, Avery didn't know.

Techno music and flashing neon was the theme. The beat was sporadic but that didn't stop people from dancing. It was still early for the club scene, giving Avery the ability to walk around the people without having to touch them.

She started with the bartender.

Model beautiful, the woman dropped a napkin on the counter. "What can I get ya?"

Avery waved her off. She turned her phone around. "Have you seen this guy?"

She glanced at Avery's phone. "Not sure."

"What about this?" The picture of the tattoo.

"I would have remembered that. Sorry. Why?"

"Douche stiffed me with the bar bill last weekend in midtown. Said he came in here once in a while."

"Did he have a name?"

"I was drunk."

The bartender nodded like she'd been there.

"Can you ask the other guys?"

Avery handed her the phone.

She watched as the woman showed it to the other guys behind the bar. One by one they looked up toward Avery, shook their heads, and continued with the drinks they were mixing.

"Sorry."

Avery meandered around the room, stopping the cocktail waitresses, giving the same story. It was easy to gain information from the women when you bonded over a douchey guy.

Thirty minutes later, she was back on the street and walking her way to the next club.

The second club was nearly the same routine, only a little harder to gain the attention of the bartenders since the clubs were filling up. Less techno and more hip-hop. The dance floor was packed.

Avery expanded her conversations to small groups of women.

The same reaction.

When she reached her third club for the night, rap dominated the playlist, and her butt skirted past sweaty bodies everywhere she walked. She would bet her next paycheck the room was way over the FDNY capacity limit. But until something went desperately wrong, laws often didn't get enforced. The bar was three deep. She looked to the far end, found a couple of guys, and moved in.

"Excuse me." Flip the hair, smile. "It's so crowded over there. Hope you don't mind me barging in."

The older, taller, and more slender of the two had no problem letting his eyes rake down her skirt and back up to rest on her chest.

"Beauty like you is never barging."

She let her smile linger and motioned for the bartender.

"Can we buy you a drink?" The younger guy held her gaze and wasn't foaming at the mouth. Avery wondered if he knew that he'd get further with girls by looking them in the eye.

"I got it."

The bartender tilted an ear and waited for her order.

Avery moved through the same routine. Phone out . . . "Have you seen him?"

The guys she stood by overheard her by design.

"Stiffed you for drinks?"

She grinned. "Yeah. I wanted to return the favor."

Tall and Sleazy said something under his breath. The polite guy reached for her phone. "Doesn't look familiar."

Yeah, she was looking for a drop of rain in a pond.

"Is that a tattoo?"

She nodded.

He leaned forward so she could hear him. "Do chicks like that?"

Avery found herself smiling. "No."

"Sure I can't buy you a drink?" Polite Kid asked.

She shook her head and leaned closer to his ear. "You might want to ditch Sleazeball here. Chicks don't like being eye raped."

Mr. Polite looked over her shoulder, then back.

Avery winked and walked off.

"If you change your mind . . ."

Avery waved and walked away.

By the fourth club, defeat had settled in.

The bartenders hadn't seen him. Most of the waitresses were too busy to look. And the music sucked. It was an uptown club that felt downtown to her. There was some serious drug action going on in a dark corner. Some didn't even bother hiding the lines on the tables.

At almost one in the morning, she was done.

"Hello . . ."

Avery smiled, not feeling it. "Hi." What she really wanted to say was *not in this lifetime*. But she was an adult these days, and talk like that caused trouble.

"What are you drinking?"

"I'm good."

"Yes, you are."

Just a kid. One that didn't mind a weight room, but a rich kid if she ever saw one. "Lines like that work for you, stud?"

"You'd be surprised." Clean-cut, money, if the watch he was wearing belonged to him.

"Eventually the women will be older, and that will result in a drink to the face."

He leaned back and his smile left the room. "Bitches better think twice before ruining my shirts."

Tough guy . . . great. Avery turned as a cocktail waitress holding a tray of shots was walking by. She stopped her, tossed a ten on the tray, and picked up a drink.

Rich Kid stared at her, daring.

Her fingers itched.

She stared back.

Avery tipped back the shot and returned the empty glass to the tray.

He found his smile again. "That was hot."

She couldn't stop herself. "Not in this lifetime." She turned to walk away, and he grabbed her arm, hard.

Instant heat shot through her. A twist, a turn, and a shove and his arm was disengaged, and Rich Kid stumbled into the tray the cocktail waitress was holding. Tiny drinks all over his shirt.

Avery thought that would be it.

It wasn't.

He marched up, hands ready to shove.

She pivoted and brushed his hand away with her forearm. The force was enough to leave a bruise on both of them. He sailed past, stumbling again.

By now a small crowd had stopped dancing.

"Dude, let it go." This was yelled by a bystander.

He charged again. Avery raised her hands, palms out. "I want nothing to do with you," she yelled. While the stance looked as nonthreatening as it got, her legs were in position and her hands were up, protecting her face.

Someone stepped between the two of them. "Fuck, dude. She's a girl. Hands off."

"Bitch pushed me."

"You grabbed her." The cocktail waitress stepped in.

Rich Kid glared at her, lifted his chin.

By now security was barging their way in.

Avery felt adrenaline dumping into her system.

"You okay?" the guy who stepped between them asked her once security was escorting Rich Kid to the door.

"I'm fine." She pulled her skirt down and dusted her hair off her shoulder. "Done for the night."

"Might wanna wait a few minutes before taking off. That guy is in here all the time. Pure asshole. Wouldn't put it past him to wait at the door."

"Thanks."

She worked her way to the women's bathroom and bumped through the women to wash her hands. A small trickle of blood ran down her arm. She must have caught the guy's watch. She rinsed it off and dabbed the scratch with a towel. The attendant in the bathroom smiled and offered her a mint.

Avery took one and pulled a five from her pocket. It was the smallest bill she had.

Expensive mint.

Back in the club, she made her way to the door.

The bouncer recognized her and moved to her side. "How about a taxi?" He glanced across the street and sure enough . . . Rich Kid watched.

The bouncer stepped into the street and hailed a cab. When the car stopped, Avery climbed in the back. The bouncer tossed a few bills to the driver. "You come in anytime, little lady. No cover, drinks on me."

She smiled. There were some nice guys out there. Unfortunately the world was laced with assholes, too. "Thanks."

Back at her hotel, Avery flicked on the lights in the bathroom and looked at herself in the mirror. Her eyes fell on the bruise forming on her arm where the guy had grabbed her and where she'd blocked him.

Warriors bruised but they didn't break.

Avery wiggled out of her skirt and turned on the shower. By the time she got out, the room was full of steam and her mind had finally started to rest.

When her cell phone rang, she picked it up from habit. "Hello?"

"You're answering your phone. That's new." It was Lori.

"Hey. It's late, what's up? Is everyone okay?" Avery wiped the mirror. Mascara ran down her face.

"How is New York?"

She paused. "How did you know I was in New York?"

"Well, let's see. Liam dropped by, worried sick. Said you'd blown off work, him, and your newfound love to fight for exercise."

Avery shook her head. Looked like her tangled web was starting to crumble.

"Care to offer a denial?" Her friend was pissed.

She really didn't owe her an explanation. "I'm working through some crap right now." Which was true.

"So you return to the scene of the crime?"

"We all work through our shit differently. I need some time. Need to be alone. I'm sorry I worried you."

"You're worrying all of us. We love you, Avery. You can't just disappear like that. I had to pull Liam back from booking a flight there tonight."

Oh, no. Then they all would learn about Spider being alive. They'd all get involved. Everyone would be in her face again.

"Thanks for stopping him. I can't deal with him right now."

Lori lost some of the fight in her voice. "Is this about him? Or is this all about last year?"

"Both. I-I need to deal with this. And I need to do it alone. I can't have you, or Liam . . . or Reed and his gang doing it for me."

"What do you hope to accomplish in New York?"

"I need to remember."

Lori sighed. "I hate this."

"Now, how did you find me? If Reed has some kind of tracking device on me—"

"No. Trina told me."

"You bugged her on her honeymoon?"

"I'm worried."

"Well, stop. I'm a grown woman. I can take care of myself. I'll let you know when I need a friend or my lawyer."

"Don't be pissed."

"Too late. Go to bed, Lori. I'll call you." Avery hung up the phone.

She moved into the living room of her suite, wearing a bathrobe. First thing she did was disable her Friend Finder app. Second, she dialed Liam.

Chapter Twenty-Six

Liam saw her name on his phone and answered it with a request. "Tell me you're okay."

"I'm okay."

He'd been hitting his fist against a wall ever since he'd gotten back from Lori and Reed's.

"Tell me what I can do. I want to help."

"I assume they told you about last year."

"Reed did. Why didn't you tell me?" he asked as gently as he could.

"Because it didn't matter. And the subject never came up."

"If it didn't matter, you wouldn't be in New York, chasing shadows."

The line was silent.

"You're right. But they're my shadows to chase."

"Let me help."

"I can't."

He shook his head. "You won't."

"Right. I won't. I won't be responsible for anyone getting hurt or missing out on work or their honeymoons or their lives while I deal with my baggage."

"How is anyone going to get hurt?"

"Everyone is already butt hurt, and all I did was leave town." Her voice rose a level.

"Because you're lying about what is going on. People care. Stop lying. Talk to us. Talk to me."

"Making demands, Liam?"

"It's a request."

"Listen, I told you I sucked at relationships. You're the one pushing it."

She was spoiling for a fight. He was *butt hurt* enough to give her one.

"Well, you have one whether you like it or not. You haven't been far from my thoughts since the day we met. That means I get to care and worry. I don't deserve you lying about important things."

"You're right. You don't deserve it. So let me help you out."

The line went dead.

"Damn it, Avery!" Liam literally banged his head against the wall. He couldn't have screwed that up better.

Lori had Trina and Shannon on a conference call the next day.

"She removed the app. I have no idea where she is." Trina sounded stressed.

"Probably still in New York. I'd call her but she won't answer. I'm not on her friend list right now."

"Because you care and called her on it?" Trina asked.

"She's stressed," Shannon told them both. "Liam is making her take a good look at herself and life with someone other than herself. It's scary."

"It doesn't have to be scary," Trina said.

"She doesn't think she can hold on to him or anyone. So love and lose, or never love at all? I don't have to remind you how I feel on the subject."

"Okay, but Shannon, would you just up and leave like this? 'Screw everyone, I need to disappear'?"

"I don't have to go anywhere to disappear," Shannon said. "Avery's the life of the party, she's the one everyone sees. For her to get away, she needs to leave."

Lori sighed. "She said she'd call if she needed a friend or a lawyer."

"Sounds like her," Trina said. "Ironic, considering she harped on me for missing a club meeting last year. But I do understand the need to figure things out on your own. I think we all should send her a message saying we're here for her."

"Agreed," Shannon added.

"Do you think I should come home early?"

"Hell, no. She'll never forgive me if you nix your honeymoon early because I bugged you." Lori glanced at the clock. "I have to go. Any news, we call each other. Promise?"

They agreed before hanging up.

Reed stood by with a coffee cup in his hand, a smirk on his face.

"What are you smiling about?" Lori asked.

"I'm just wondering what you would do to have a spy on Avery to ease your mind."

She shook her head like he was crazy, then stopped and stared. "You can do that."

"I could. But I'm not going to."

"You walk a fine line, Reed. Reckless since I'm PMS-ing."

He tried not to laugh. "I'll be sure and come home with chocolate and wine."

She grabbed her briefcase and pointed at him. "You do that."

He kissed her before she could walk away.

Armstrong walked into the downtown main precinct with his badge on the outside of his plain clothes.

"Officer Ferrero?"

"Detective now, promotion went through five months ago."

"Congratulations."

Armstrong shook the hand of a man he'd met in person only one time before. "Thanks for meeting me today."

"No problem. Sit. What can I do for you?"

"I reopened the Grant case you signed off to me last year."

"I saw the e-mail you sent. I was surprised. I thought the main suspect was dead."

"We did, too. Our only witness came up with new information."

"A year later? That's unusual."

"If you remember right, Ms. Grant was pretty jacked up. Head injury. Anyway. I wanted to make sure the description of this guy isn't buried on a desk. I'd really like to bring him in."

Ferrero nodded. "His picture is on the board. I'll make sure he is mentioned in all call."

"I appreciate it."

They stood.

"I thought I would do a little legwork while I'm in the city. Any suggestions on tattoo parlors that might have done the work on our suspect?"

"Several. But I'd start with Van Lynch. He's the top insect guy. He's up on Fourteenth."

Ferrero walked him out. "Mind if I ask you something?"

"No, no. Go ahead."

"Is this personal? It's just an assault case."

Armstrong turned to shake Ferrero's hand at the station door. "Yeah, a little. I don't like it when I make the wrong call and let someone like him off the hook. I don't want to see an innocent person go down because of this guy."

Ferrero smiled. "I'll call if anything shows up."

"Appreciate it."

⌒つ

"You're back."

Avery smiled and reached out her arm. "I want a tattoo."

Zelda smiled. "Do you have a drawing?"

Avery removed the design she had Monique make that morning. Avery was pretty sure the three art students were camped out at the coffee shop daily now that she was constantly handing out hundred-dollar bills like they were Monopoly money.

"Cool. Come on in the back."

Avery followed her behind the desk and sat in the chair Zelda pointed to.

"Have you thought about your boyfriend's artwork?"

Avery swallowed hard. "I think we broke up."

"Oh. Is this a breakup tattoo? Because I have to caution you . . ."

"No. This is for me," Avery quickly said.

"Good. Get comfortable. I'll get the paperwork."

It took Avery sitting on her hands that morning to not call Liam and apologize for being such an asshole. But to what end? They would be right back where they started. Him wanting to fix her problems and her not wanting him involved in however this ended up. Her life, her way, her demons. The therapist she'd seen all of four times after the incident had told her that no one could go through the emotional process for her. How right she was.

Less than thirty minutes later Zelda pushed her seat back with a satisfied smile. "What do you think?"

Avery looked down at her stinging arm. "I like it."

"The spider dripping off the word is a nice touch."

"I thought so, too."

Zelda applied ointment and a bandage. "Tell me, is there a boyfriend who wants a spider tattoo?"

Avery looked at the top of Zelda's head and thought . . . *Why lie? Stop lying.* "No."

"That's what I thought. So what was up with the art you showed me?"

"The guy with that tattoo jumped me in a garage on Fifth Avenue last year. Messed me up pretty bad. Up until last week I thought he was dead."

Zelda once again pushed her rolling chair back. "That's rough."

"It hasn't been easy."

She nodded toward Avery's forearm. "Obviously. You find that dude and then what?"

"I don't know. Can't say I've really thought it that far out. Chances of me really finding that guy aren't looking very good."

"In this city, it's right up there with a needle in a haystack."

Avery sat up and put on her jacket. "I still have to try."

"I get that."

As Avery paid the bill and pocketed her aftercare instructions for the tattoo, Zelda offered to ask around about Spider. Avery left her cell number before walking away.

Armed with a wad of ten-dollar bills, enough to buy anyone who would talk to her a beer, she set out for a sober bar crawl.

∽

There was no point in trying to hide he was a cop, so Armstrong waltzed up to the tatted up clerk and dropped his badge on the counter. "How you doing today?" he asked the kid.

He glanced at the badge, smiled. "Fine. What can I do for you, Officer?"

232

"Detective."

"Detective," the clerk mimicked.

"I'm looking for someone who might have had a tattoo done here."

The clerk grinned. Armstrong had seen that smile before. It said he wasn't going to find anything. "Lots of people get tattoos here. It's what we do."

He removed the picture of Avery's spider and turned it toward the clerk.

While the clerk glanced at the image, Armstrong studied the kid.

Recognition lit in his eyes. His breathing shifted pace, and a tiny twitch behind his left eye screamed *BINGO*.

"Van specializes in everything that crawls."

"Have you seen the guy who has this tattoo?"

"No." The clerk seemed amused with his denial.

"What's so funny?"

"No wonder our tax dollars are so high."

Armstrong rested both hands on the counter. The movement always opened his jacket, and anyone looking would see his concealed weapon. Outside of his tiny badge, it was often the only thing that reminded people he was a cop. "Mind explaining?"

"Sure. Your partner, she was already in here last week."

"My partner?" *She?*

"Yeah. Showed me the exact picture and gave some bullshit story about wanting to get one for her boyfriend but didn't want a similar tat out there. Had we done this one before? I'll tell you the same thing I told her. Bugs, it's what we do. Can't say Van did that or didn't. We don't take pictures of all the art we do."

Avery!

"This partner of mine . . . blonde, about yea tall?" He waved his hand in the air at about his shoulder height.

"Yeah."

Armstrong pulled a picture of the suspect. "This guy? You see him?"

The clerk smiled. "Half a face. Could be anyone. He doesn't look familiar."

He shoved the papers back in his pocket after tossing a card on the desk. "You see this guy, call me."

The clerk offered a short salute as Armstrong walked out.

~~~

Nothing good happens after midnight. Her mother's voice rang in her head. On this, she had to agree with the woman.

Someone handed Avery a bag of ice. She placed it on the side of her face where her cheek had caught someone's fist.

"What's your name?" The police officer wrote in his tiny notepad while several of his brothers did the same with the half a dozen people gathered outside the club.

Avery glanced to her right and then the left. Yup. She was the only woman outside of the cocktail waitresses being questioned.

"How did this start?"

Avery pointed through the crowd. "That guy grabbed my ass."

The officer stopped writing and looked at her outfit. "And you didn't want that." It wasn't a question.

"No."

"What did you do?"

"I removed his hand from my ass. Then I told him it wasn't polite to touch unless invited."

"*How* did you remove his hand from your *ass*?"

"Assertively."

The officer questioning her smirked.

"And then what happened?"

"One of his friends, the guy in the jean jacket"—she pointed him out—"jumped in front of us and shoved me."

"Uh-huh . . . and then?"

"Not really sure. I heard someone tell those two to pick a fight with a man instead of a woman. The next thing I know, chairs were skidding across the floor and people were throwing punches."

"Right." The officer was bored. "And did you throw punches?"

The side of her face started to sting. "I'm more of an elbow and knee girl when someone hits me first."

Yep, the cop was smiling. "Well . . ." He glanced at her ID, which he had in his hand. "Avery Grant. Stay right here."

Since he left with her ID, she didn't really have a choice.

The bouncer, pure New Yorker, walked over. "Hey."

"Hey."

"What was that back in there?" he asked. "Some kind of martial arts?"

"Krav maga."

He smiled, lifted his fist for a bump.

Avery obliged.

How things had changed. She used to visit clubs and gain the admiration of the bouncers, tip them heavily, and avoid comments when they stared. Now she earned it by defending herself.

The cop returned, looked at her ID again before handing it back. "Is that your current address?"

"Yes."

"Are you visiting us or moving here?"

"Visiting." Avery kept her answers short and didn't elaborate. Somewhere in her years of friendship with Lori, she'd heard that offering information never boded well if there was a chance you could be charged with a crime.

"Where are you staying?"

"The Ritz-Carlton, Central Park."

He paused. "Fancy hotel."

She shrugged. "I'm a fancy girl."

"What are you doing down here? In the *less* fancy part of town."

Avery glanced up at the sign for the club. "I was thirsty."

He wasn't buying it. "I think the waitress has had more to drink tonight than you."

She was getting cold now that the heat of the bar had left her skin and the night air had dipped into the high forties. "Am I being charged with anything, Officer?"

"Let's see . . . could be assault, battery . . . inciting a riot."

"I didn't realize a bar fight was considered a riot."

The officer stared at her as if contemplating the key to a Rubik's Cube. "No one is going to jail tonight, Miss Grant. Only because the gentleman whose hand needed reminding not to wander isn't pressing charges on you."

That was rich. "And if I'd like to press charges on him?"

The officer put his hands in the air before returning them to his belt full of tools and a gun. "Then we can pull you both in and put you both through the process. Your call. I assure you, the Ritz has much better accommodations."

Avery glanced over her shoulder to the fist-bumping bouncer.

He shook his head and made a back-and-forth slicing motion at his neck.

Thirty minutes later, Avery stood in a hot shower. Even though everything but her toes was hurting, she started to laugh. "Hey, Mom . . . guess what? Your dream came true. Can you come bail me out of jail?" Adeline would have a stroke.

Avery bit her lip and continued talking to herself. "Lori, what's up? About those lawyer services?"

Brenda would be all, *How did he get close enough to punch your face?*

And Liam.

Avery's smile started to fade when she thought of him.

There wouldn't be a Liam to call.

Oh, well. At least she wouldn't disappoint him.

Again.

Chapter Twenty-Seven

"You're probably deleting these messages before listening to them. That isn't going to stop me from trying. I'm sorry I cornered you. I know you're going through a hard time, and I want to help. Please, Avery. Let me help. I miss you and I'm worried." Liam hung up the phone and leaned against the bed of his truck as he stared down his new project in Santa Monica.

Never in his life had he made this much of an effort to stay attached to a woman. Not that he was the one to bug out at the first sign of conflict in relationships, but Avery all but told him to go to hell by hanging up and not returning his calls.

He felt marginally better when his daily check-in with Reed told him no one had heard from her.

Liam booked a flight to New York that would leave on Sunday. He'd given her enough time alone.

He wouldn't let her work her way into another week of this journey without him.

Avery checked three more clubs off her list.

Maybe she was going at this the wrong way. Although, there had been a few people she'd asked who said they had seen a similar tattoo but didn't remember the face it belonged to.

"Here ya go." A waitress slid a full plate of food in front of Avery, refilled her coffee, and scurried away.

She was starving. Her nights had been too busy for her to think about food, and her lack of a breakfast habit was making her weak.

Avery looked at the eggs, potatoes, bacon, and toast like she'd not seen such a delight.

Digging in like a trucker, she felt her energy seeping back into her veins. Her fork was halfway to her mouth when she felt a hand grab her shoulder.

She jumped, dropped her fork, and looked over her right shoulder as her elbow swung up. It stopped less than an inch from Detective Armstrong's chest.

"Easy, tiger." He took a step back and looked down at her.

"Not smart to sneak up on people, Detective."

"I can see that." He slid into the chair opposite her without invitation. His eyes found the bruise on her face. "New makeup fad?"

She didn't dignify him with a response. "Did you find him?"

"No. Did you?"

Again, she sat silently and picked her fork back up. "Seems you had no problem finding me in this ocean of people. You should channel that energy into finding Spider."

He leaned forward on his elbows. "Funny, it wasn't very hard learning where you were. Would you like to guess why?"

He was here to lecture her. If there was something she'd gotten used to since she was a teenager, it was authority dominating over her. She wasn't going to escape it, so she kept eating and let him rant.

"Apparently there was a bar fight on the East Side the other night, and guess whose name came up on the list of participants?"

The potatoes stuck in her throat. She washed them down with coffee.

The waitress stopped at the table, and Armstrong encouraged her to pour him a cup of coffee.

Great, he wasn't yelling and then leaving promptly.

Avery kept eating, no longer tasting her food.

"What do you hope to accomplish, Grant?"

"Unlike you, I'm going to find him."

"By kicking the shit out of everyone you come across in the process?"

"I haven't shit kicked yet." She shoveled a forkful of eggs. Although the last fight did give her the opportunity to throw a few punches. Catching a couple was to be expected.

"What happens when you take a knife to a gun fight?"

"I don't carry—"

"Not my point and you know it! I don't see any of this ending well for you if you keep this up."

She placed her fork aside and knew she wouldn't be able to finish. "Asking around in a few clubs isn't a crime. Stopping someone from touching what doesn't belong to them isn't a crime."

"It is when people get hurt and property is damaged."

"I think it was you who said jail time for assault was laughable."

"That's not what I said—"

"No, but that's how it translated in my head. So I'll take my chances and defend myself if I have to."

"Defend yourself? Is that what you call picking a fight and then rearranging men's testicles?"

"They touch my ass, I touch their balls. Sounds like a win-win to me."

"You won't be happy until you're in jail, will you?"

"Maybe I'll find a lead there."

"You're going to end up in the hospital again. You know what happens to people when they go around searching for a bad guy?"

She was getting pissed now. "Oh, I don't know . . . find him?"

"They put a target on their backs. If this guy is out there and he learns of you kicking up smoke, there is no telling what he'll do to you this time."

She couldn't stop the smile from reaching her lips. "I'd like to see him try."

Armstrong leaned closer and lowered his voice. "Then there is the guy that sees a pretty little thing like you asking questions and he's all, 'yeah, baby . . . I know where he is.' Or the guy that has a similar tattoo on his arm and thinks you're looking for him. Only he has a gang of ten on his side. What about that guy, Avery?"

Those things hadn't happened.

She clenched her jaw and hid the fear he put in her head.

"I'm going to offer some free advice." He stared her in the eye. "Go home. This man stole a year of your life. Don't give him the power to take the rest of it. Let me do my job."

"What have you done other than lecture me?"

Armstrong sat farther back. "His ink isn't coming up in our database."

"What does that mean?"

"Any number of things. He's never been arrested. Due to the brutality of your attack, I have a hard time believing that. So he isn't from around here. Probably not even in the city."

She smelled smoke. "You just want me out of town."

Armstrong nodded. "Absolutely right. I want you back in your cozy life in LA, where I can look for this guy and not look after you."

Avery rolled her eyes. "I can clearly look out for myself." She swung her legs out from under the table and dropped some bills on the surface. "Thanks for the pep talk. I'll let you know if I find any leads."

"Damn it, Grant."

She ignored him and walked out.

∽

Armstrong glared at her uneaten food. He couldn't do anything but wait and watch for the pieces to fall around her. Protecting her from herself wasn't on his job list, and he was way out of his jurisdiction.

What he needed was backup.

Where was her posse of friends that had been so attentive a year ago?

He retrieved his phone from his pocket and started scrolling through phone numbers. He found the one he was looking for and put the phone to his ear.

"Hello?"

"Is this Reed?"

"Who is this?"

"Detective Armstrong. We met last year."

"Oh, shit."

"Yeah, 'oh, shit.' Where the hell are you guys?"

⌒⑨

Liam met Reed at a coffee shop a few blocks from the condominium complex.

When the text came through that Reed had information about Avery to share, Liam dropped his work in Carlos's lap and left the job.

"Is she okay?" Liam asked the question the second he noticed the drawn expression on Reed's face.

"Yes. Before I start, know I already have boots on the ground in New York. My critical player will be there in a couple of hours."

Liam kept his fear in check, his jaw clenched.

Reed took a deep breath and began. "Avery's memory of what happened to her last year came back."

"That's a good thing."

"Normally, yeah. Except the details she remembered about the guy who attacked her didn't line up with the dead man pinned as her attacker."

Liam turned an ear toward Reed. "Come again?"

"They had the wrong guy. The one who attacked her is still out there."

His fist clenched. "Oh, no."

"Avery is running around Manhattan with a picture and asking questions. According to the detective that was on her case last year, she's searching the nightclubs, from sleazy to snazzy. At the same time, she's making quite the name for herself. While no one has seen the guy she's looking for, everyone has seen her. She's making enemies daily," Reed said.

"You mean she's kicking ass." Liam recalled the first time he saw her at Pug's. It didn't take an expansive imagination to see her doing that all over New York City. He itched to leave the table and drive straight to the airport.

"Yeah. Armstrong said it isn't without a toll on her."

"Armstrong is the detective?"

"Yes. He said Avery looked a little rattled, a lot bruised, and thin."

"I need to go." He pushed back from the table.

"Glad to hear you say that. You won't be able to force her back, but you can keep her from making a lethal mistake. My guess is she thinks this is her fight and her fight alone. If it were you or I, I'd agree. But I have a strong aversion to men beating on women. Even if the woman can take him."

"No one is going to touch her. I'll make sure of that."

Reed smiled. "Perfect. You take care of Avery, we'll find her attacker."

"If the police can't . . ."

The expression on Reed's face shut Liam up.

"It's what we do. If he's there, we will find him."

"I thought you were in private security."

"I am. Sometimes security means being a PI and neutralizing threats before they attack."

"That sounds illegal." And while that would have made him question Reed in the past, Liam was willing to look past it now.

"Nah . . . my goal is to find him and offer Avery the closure she needs. We make sure he can't hurt her, and she doesn't hurt him and end up on the wrong side of the law. I want this cleaned up before the women find out what's going on."

"The women?"

"Lori, Trina—"

"And Shannon," Liam finished.

"Yeah. Keeping them out of the mix will be impossible." Reed looked at his watch. "I'm giving this seventy-two hours before everyone is on their way home and sleeping in their own beds."

Liam liked his confidence, found it contagious. "Are you calling the SEALs?" Liam joked.

"Not quite." Reed reached into his jacket and removed an envelope. "Your plane leaves in three hours—"

"I bought a ticket to New York that leaves on Sunday."

"Cancel it. Use this one." Yeah, Liam liked that idea better.

"I'm sending you a link. Click it and we will have you tracked at all times. I haven't forgotten what this guy did to her, so if there is any safety threat at all, the rules change."

"How can you know there isn't already a threat?"

"Because Avery is still vertical and she's been there over two weeks." Reed stood. "Three hours, Holt. Click on the link. I'll be in touch."

Chapter Twenty-Eight

Either Armstrong stripped her confidence and single-handedly made her paranoid or Avery was being watched.

She supposed it was entirely possible that the detective put someone on her, but she couldn't imagine the limited resources the police department had would warrant that.

Still, the tingle up her spine and the need to turn around and find the eyes fixed on her was a constant cloud as she walked around Manhattan. It was midday and the streets were packed.

She stepped away from the curb and lifted her arm for a passing cab. Avery opened the back door and jumped in. "Times—" Someone holding her door open stopped her. "Sasha?"

"Scoot over, sweet cheeks."

Avery released a frustrated breath and slid across the seat. "How long have you been following me?"

Sasha wore black. Her sleek, dark hair was tied back in a ponytail and nearly reached her waist, dark sunglasses hid her eyes, and olive skin and near perfect features made you think she was famous. "Ten minutes," she said.

"Not possible. Someone has been on me all morning."

Sasha's curt accent, one born in Germany and honed by spending much of her childhood in eastern Europe, demanded attention. "I've been on you for ten minutes. I have no idea about the others."

Avery looked out the back window of the cab. "Damn it."

"Hey, ladies. Where yous goin'?"

Sasha managed to pierce Avery with her eyes, through her sunglasses. Yeah, her presence was that huge. "Well?"

Avery leaned forward. "Times Square."

The cab took off to a blare of horns behind.

Sasha's presence meant only one thing. "They all know he's alive."

"Not everyone. But that is only a matter of time."

"Trina? Please tell me she hasn't—"

"No. If you want to keep her away from this, we must find your Spider Man before she's told."

"We?"

"We."

Avery didn't try to argue. Since Sasha worked with Reed, it stood to reason there were other security guards hidden in the crowd.

For a couple of blocks, Avery stared out the window and worked through the quick change in events. "You're not going to tell me to go home. Tell me my search is in vain?"

"I know a thing or two about revenge."

"I guess you would." Considering the woman's father had killed her mother and nearly killed her. Sasha was a poster child for a life bent on revenge.

"I applaud your tenacity, but your execution is pathetic."

"Hey, I don't do this as a lifestyle."

"Based on the bruise on your face, that's obvious."

"Battle scars."

Was that a smile on Sasha's face?

No, couldn't be.

The cabbie dropped them off once he reached the tourist mecca of the city.

"What have you learned? Two weeks here, there must be something." Sasha walked with long strides, forcing Avery to keep up.

"The best tattoo artist in the city is in the Meatpacking District. Very expensive and months out on appointments. But the parlors I've been to point the finger to him being the guy who did the art on Spider."

"You call him Spider?"

Avery followed Sasha as she crossed the street without heeding the light.

"Spider-Man is a superhero."

"You're sure of this artist?"

Much as she would have loved to say yes, she couldn't. "No. But it's the only solid anything I've found."

Sasha opened the door to a diner and stepped in.

"What are we doing here?"

For the first time, Sasha removed her sunglasses and looked Avery in the eye. "You look like shit. What have you lost, two, three kilograms?"

"Yeah, maybe a couple of pounds."

Sasha glared and took a seat in a booth as far away from people as she could. "We'll talk while you eat."

Since Armstrong had stolen her appetite at breakfast, and it was getting close to dinnertime, Avery's stomach growled.

Avery tried to order a soup and salad, but Sasha interrupted and ordered two hamburgers, loaded, soup instead of fries.

"I feel like I'm having lunch with my mother's evil twin."

Sasha did have a smile. Brief, but it was there.

"Tell me everything about Spider. Every tiny detail you remember."

Avery started from the beginning, adding little things that had come to her over the past two weeks. The meal came and Avery continued to talk while she ate.

By the time she finished her meal, nothing but the pickle was left on her plate, and she was out of information to share.

"Do you know anything of the man my father sent to kill you? The man who the police said attacked you?"

"Not really. I called him Scarface. He went by Krueger when he was alive."

Sasha nodded. "He was an amateur. Liked dealing drugs more than killing people. My father's resources were not unlimited, and hiring a professional would have meant you'd be dead, and your killer would never be found."

Avery swallowed the chill. "I'm happy Daddy was hard up for money."

"Why did you decide to search nightclubs?"

"Because the guy seemed young to me. A punk. The tattoo was expensive and his shoes were new. He's like the guy you see at a bar where you move down four stools and squeeze between two strangers because you don't want him hitting on you."

Sasha tapped a perfectly plain manicured finger on her water glass. "What did he smell like?"

Avery sat back. "Smell. I don't know. I didn't . . ."

"You said he wore pants that were too big, frayed. A sweatshirt, but the sleeves hung down and easily displayed his tattoo when he grabbed you."

"Yes."

The waitress stopped at the table. "Anything else?"

"A bag, please." Sasha pulled money from a pocket.

Avery noticed her uneaten burger. "You weren't hungry?"

"Breakfast is the most important meal of the day."

They exited the diner and immediately left the tourist block and moved down an alley.

"Tell me what you smell," Sasha demanded.

That was easy. "Garbage."

They stepped around puddles of unidentifiable liquid, past an abandoned cardboard box that looked like it had been someone's home.

"And now? What do you smell?"

"Urine. Why?"

"Humor me." Sasha led her down a few more blocks. While there were still people everywhere, they weren't shoulder to shoulder.

For what felt like no reason, Sasha stopped walking and stepped off of the sidewalk and against a building. "That man. What do you see?" She pointed to a sad staple that plagued every major city in the country.

"A homeless man begging for change."

Sasha sighed. "I see hunger, despair. Someone who has given up on life."

She pushed away from the building, and they crossed the street to the man she was talking about. When she reached him, she leaned down. "Are you hungry?" she asked him.

His eyes tracked her with caution, his gaze shifted to Avery.

"Yeah."

Sasha handed him the bag holding her uneaten hamburger. She then said something in Russian before standing up and leading Avery away.

"This woman," Sasha said as they walked by yet another homeless person. "What do you see?"

Avery suddenly felt like she was being walked through a living documentary of the human existence. "Mental illness to the extreme."

Sasha again stopped and looked behind them. "The woman is ill, but also on something. What did you smell when you walked by?"

"Body odor."

They kept walking.

When Sasha slowed her pace, Avery searched out the next demographic. Two guys sat on a fence, smoking a cigarette. They were both thin, drawn.

"On drugs," Avery said before Sasha could ask her.

"Homeless?"

"Probably."

"How much do you know about drugs?"

Avery smirked. "I know not to take them."

Sasha looked out of the corner of her eye at her, disapproving.

"My rebellion included a little pot and a lot of teenage drinking," Avery clarified.

"But you had access to other things."

"Yeah, of course. What kid doesn't?"

They started across the street toward the boys.

"Do you know anyone who had a more experimental rebellion?"

"No one I was close to. There were always those that got hooked on something stupid in high school, early college. Snorted their tuition money up their nose. I blew my tuition on Cancun."

Sasha chuckled and marched right up to the kids. "Gentlemen?" She managed to get their full attention with one word and a smile. "I was wondering if you could help me out."

One of the kids sitting on the iron fence slid off, pulled himself up straight with a jerk, and nodded. "I can help you with whatever you need."

He was definitely high, but he was hetero and liked what he saw, Avery observed.

"I need to know if you've seen someone."

Avery stood back and watched the kids.

Neither of them could hold their hands still. One realized he was twitchy and slammed his hands into his back pockets, attempting to keep his eyes on Sasha.

"Yeah, hey . . . we see people walk by every day."

Sasha pulled a picture out of her back pocket, but before she showed it to the kids, she said, "Twenty bucks each, to the both of you, if you tell me the truth. You lie, you get nothing."

"Yeah, lady. Okay. I could use twenty bucks."

The image of Avery's sketched suspect sat in Sasha's hands.

The guys looked at it.

Sasha watched the kids.

Avery saw everyone.

"That could be anyone," the kid on her right said. "I wanna say I have, but I don't know."

"And you?" She moved the picture closer to the second kid.

He shook his head.

"What about this?" Spider's tattoo was in the next picture.

Both of them shook their heads.

Sasha stashed the pictures and handed them the money.

"They're just going to buy more drugs," Avery said as they walked away.

Sasha shrugged. "Until they hit bottom or die." She glanced over her shoulder. "Twenty bucks won't change their course."

"That's cold," Avery said.

"Truth often is. Come on."

When they had circled back to Times Square, Avery finally stopped Sasha's pace by grabbing her arm and turning her around. "Much as I liked the garbage-filled path through the decay of the homeless population, was there a point to what just happened?"

People walked around the two of them like they were rocks in a stream while they talked.

"Spider is young, agile. New shoes, old clothes. If he's homeless, he wasn't for long before you. His clothing, while worn, did not smell like Homeless Man Number One. Spider completed a task and spoke coherently, so not like Homeless Woman Number Two. Homeless Examples Three and Four, once hooked on something much stronger than what they can afford now, is who we are searching for. Two for twenty couldn't stop moving. They wash their hands because of nerves and because their veins itch with need. They only stop at the peak of their high or when they are too sick to move during their low. They spend the majority of their day searching for means to maintain their level of stupid. Junkies don't spend money on tattoos, so our guy was new to the game."

Avery felt a rush from Sasha's words.

"We know for a fact Krueger's day job was selling drugs, and his night job was taking out kneecaps or putting people in the morgue. My father paid Krueger to kill you. In turn, Krueger paid your Spider to do the job. Why? Because Krueger sees an opportunity to get paid for a job without the risk of going to jail for it. Spider's rapid descent makes him say yes. He knocks you down, hesitates, then uses his feet. Why? Because his hands would be too personal. Even though he's higher than a rocket to the space station, he knows somewhere that what he is doing is wrong. 'Don't look at me.' His words. Not because he doesn't want you to see him, but so he won't see your eyes."

Avery ran a hand through her hair. Everything Sasha was saying made sense in a twisted, fucked-up way. "So I've wasted my time searching nightclubs."

"No. Not entirely. You know where he isn't. We know he isn't in jail. What did I say about Homeless Men Three and Four?"

Avery had to think for a minute. "That they would buy drugs until they hit rock bottom or die." Jesus . . . was she chasing a dead man?

"We stop searching clubs and start searching rehabs and morgues."

Avery held a staring contest with Sasha. "You knew all of this before we sat down to eat, didn't you?"

"I suspected. Between what you've told me and what the police have found . . . or more importantly, haven't found, I've drawn my conclusions."

"Then why waste time with all of this?" Avery waved her hands around her, as if including the entire city in her argument.

Sasha stepped closer, her face nothing but harsh lines of sobriety. "Because you need to learn who this man is on your own so you can accept whatever it is that we find. Me telling you who we are looking for will always raise doubt in your head."

Avery sighed, ran the back of her hand against her chin. God, she was tired. With a deep breath, she asked, "Okay. Where do we start?"

Sasha stepped back. "Tomorrow."

"But—"

"You need to eat again and sleep. Warriors only enter a battle rested and fed."

Avery glanced at the tattoo on her arm and resigned. "Okay."

Sasha glanced behind Avery. "Take her back to the hotel. I will call on you in the morning."

"Yes, ma'am."

Avery turned around so fast her head spun. "Liam."

Chapter Twenty-Nine

Liam had to force a smile to his face.

He'd been tracking Sasha's location via Reed since he landed. He dropped a bag off at Avery's hotel and taxied to Times Square. Having never been to New York before, he found himself turned around more than once while GPS tangled with the tall buildings and sometimes had him on the wrong side of the street.

The two of them walked into his line of sight, and Liam stopped behind Avery right as Sasha described Avery's attacker. Even though he stood right there, Sasha's eyes never left Avery.

Slowly, as Sasha's conclusion settled in Avery's head, Liam noticed her entire posture sink. For a brief moment, he thought she might just slump to the ground right in the middle of Times Square.

Now Avery was staring at him, and they were the clog of traffic as people walked by.

Eyes hollow, lips swollen . . . Liam reached out and traced a hand to the bruise on her cheek. His simple touch and she closed the gap between them and pressed her face to his chest.

"I'm sorry," she choked out.

Liam wrapped his arms around her and buried his head in her hair. "It's okay."

"I was such a child."

"It's okay, Princess."

She hugged him tighter.

Liam closed his eyes and held her. "I'll get her back—" He glanced up and Sasha was gone.

Avery disengaged long enough to look around.

"Where did she go?"

Avery shook her head. "I'm sure she'll be back."

Liam brushed a hair behind her ear and cradled her cheek in his hand. So many words needed to be said . . . instead, he brushed his lips against hers.

She kissed him back with a sigh.

"C'mon. Let's get you back to the hotel."

Liam kept an arm around her and signaled for a taxi.

Thirty minutes later they were in her room and he'd ordered room service.

"I had to come to New York," Avery started.

"I know that. You have me now, you didn't need to come alone."

A small dining table stood on one end of the suite. The two of them sat across from each other. Liam kept both her hands in his as they talked.

"It's hard for me to depend on other people."

"I put that together," he said with a slight smile. "Here is the beauty of a truly committed relationship. You're allowed to depend on someone else. When you're hurting, they hurt, so it's on both your radars to fix the problem. Just because you zone out doesn't stop the other from caring."

"The last thing I wanted was to hurt you."

He squeezed her hands, saw her eyes glisten with unshed tears. "Finding out that your girlfriend is three thousand miles away chasing this Spider guy all by herself wasn't painful, it made me feel helpless. I'm here. You don't have to do any of this alone."

"I see that now. I'll try."

"Do or don't do. There is no try." His words were there to make her grin. They succeeded.

"You're quoting Yoda?"

"Whatever it takes to make you smile."

She brushed away a tear. "I'm so tired."

He summoned her with a crook of his finger, and she slid out of her chair and onto his lap. His hands traveled once again to the bruise on her cheek. "How many more scars am I going to find when I undress you?"

She rocked her head back and forth. "A few."

He somehow thought that meant a dozen.

The thought of anyone hitting her made him boil. He downplayed her bruises so that he could keep from losing his shit. "You let them get close enough to punch you?"

Avery's laugh started slowly. "Have you been talking to Brenda?"

"It does sound like something she'd say."

She placed her palm to the side of his face. "I feel so much better with you here."

"Good thing."

"Don't let me run off again."

Let her?

"Is that a demand?" he asked.

"It's a . . ." She caught herself. "Yeah. It is."

He grinned and leaned in for a kiss. "You got it, Princess."

Hours later, after he'd seen Avery eat more than he'd seen any woman consume before, he drew her a bath, counted her bruises. He poured her a glass of wine while she soaked in the tub, and then sat on the edge of the thing, rubbing her feet.

And they talked.

She told him about the beating. In her words, it was as if he felt every blow and every needle from the hospital. But her delivery of the attack lacked the heat he expected. A testament to her tired state. He imagined that she'd be fired up about Spider after a night of rest.

Liam, on the other hand, poured himself a drink from the minibar to keep from searching every street in New York to find the guy. Not to mention the assholes from bars two, three, and four.

"More people stood up to help than stood back to watch," she told him when talking of the last fight.

"No more New York nightclubs without me," he told her.

"Is that a demand?"

He smiled and without hesitation said, "Yes."

"One for one." She moved her hand along the bubbles hiding her nudity.

"I have another demand," he said.

"Pushing your luck."

He took a drink from his cocktail and leaned his head against the harsh porcelain of the hotel wall. "No more lying. If you don't want to answer the question or tell me something, then tell me that. But don't lie."

She nodded. "I'll try."

He hiked a brow.

"I will," she amended.

Liam pushed off the edge of the tub. "Finish your bath. I need to call Reed and give him an update."

"I'm sure Sasha already has."

"What Sasha is going to say to him won't keep your gaggle of friends away. What I'm going to tell him will."

"Liam?"

He turned at the door.

"Thank you for coming."

He crossed the room in two steps and kissed her quickly. "Always."

By the time Liam made it back into the bedroom of the suite, Avery was curled up in a ball on the bed, asleep.

Liam stood at the door and watched her.

He loved this woman. With every ounce of baggage and bundle of insecurities she had, he loved her. The sassy mouth, the attitude, her independence. He loved all that, too. He couldn't help but feel like they'd gotten over the biggest hurdle and now all he had to do was keep his promises and show her she could depend on him.

All she needed to do was let him love her. He'd do all the rest.

He moved around the room, turned off lights, stripped his clothes, and slid into bed beside her.

She turned into his arms the moment he settled, and draped a bare leg over his. "I missed you," she whispered.

"Shh, go to sleep. You need to rest."

Her hand resting on his chest started to move. "I do need to sleep. But I need you more."

She lifted her hazel eyes to his.

"Are you sure? You've been on empty."

Velvet fingertips fresh from the bath brushed against him, and his cock jumped into her palm. "I'll let you do all the work."

He kissed her softly, slowly.

Her lips moved over his as if drinking him in.

"I thought I was losing you," he whispered. He traced her back, careful of the places where he'd seen her bruises. Felt the tips of her breasts against his chest.

"I'm here and I want to feel you."

Her words were all the invitation he needed. Liam rolled her gently on her back and held her arms spread out, intertwining their fingers. His lips lingered on hers, and he tasted the soap from her bath, drew in her scent as he dipped his way down her neck, her shoulder.

The tips of her breasts were already tiny nubs, asking to be licked. When he pulled one into his mouth, she arched against the mattress, her fingers squeezing. He spent time on one, moved to the next, and moved gently over her bruises, tiny kisses meant to soothe the pain she must have felt when receiving the blows that caused the colors to erupt.

Avery wiggled her hips and opened her legs as he settled in lower. She twisted her hands away from his and threaded them through his hair. So damn soft, this spot, the one where her hip met the top of her thigh, loved the feel of his tongue. He sensed her need even before he felt her lift one knee and place her foot on his back. Oh, yes . . . this was his. All his, so he kissed and nibbled until he found the place inside her that made her grab the back of his head and keep him exactly where she wanted. She tasted like sunshine and smelled like dreams.

"Oh, please . . . more. Liam, more."

Her breathy request was all he needed. If she wanted more, she'd get more until she told him to stop. Much as he wanted to make love to her all night, he wouldn't be that selfish. He pulled her swollen flesh between lips and tongue, found the right angle, and found her rhythm. When she was close, he moved his fingers inside of her until she stiffened under him, and he tasted everything she had to give.

"Liam." His name was a cry.

He kissed her aftershocks, felt her thighs quivering next to his cheeks.

"Come here," she said, looking down at him.

Crawling up her body, he captured her kiss, his erection screaming.

"Inside. I need you inside."

He smiled into her kiss. "Demands?"

"Hell, yeah."

Reaching down, he found his pants, unearthed a condom from his wallet, and pulled it on.

Avery smiled and drew him closer.

"I'm a lucky man," he told her as he gave her what she demanded.

So warm.

Like home.

"Take me," she told him, her legs wrapped around his waist, and he shifted his angle to move deeper.

"So good," he managed as his thrusts became quicker, her tiny cries became a sharp inhale and a word of encouragement for more . . . everything. When everything inside of her gripped all of him, his rush of release rivaled hers.

A satisfied smile met him when he opened his eyes. He collapsed back onto the bed, careful to not crush her.

"We do that really well together," she said in his ear.

"Imagine how much better it will be when I learn every spot, and every desire."

She wrapped lazy arms over his back and kept her legs entwined with his. "We're already off the charts, I'm not sure it gets better."

"That's a challenge I'm happy to accept." Her laughter warmed his heart. "I love you, Avery."

Her smile waned but didn't disappear altogether. "Liam, I'm not ready to—"

"I know, Princess. You don't have to say it back right now. I know the words don't come easy, which just means that they mean more when you do say them. I can wait. I'm not going anywhere. I need you to know how I feel so that when you do tell me you love me, I know we're all in."

Her smile softened, and he knew he'd eased her into the thought of loving him completely.

"How is it you know me so well already?"

He lowered his lips to hers again. "Because I love you."

"Is that going to be your ending statement from here on out?"

He nodded. "Yup."

Chapter Thirty

"If he's dead, he didn't come in as a John Doe," Armstrong told Reed when he called first thing the next morning.

"Thanks for looking into that for me."

"That part's easy. Anything else I can do for you?"

"Not unless you're willing to hack into hospital databases."

"Ha. No. I actually like my job. What are you looking for?"

Reed sighed.

"On second thought, don't tell me. I don't need any marks on my record."

Reed laughed. "Probably for the best."

Armstrong smiled. "How's Avery?"

"Better. Still in New York, but no longer searching the gutters. Her boyfriend is with her."

"Boyfriends tend to do the most damage when suspects are caught."

"Depends on the size of the fish we pull from the ocean. He's levelheaded."

Armstrong leaned on his desk, tapped his pen to the notebook in front of him. "Anyone else I need to worry about?"

Reed sighed.

"You know what . . . you're right. I don't need to know that either. You call me if you need any legal information I can share, and let me know how it all works out."

"That I can do. Thanks again." Reed hung up.

Yeah, Armstrong really didn't want to know how Reed and his group operated.

∾

Sasha knocked on their hotel room door at ten in the morning. Good thing, since Avery slept until eight and had finished her breakfast right before.

Sasha wore tan slacks and a silk blouse. Her conservative outfit made Avery pause. "Are we going to church?"

She shook her head. "Visiting hours. Go change. I'll wait."

Avery didn't argue.

After she'd woken up that morning feeling like the hundred-pound weight on her chest had lifted, much of the fight had left her system.

She'd cried. While it might not have seemed like much to the average person, the reality was she hadn't shed one tear over herself since everything had gone down. The tears, she realized after she'd woken up, weren't over Spider, but Liam. She almost lost him.

There was no reason for him to chase her to New York, but there he was. She saw the look in his eye when she took off her shirt and he took in the footprint size bruise on her hip. What he had said about her pain being his . . . she got that now. Later, when he made love to her and cherished every piece she allowed him to take, he awakened something new inside.

I love you, Avery.

The words echoed in her mind all night. Not that she had to wait long to hear them again. Liam meant it when he said they were his ending statement. When he saw the worry on her face, he kissed her and said he knew how she felt.

Before she took her morning shower, she sent a group text to the First Wives. I'm feeling much better. Liam is here and helping me through this. I love you all.

The replies were rapid and all held the same sentiment. We love you. We're here. Call if you need us. Come home soon.

Avery returned to the living room of the suite.

Liam smiled and Sasha sent a look of disapproval.

"What?"

"Boots?"

"Yeah, why?"

She shook her head. "You're disappointing me. You need a purse."

Avery sent Liam a look that said *What the hell?* and *okay* at the same time.

She returned with her purse.

"Chloé, good." Another scan from Sasha. "Did you bring any jewelry with you?"

Avery stalked back into the room, wearing the earrings and bracelet she'd bought to wear in the clubs.

Sasha released a frustrated sigh and they left the hotel. Instead of getting in a cab, they walked across the street and straight into a department store. Sasha marched them into the men's department, picked up a Friday casual jacket, and shoved it in Liam's hands. "Put this on."

Liam shrugged into it.

Avery had him turn around. Not only did it fit, it managed to kickstart a flutter in her chest. "Looks good."

"Why are we dressing up?"

Sasha didn't answer. She took the coat from him and moved to the service desk.

Liam reached for his wallet, but Sasha had already swiped her card.

After the clerk removed the security tag, Sasha took the jacket from her hands and gave it back to Liam.

"No one has bought me clothes since my parents," he told them.

Sasha stood to his side, smoothed out the arms. "It's two thousand dollars, feel free to pay me back. Or don't."

Liam's jaw dropped.

Avery grabbed his hand and they continued through the store.

Sasha stopped at a makeup counter, flagged an attendant, and pointed to Avery's face. "Fix this."

Okay, just because Avery hadn't brought all her concealers and moisturizers didn't mean she needed fixing.

Only with one look in the tilted countertop mirror, she realized she did.

Sasha pointed to Avery's feet. "Size?"

"Six and a half. I can buy my own shoes."

Without comment, Sasha walked away.

Liam leaned in. "What the hell is she all about?"

"Efficiency."

The woman working on her makeup smoothed something under Avery's eyes that felt like heaven. "Have you been sick?" the stranger asked.

Avery closed her eyes. "I'm getting over it."

Liam rested a hand on her shoulder.

Twenty minutes later, wearing an edgy jacket in a rust orange color with matching Prada on her feet, Avery felt a little like her old self. Because she couldn't leave the makeup lady without buying a few things, Avery held a bag with her boots and five hundred dollars' worth of makeup.

Apparently Sasha didn't approve. The second they were out of the department store, she grabbed Avery's bag and handed it to the first petite homeless woman she could. "Merry Christmas."

Avery's jaw dropped. "Those were Stuart Weitzmans."

"I'm sure Stuart has others. Come on. We're late."

Sasha stopped in front of a black SUV double-parked outside the department store. "Liam, you're in front."

Avery scooted in the back with Sasha and glanced at the driver. "I know you," she said, slightly surprised. "You're part of the Alliance team."

"That's right. Cooper. How are you, Avery?"

"I'm fine. This is Liam. Liam, Cooper works with Reed."

Sasha clapped her hands like she was starting class. "Okay, kids, listen up."

Liam shot Avery a grin.

"It's really very simple. Today is visiting day, and the two of you are searching out a facility for your desperate younger brother who is snorting his tuition up his nose. Your brother's name is Cooper."

From the driver's seat, Cooper offered a thumbs-up as he cut through traffic.

"My name is Mary. Think virginal."

It took everything to keep Avery from laughing.

"What's my name?" Avery said with a lift in her voice.

"Avery. And he's Liam. IDs will be checked at the door."

"Wait, your name is really Mary?"

Sasha looked at her like she was crazy. "Are you new?"

An invisible hand hit Avery upside the head. *Fake ID*. Okay. "But why do *you* need a fake ID?"

Again, Sasha blinked and kept silent. "We'll walk in separately. Mingle. Liam, you stay with Avery. Take your time. Look in open doors, ask questions about the facility, talk to the patients, the counselors, the doctors. Avery, you're exceptional about keeping your lies together. You do the talking. Liam, your job is to offer those big shoulders to help."

Avery glanced at Liam. "My pact to tell the truth lasted less than twelve hours."

Liam winked.

"Do not, under any circumstances, ask about Spider. Rehabilitation facilities will bounce you out the door if they think for one minute you're there to find someone. Just because you don't see Spider doesn't mean he isn't there."

Avery's smile sobered. "What if he is?"

"We'll cross that when we get there."

"*If* we get there."

Sasha lifted Avery's chin with a finger. *"When."*

Cooper stopped the car.

"Okay, kids. First act is on you. Cooper, drive me around the block."

Avery opened the door, and Liam was there to help her out.

"I'll see you on the inside."

Chapter Thirty-One

Avery glanced up at the sign above the door. "'Tranquility Springs.' Sounds like a spa."

Liam tugged on his jacket. "Looks expensive."

Avery put her hand in his. "So do you."

They walked up the steps together and opened the front door. Zen meditation music greeted them, along with a perfectly polished feminine man behind a mahogany reception desk. "Good afternoon. Welcome to Tranquility Springs."

"We're here to look around. There is an open house today, right?" Since the lobby was free of people, she was starting to wonder if Sasha had her facts wrong.

"Of course. I just need you to sign in."

Avery's hands actually started to sweat. She signed her name to the registration log and turned the pen to Liam.

"Your ID, please."

"Of course." She fished in her bag for her ID and handed it to him. "I'm so nervous. My brother has been so sick. I don't know what else to do for him."

"We here at Tranquility Springs understand. If you'll follow me, I'll find you a guide."

He led them through a set of double doors and around a corner. He punched in a set of numbers at the locked door. "The lock is to keep people out, not in."

"Oh." Avery glanced at Liam.

He shrugged.

"Wait here."

They were in a common room with other people milling about. Some were couples, but the majority were lone women. Single mothers, or maybe the wives of men who gave up. Everyone appeared to have deep pockets, based on their style of dress and jewelry.

Liam whispered in her ear, "I like my new jacket."

She smiled and felt some of the tension leave her shoulders for the first time since they'd walked in.

A smartly dressed woman, similar in size and frame to Avery, walked up to them. "Hello. Welcome to Tranquility Springs. I'm Evita. Is this your first time here?"

"Yes." Avery held out her hand for the other woman to shake.

"Welcome. Let me give you a tour, and then feel free to roam around. Everything is open but the top two floors. We have guests that don't care to be interrupted during their day. But know that the second and third floors are a duplicate of this one. Mainly private rooms and a couple of intimate group rooms."

Evita walked through a hallway and started her tour. "We like to create an inviting home environment. Which means group meals and common areas like the living room we just left." She walked them into a dining room that looked as if it could seat fourteen comfortably. Not an easy task in a Manhattan home.

They walked through a state-of-the-art kitchen. "Our chefs create nutritious menus to suit every allergy, dislike, and diet. We like to refer to anyone here at Tranquility as a client or even guest, if they prefer. Our guests have full run of the kitchen. Again, this is their home, and they are welcome to take anything they need."

This was nice and all but not helping Avery find Spider.

They walked through another set of doors and into what looked like a private room in a hospital. "Some of our clients come to us directly from the hospital. We have a full team of medical doctors and nurses on call twenty-four seven."

She walked by three large, open rooms: two had people inside, talking, and one was empty. Evita drew their attention across the hall. "Group therapy. Our counselors' offices are open when we're not hosting an open house. For our clients' privacy, they are locked today."

They walked by a full gym and yoga studio, then past rooms that looked like luxury apartments, until finally they dumped out into a courtyard with plants and trees and a meditation pond, as Evita called it.

Finally Evita paused her tour and asked a few questions. "How long has your brother been using?"

"Late high school. It got worse in college, and now he's out of control. Our parents are beyond themselves and giving up. But I can't do that. He needs help."

Liam placed a hand on Avery's shoulder. "What is the recovery rate here?"

Evita offered another smile. "We are one of the top rated addiction recovery centers in the country. Nearly seventy percent of our patients return only to continue their outpatient therapy or to offer assistance to new clients coming in." Evita looked over their shoulders and made her excuses. "Feel free to walk around. There is a small reception in the room opposite of the one you entered through. Please feel free to talk to anyone here. No one is offended if you ask if they are a client or staff."

"Great, thank you."

Avery sighed and took Liam's arm. "I thought she would never leave."

"This place feels like a country club," Liam said.

"Let's start circulating."

They traversed the courtyard space quickly. While it was an outdoor private garden, it was in the middle of Manhattan, so it wasn't huge. Avery caught Sasha out of the corner of her eye, talking with Evita. Only Sasha was the one walking in front of the staff. Listening to the woman talk about the facility was obviously not something she wanted to deal with.

"There were more people in the group rooms."

Liam held her hand as they walked their way back inside. There were half a dozen people talking in the first group room.

Avery looked at the men who appeared to be either staff or clients. Two couples were standing with two men that were part of the staff. "I see a theme," she whispered to Liam.

He was looking at the testimonials on the wall. "What's that?"

"Staff and patients are wearing long sleeve shirts and casual pants."

Liam glanced in the other room. "I think you're right."

Avery looked at everyone now a little differently. Every man in a long sleeve shirt without a jacket became part of her mental lineup. Too tall, wrong nationality, wrong build . . . she didn't rule out thick or thin, because a year could change that. It was while walking through the main living room that she started to realize exactly what she was seeing.

"Are you okay?" Liam asked. "You look pale."

She placed her lips close to his ear and whispered, "If he is here, he's like these people. No one is raving mad and crazy."

"We don't know what is happening on the top floors."

Avery needed more. She walked up to the first collared-shirted man and smiled. "I'm sorry, do you work here?"

"I do." He extended a hand. "I'm Duane. One of the counselors."

"I'm Avery and this is Liam. Can I ask you a few questions?"

"That's why we're here."

"My brother, he's been using for a long time. He's kind of a mess. He has hit our mother a couple of times. Everything here seems so orderly and balanced. Am I looking at the right facility?"

"We work with all types of addiction, and sometimes the initial phases of detox involve violent tendencies. We do everything in our power to talk patients down and provide a safe environment for everyone. The fact that you're here, looking for help, is a positive step. But I'm sure you know he has to be the one to walk through the door. No one is forced to stay here. Is your brother ready?"

"I don't honestly know." Her lies about a fictitious brother came easy.

"How old is he?"

Avery thought about the approximate age of her attacker. "Twenty-six."

"College?"

"He used the money for college on his habit."

"Not uncommon for our clientele."

Yeah, kids with money had more to blow . . . literally.

"Thank you for speaking with me."

He reached a hand out and placed it on her arm. "I look forward to helping your brother beat this and taking that look out of your eye. Addicts often don't understand the pain they dish out to their family every time they use. He can earn your trust back. I see it every day."

Duane walked away and Liam whispered, "You're a little too good at lying."

Avery held her smile back. Across the room, Sasha made a nodding motion to the courtyard.

They slowly made their way back outside.

"Did you recognize anyone?" Sasha asked quietly.

"Everyone looks *normal*." *Normal* didn't fit the image in her head.

Liam placed a hand over her shoulders and kissed the top of her head. "We'll find him."

"You wait out here. I'll do another pass and signal when I'm leaving."

"Do you have what you need?"

Sasha's only confirmation was a slight nod.

Liam guided Avery to a bench and took her side. "What do you think she needed?"

Avery sighed. "Their records, registry for the patients?"

"You think she hacked into their computers in the time we've been here?"

"I wouldn't put anything past her, from the stories I've heard."

"I can't wait to hear them."

She stared down at their intertwined hands. "It feels like we're wasting our time."

"We waste as much as you need." He pulled her hand to his lips and kissed her fingertips.

Yeah, but what if every day was like this? Hype and hope followed by disappointment.

"Excuse me?"

Avery and Liam looked up.

"Duane suggested I come over and talk to you." He pointed to his chest. "I'm one of the clients here. He thought you might want to hear about how this facility helped me."

Twenty-five, maybe, clean-cut with a polite smile.

Avery blinked several times, forgetting the string of lies she'd managed since walking through the door.

"That would be great," Liam said.

He pulled an empty chair from behind him and sat facing them. "I'm Cedrick Palmer." He reached out to shake Liam's hand.

From the edge of his sleeve, peeking out from under the material, was one spiny leg.

Avery brought both hands to her mouth to keep from crying out. *It's him.*

Liam swiveled his gaze, then turned back to the man whose hand he just shook.

She noticed the second Liam realized what was happening. His arm tensed.

Avery grabbed his leg and kept him sitting.

Cedrick started to push his seat back. "Are you okay? Can I get you some water?"

She started shaking. "I'm fine. You, ah . . . you look like my brother."

He looked over his shoulder, and she saw the memory in vivid color. He'd put on twenty pounds, his eyes weren't wild.

"How old is your brother?"

Avery opened her mouth and nothing came out. *He doesn't recognize me.*

"Twenty-six," Liam said for her.

"How old are you?" Avery found her voice.

"Twenty-four. I came here eleven months ago. I'll be getting my one-year pin next month."

Avery didn't know if she wanted to hear this. The man, the kid who haunted her while he was sobering up, was talking to her without an ounce of recollection in his face.

"What made you walk in the door?"

Liam's hand was in hers. She wasn't sure who was holding on tighter.

"I hit bottom. My parents reached their limit with my addiction, lies, and stealing. Because I had been a good customer for so long, and my dealer didn't think my parents would completely cut me off, he offered a line of credit."

Krueger.

"Only his drugs weren't cut the same. Or maybe my body simply rebelled. My high was shorter and life in between was longer. I was on these streets, walking past clubs I used to go in and buy the rounds. I had been reduced to standing by the back door, hoping to see an old friend who could hook me up."

"That was your rock bottom?" Liam asked. "Living on the street and begging for handouts?"

"I wish." Cedrick shook his head. "My dealer was tired of waiting for money and told me I could earn everything if I did a job for him."

Avery's skin tensed, her breath shallow. "What job?" Her voice was tight.

"I don't know. He gave me a hit when we met up. Some crazy shit I had never had before. I remember walking with him, feeling surprised I was standing up. It was like I was on the outside of my body, looking down, saying, 'Dude, you should be facedown in a ditch. And not in a high, party way, but just die already and get it over with.'"

He doesn't remember anything. His tone, his manners . . . none of it was what she was prepared to see.

"The next day I woke up in an alley with someone else's clothes on my back. I have no idea what happened that night. I learned later that week that my dealer overdosed on his own shit. I knew that could have been me, that I was next. I stopped using for three days, easy to do when you don't have money and your dealer is dead. I went to the emergency room and told them I wanted to kill myself. I didn't. But I knew it would give me three days of medical care, food, and a bed. When I left, I went to my parents' house and begged them to check me in here."

"You don't remember anything? Nothing at all?"

"No. It haunts me sometimes. Like I should. In here I realized that I only had a few nights without any memories. Some of these guys have forgotten years. But I'm doing much better now. I'm six months from finishing my bachelor's degree and starting my master's in psychology, specializing in addiction. I was given this path, and I need to help others get out. I have to give back and make up for everyone I've hurt."

Avery closed her eyes and tilted her head to the sky.

"What do you want to do?" Liam asked her.

She opened her eyes to find Liam poised and ready for whatever she needed. Beyond him, Sasha stood beside Cooper.

Cedrick sat with his fingers crossed in his lap. Forcing him to remember would do what? It wouldn't bring back her year, wouldn't erase the past.

She slowly let her lungs fill with fresh air.

Avery smiled at Liam, touched the side of his face, and shook her head.

She stood, her legs a little less than stable.

Liam kept an arm on her elbow.

"You've been very helpful, Mr. Palmer."

He stood with them and smiled.

Avery's hand moved out slowly.

He took it without hesitation.

His gaze fell to the tattoo on her arm. "What does that say?"

She lifted her chin and brought her arm up.

"Warrior. Nice. I like the spider." And without a thought, he rolled up his sleeve to show her his tattoo. There it was, the image of her nightmares. "I need to touch this up. The eyes freak even me out."

"That would give anyone bad dreams," Liam said.

Cedrick smiled. "Why *warrior*?" he asked Avery.

She looked her past in the eye and let it go. "Because it was better than *survivor*."

Something flashed in his eyes for a moment, then was gone.

"Congratulations on your one-year pin, Mr. Palmer."

"Thank you."

Avery walked out of Tranquility Springs flanked by security and in a cloud of peace.

Liam took the back seat with her.

"What are we doing?" Cooper asked.

Sasha looked over her shoulder.

"You knew he was in there all the time, didn't you?"

Sasha sighed. "No. Palmer's name came up in Van's tattoo parlor's database with a description of the spider. The profile was exactly as you said. A young man with money who hadn't been in since the tattoo was put on his arm. Palmer wasn't on the police radar. No criminal activity. He did turn up on the dean's list at his current college. There was a link to a term paper on drug addiction and recovery. Without a current address, it was safe to say he was still residing in a private rehabilitation facility. By two o'clock this morning our team narrowed it down to this facility or another one across town. This being the most likely."

"You could have just told me."

Sasha shook her head. "No. I could not give you what he just did."

Avery closed her eyes.

"Babe?" Liam asked. "Are we calling Armstrong?"

She shook her head and leaned into his shoulder. "Take me home."

Chapter Thirty-Two

Armstrong answered Reed's call as he was walking out to his car.

"Armstrong?"

"No bad news, please. My wife hasn't seen me in a week."

He heard Reed laugh on the line. "Avery is on her way back to California."

"Thank God. We will eventually find this guy. Assure her of that."

Again, Reed laughed. "I sent you an e-mail. The file is encrypted. Use it if you need to. Avery Grant wants to put this behind her at this time. She's not going to pursue him."

Armstrong leaned against the hood of his car. "Son of a bitch . . . you found him. How?"

Reed was silent.

"Yeah, you know what? I don't want to know."

"Enjoy your evening, Detective. If you're ever in LA, drop me a call. We'll grab a beer."

"You're on. Thanks, Reed."

Armstrong looked at his phone, laughed, and shoved it in his back pocket before pulling out of the parking lot.

Sally was going to freak when he came home early.

Liam had his sister drop off a duffel full of his clothes and a few days' worth of groceries while Avery was sleeping.

They'd returned to her condo after midnight, and at nearly noon, she finally emerged from her bedroom. The fact that Avery stepped from the shower with wet hair and a lack of makeup was a testament to where they were in their relationship.

Liam swiveled the stool he was sitting on by her kitchen counter and opened his arms for her to walk into. She sank into him like an extension cord into an outlet. "Good morning," she said against his lips.

Such sweet words. Yeah, she could probably say anything and he'd call it something flowery.

He accepted her kiss and gave one of his own. "Good afternoon."

He pulled her to sit on one of his legs, and she looked down at his laptop and what he was working on. "What's that?"

"Invoices, paperwork. Things I've been slowly getting behind on."

"Because you're chasing your girlfriend around all over the country."

He knew he was sporting a shit-eating grin. "You said *girlfriend* without stuttering."

She placed a lazy arm on his shoulder and moved a strand of his hair more to her liking. "I'm evolving."

"I approve of your evolution."

She kissed him again, a little slower this time. "Thank you for being here. For chasing me. I rolled over a couple of times last night and felt you there, all I could think was *you're still here*. You didn't run away, even though I gave you an out."

"You aren't getting rid of me that easy, Princess."

He sealed that promise with a kiss.

She smiled when she pulled back.

"How are you feeling about yesterday?" he asked. The trip home was void of all conversation about Cedrick Palmer.

"Resolved. I went to New York searching for revenge, and look how quickly I let it consume me. I stepped on the scale today. I lost eight pounds. That never happens when I want it to."

Liam squeezed her thigh.

"I didn't realize how dim everything felt until I woke up today. I saw the light coming in, heard you in here . . . and the shadows of the past were gone. Vanished. Then I looked at this and thought"—she lifted her arm with the tattoo and traced it with one finger—"I'm really glad I didn't get anything bigger."

They both laughed.

Her smile lit up her face.

"You can always have it removed," he told her.

"No. I want it. A forever reminder to learn from the past and let it go. From my parents and the things they did to make me spend money on a therapy couch, to Cedrick's walk on the dark side, where I was caught in the cross fire."

"Past relationships that keep you from entering a new one . . . like your previous marriage?"

"Oh, hon . . . no. That has nothing to do with my resistance to all things relationships."

Liam fixed her with a questioning look. "You were married. That had to have some impact on you."

Avery placed a hand to the side of his face. "What's my ex's name?"

He opened his mouth to respond, closed it. "Mr. Grant?"

God, he loved her smile. "No. I never took *Bernie's* last name."

"Bernie?" *What man had that name?*

She slid off his lap and grabbed the phone on an opposite counter. Who was she calling?

"Bernie. It's Avery."

Liam sat dumbfounded. She was calling her ex?

"Well, of course you know my voice. Everyone should remember the ex-wife's voice." She smiled at Liam as she spoke. "Listen, I don't have a lot of time . . . no, no. I'm doing well, but thank you. Yes, I know."

Had Liam ever heard an ex talking to an ex as happily as he was witnessing right now?

Nope.

Right on up there with never.

"I met someone." She was silent for a beat. "No. Stop. He's important to me, and I wanted you to meet him."

Liam lifted his hands in the air and mouthed, *What?*

"Next week would be great." Her eyes lit up. "Seriously? Congratulations. She's not after your money—"

Liam felt he needed popcorn for the conversation he was witnessing.

"Okay, if you say so. But I can kick some ass these days." She laughed. A wholehearted belly laugh Liam wasn't sure he'd ever seen her do. "Perfect. I'll see you then. I adore you, too."

Avery hung up.

"What the hell was that?"

"Bernie's getting married. I can't believe it."

Liam watched her pour a cup of coffee. "You set us up on a double date with your ex?"

"Sure did. Because as your *girlfriend*, I get to do that."

"But your ex-husband?"

Avery leaned on her elbows across the counter and took a sip of coffee. "I married him as a means to get out from under my parents. He married me because he wanted a trophy wife and the confidence it gave him. He gave me money. I helped him find his backbone." She took another drink. "We never slept together."

"Holy shit, you really did marry him for his money. That wasn't a joke."

"Not a joke. Not a lie. He just asked me if I needed more. He is *that* guy. I think you two will get along great."

"This is surreal, you get that, right?"

"Yup. Even more odd is that you will meet him before my parents. Maybe he can convince you how they are so you don't hold it against me when my mother disapproves."

"Mothers love me."

"If you look up *pretentious* in a dictionary, you'll see her picture. So unless you're hiding a couple hundred million somewhere, be prepared."

"Can't say I am."

He paused and watched her drink her coffee.

"Is that going to be an issue?"

Avery narrowed her eyes. "What?"

"That I don't have that kind of money."

She lowered her cup from her lips and set it down. "Is it an issue that I do?"

He saw her point and smiled. "No."

She released a sigh. "Good. Because I really don't want to throw it away. In fact, I have some serious retail therapy to do as soon as the Brentwood project is tied up. If I still have that job, that is."

"I'm sure a truthful explanation will keep you in good standing with Lankford."

"We'll see. What's done is done. I'm not going to stress about it."

He stood and moved to her side of the counter. "Now sit down and let me make you something to eat. I need to get some of that meat back on your bones."

"Oh my God, you're going to cook for me again? I feel like I hit the jackpot."

He kissed her, hard, and pushed her into a chair. "You haven't seen anything yet."

$\mathcal{C}\mathcal{I}$

Two weeks later Avery stood outside the Brentwood estate as the last of the Lankfords' belongings were shipped off to Goodwill. Many of the estate's treasures were at auction houses, sold, or now just given away. But outside of collecting a check when everything sold, Avery was done. Three weeks behind schedule, but that didn't seem to matter.

"So that's it?" Sheldon asked when he walked out of the empty house to stand by her as the Goodwill truck pulled out of the driveway.

"That's it."

Avery had heard a sigh like that from her own lips just a few weeks before.

"Sheldon." She pulled her nerve in and lifted her eyes to his. "I found some pictures a while back, hidden in your father's desk."

He stared down at her, blinking.

He said nothing.

"I left his desk in the office, in case you wanted to see where they were. I removed them so they wouldn't end up in the wrong hands. I'm not sure if you want to see them, or—"

"What kind of pictures?"

She picked up her oversize purse and removed an envelope and handed them over. "I think your dad had an affair."

Sheldon seemed unfazed as he removed the old photographs and barely gave them a look. He turned his head and stared blankly at the disappearing truck.

He knew.

"I'm sorry," she said, laying a hand on his arm.

Sheldon attempted to smile. "Don't be. I always assumed he had other people in his life. He always had time for everyone other than me."

It was sad to think the man went to his grave never changing his relationship with his chosen son.

Noise from the drive had her turning around.

Liam and two of his workers pulled up in trucks. When her boyfriend stepped out, she couldn't stop her heart from reaching her smile.

"Liam is a lucky man," Sheldon said.

"Thank you."

Holding a sledgehammer, Liam climbed up the stairs. He dropped a quick kiss to her lips and shook Sheldon's hand. "Good morning. Ready to get started?"

"Nope," Avery said. "I have some shopping to do."

Liam and Sheldon both laughed.

"We're going to start the demo. Lots of noise, dust, and trash." He offered the sledgehammer to Sheldon. "Some of my clients like to take the first swing."

Sheldon immediately shook his head. "I'll leave that to the profess—" He paused and accepted the tool. "On the other hand, there's a desk I wouldn't mind taking a hammer to."

With that, he walked back into the house.

⁓

"First Wives Club meetings shall always include shopping, shoes, and champagne." Avery lifted her glass to the other three club members as a toast.

"Cheers."

Their club meeting was being held at the Hotel del Coronado in San Diego.

"I needed this!" Avery exclaimed. "I can't remember the last time I managed any serious shopping."

Their bungalow looked out over the Pacific Ocean with endless sunshine. They sat on a private deck, enjoying the last rays of heat as the sun started to set.

"Wade and I did our share of damage on our honeymoon," Trina told them. "I've never known a man who likes to shop more than him."

"That's because he's loaded," Avery teased.

"It's because he looks good in everything he puts on." Everyone turned to stare at Shannon.

"Is it possible the woman who seems impervious to the male species is finally starting to open her eyes?" Avery asked.

"I fall hard, and fast . . . and for the wrong men. You flitter from one flower to another until a Venus flytrap grabs your leg to keep you from running away."

Lori tilted her flute glass Avery's way. "She has a point."

"So are you dating?" Avery asked Shannon.

"Not yet. Before you ask, yes, I've been going out a little more. I'm not sure I want to date in LA."

"What does that mean? Where would you date?"

She shrugged. "I'm thinking of selling the house and moving."

"What? Why?"

"Because Paul bought it for me."

"That was part of your agreement," Lori said.

"I'll use the money from the sale to buy something else. Granted, he didn't have much to do with the purchasing process other than writing a check, but it still feels like it's part of him."

"Hey, anything you can do to move on, sista." Avery clinked her glass to Shannon's.

"Where would you move?"

"I'm not sure. I like the beach."

"Just don't move too far," Avery suggested.

"Hey, I moved to Texas," Trina said.

"You fly here all the time." Avery set her glass down.

"True."

"So, Avery, how is everything going with Liam?"

"He is an unexpected pleasure in my world."

"Has he told you he loves you?" Trina asked.

Avery knew her cheeks were blushing. "Yes."

Trina did the smiling chair dance.

"And you him?" Lori asked.

Avery hid her answer in her drink.

"Excuse me, what was that?" Shannon asked.

"No. I can't."

"Do you?"

"Yes. Of course. He's the best thing in my life. We laugh all the time, toss each other around in krav and in the bedroom. He keeps me grounded and safe . . . and I don't know, settled."

Lori moved away from the railing she was leaning on and sat in a chair. "So why not tell him that?"

"Because then he will move on to the next thing. It's what he does. It started with insisting that we were dating when we weren't . . . and the next thing I know I'm in a relationship. I erased all my dating profiles, my data dump of phone numbers gave my phone so much room it downloaded music all by itself just because it could."

They were laughing.

"He has a drawer at my place—hell, he took half the closet. I even have a dog bed for Whiskey. His niece is already calling me Auntie Avery, and Michelle is calling me to arrange a family dinner so everyone can meet. I can't do that, because I still haven't taken him over to the Grant home for what will surely be the dinner from hell."

"It could go well," Miss Glass Half-Full told her.

"Snowball's chance, Shannon. Snowball's chance."

"What does he do when he tells you he loves you and you don't say it back?"

Avery found herself smiling. "He tells me it's okay that I don't because he knows that when I do, I'm *all in*, that since the words aren't easy for me, they mean more. He's so damn understanding."

"Sounds like the real thing."

"I tell him I love him, and the next thing I know, you guys will be back buying more freaking bridesmaids' dresses. My condo doesn't work for the dog. I love my condo. And what happens if I get pregnant? I'm too young to be a mom."

"You're thirty-two," Trina reminded her.

"Liam will be a great dad," Lori added.

Avery thought about how he treated his niece, and smiled.

"You know what is killing me about this whole picture?" Shannon asked.

"What?"

"You know you love him. He adores you. Keeping that little word that means so much out of the mix is only prolonging what you know is going to happen. You want it to happen."

"Do I?"

Shannon leaned forward. "Close your eyes?"

"What?"

"Humor me."

Avery frowned and followed instructions.

"Fast-forward five years. Is Liam there?"

She smiled. "Yes."

"Where are you guys?"

She saw his home, the one with the yard, or one like it. There were kids' toys in the yard and a white fence. Damn, she was happy.

Avery unfolded herself from her chair. "Son of a . . ." Opened the door leading back inside.

"Where are you going?" Trina called after her.

"I have to call Liam."

They started laughing.

Avery grabbed her cell phone from her purse and hid in the bathroom. Before she lost her nerve, she leveled the phone with her face and called Liam via FaceTime.

He picked up on the second ring.

Just seeing him made her smile. "Shouldn't you be chardonnay drunk by now?" he teased.

"Probably."

He was in his backyard, under the lights of his patio.

"Is that Auntie Avery?"

Liam smiled and turned the phone toward Cassandra. "Sure is. Say hi."

"Hi, Auntie Avery. When are you gonna come back over so I can braid your hair?"

"Soon, honey. Can you do me a big favor and give me and your uncle a few minutes?"

Liam scooted his niece off his lap. "Play with the dog before it gets dark."

Avery heard Cassie's squeals and the dog barking as she ran out of view.

"Is everything okay?" he asked.

She nodded like a fool for a good five seconds and then sucked up her nerve. "Yup. I just called to tell you I love you."

Liam's smile started at his eyes, and when it reached his lips, he held it in. "Did that hurt?"

"God, yes," she exhaled.

He was chuckling.

"I promised that I wouldn't lie to you, and not saying it has been a lie by omission, so there. I love you, Liam Holt."

He peered into the camera. "Are you in a bathroom?"

"Are you going to give me crap about where I chose to say it?"

"Maybe."

She was laughing with him. "It was private."

"I think I'm going to love these club meetings of yours."

She glanced at the bathroom door, heard the ladies on the other side. "Okay, so that's it. That's all I called to say."

"Say it again."

"Is that a demand?"

"Yes." His eyes were alive with happiness.

"I love you, Liam. I'll show you how much when I see you on Monday."

"I love you, too. Thanks for being impulsive."

"A trait you're going to hate."

"So far it's working for me."

He blew her a kiss and hung up.

She closed her eyes and hugged her phone to her chest.

It was all over now.

Epilogue

Avery walked around the condo, placing flowers in the perfect locations and then deciding they didn't look right and moving them.

The caterers were busy setting up in the kitchen, and music already played on her sound system.

Introducing Liam to her parents at a cocktail party had been his idea.

Making sure everyone was at the party before her parents could arrive was hers.

Liam brushed up behind her and ran his hands up her bare arms. "You look edible."

The sleek cocktail dress didn't leave room for a bra. It came up to her neck almost like a collar and crisscrossed all over the back, which dipped low. The First Wives approved and also suggested that she double up on her birth control pills if she wore it for Liam. By the heat breathing down on her neck from the man in question, they were right.

"So we should tell everyone the party is off and go to bed early."

He chuckled in her ear. "You're not wiggling out of this."

She moaned.

The doorbell rang and her palms broke out in a sweat.

"Relax."

Not standing on ceremony, Trina and Wade arrived and immediately made themselves at home. Lori and Reed, Shannon. The Wives were there. Michelle brought a friend from class. Leslie arrived with a mutual friend from krav.

"Samantha! I didn't think you guys were going to make it." Avery kissed the side of Samantha Harrison's cheek and did the same for Blake.

"And miss meeting this guy?" Sam extended a hand. "I'm Samantha, almost everyone calls me Sam."

"My pleasure."

"This is Blake Harrison. We've been friends with Avery for quite a few years."

"Nice to meet you," Liam said.

"Are the parents here yet?" Sam asked.

"No."

Sam leaned closer to Liam. "Keep Avery away from the tequila when Adeline shows up."

"Stop. I'm not that . . ." She paused. "Okay, I was that bad."

Blake turned to Liam. "I'm told you're in construction."

"I am."

"Commercial or residential?"

"A little of both, actually."

The two of them started a conversation about work, and the doorbell rang again. Each time was like a tiny nail in Avery's side.

"Brenda?" Avery's jaw dropped. She'd invited her krav instructor, but she seriously hadn't thought she'd show.

Holy shit did Brenda clean up. Wow, she took little black dress to a whole new meaning, and the man holding her arm was African American and towered over her. Not hard, because she was kinda on the short side, but wow.

Avery excused herself from Sam's side and crossed to the door. "Look at this sexy mama!"

Brenda gave her a stern look. "Zip it, Grant, or you'll be doing burpees until Christmas."

Yeah, those words didn't scare her. "You must be Brenda's main squeeze."

"I am." Oh, and his voice was bayou deep.

"Phil. His name is Phil, not main squeeze," Brenda corrected.

Avery pulled them into the room. "Let me introduce you to some of our friends. Shannon, Lori, this is Brenda, the krav queen of LA, and her boyfriend, Phil. Brenda, you need to talk Shannon into coming to class. I think a strong wind could knock her down."

"Kinda like you when you first came to me?" Brenda was all snark.

"Delicate flowers hold the most poison," Phil said, smiling down at Brenda.

Avery barely registered the doorbell ringing, because she was laughing. Brenda and *delicate* . . . that was rich.

"Oh, dear Lord."

Avery felt the nails of her mother's voice on her childhood chalkboard.

Her parents stood side by side in stunned silence when Avery turned around.

What, is there a problem already?

A waiter walked by, and her mother snagged a glass of wine off the tray so fast the guy almost lost the whole thing.

That's when Avery looked around to see if anyone else was watching her reaction.

Phil started to laugh.

Avery looked up, then back at her mother, and shook her head.

Adeline Grant was about to have a coronary.

Because Avery couldn't help herself, she waited just a couple of beats before excusing herself to greet her parents. "Hello, Mother. Daddy."

Her father kissed her cheek. "It's good to see you. Been too long."

"Well, I have been busy."

Adeline kept eyeing the man standing behind her daughter.

"There's someone I'd like you to meet."

Avery took a few steps, noticed her mother wasn't moving, and motioned with her hand.

Turning on her heel, Avery walked past Phil and winked. He smiled back, and she moved past him and up to Liam.

She slid her arm around Liam's waist and turned to her parents. "Mom, Dad, this is Liam. My boyfr—"

"Oh, thank God!" Adeline almost melted right there in the middle of the condo.

Liam was all smiles. He looked down at Avery as if saying, *see, I told you all mothers love me.*

"A pleasure to meet you, young man. I'm Howard, and this is my wife, Adeline."

Liam shook her father's hand, met his eyes, and turned to Adeline.

To Avery's surprise, her mother leaned in for a kiss to Liam's cheek. "You cannot understand my joy right now."

Avery started to laugh.

"I've heard a lot about you," Liam told them.

"I can't say the same. I suppose that means we'll have plenty to talk about," Adeline said.

"I see where Avery gets her beautiful smile."

Avery had a strong urge to roll her eyes.

She did a double take—was that her mother blushing? "Such a handsome man, Avery. Where ever did you meet?"

"In a bar," she said, deadpan.

"At the gym," Liam said at the same time.

Lori leaned in. "Jury is still out on which one of those answers is the truth."

An hour later, when the party was in full swing, Avery had left her parents to fend for themselves and checked on the state of the caterers and supply of wine and cocktails.

She heard someone clinking a glass and the room grow silent. Turning, she saw Liam grabbing everyone's attention. Someone turned the music down.

He motioned for her to join him.

What are you doing?

"I wanted to take a minute to thank everyone for coming tonight. I like to think this is the first of many celebrations with this beautiful woman at my side. I especially want to thank Brenda, for giving Avery the skills to walk with confidence, not to mention kick ass."

Avery saw her mother's eyes. "Mom's not going to like hearing that, babe."

"It's okay, Mrs. G. I'll tell you how I first saw your daughter later."

Mrs. G?

Holy shit, her mother was blushing again.

"Reed and your crew. The weight off Avery's shoulders is like night and day." Liam lifted his glass and Reed lifted his.

"I would be remiss if I didn't thank Bernie, who isn't here . . . so glad he divorced you so I could have a chance," Liam said directly to Avery.

"To Bernie," someone in the crowd said, and a chorus went up.

Liam turned to her. "To this beautiful, strong, independent, snarky—"

Avery heard her mother laugh.

"Courageous woman who opened up her heart so I could park myself in."

She melted in his public appraisal.

"I love you, Princess. I've had a little chat with your father. So I need you to take some time and to get used to the idea of changing your name. Because the next time this group of people gets together, it's going to be with me on one side of the church and you walking my way."

Her nerves were wrecked. "Are you asking me . . . ?"

"Are you ready for me to ask you to marry me?"

Everything in her tightened. Fear? Excitement?

"I, um . . ."

He winked. "I'll ask that question in private, but with your track record, I thought it best to let everyone in the room know my intention, so if you suddenly disappear and end up in Finland, your friends here will know why. I'm going to marry you. I'm just telling you now so you can get used to the idea."

She was going to cry.

"To Avery." Liam put his glass in the air.

"To Avery," a chorus went up in the room.

Slowly the music was turned up, and their guests struck up their conversations.

"I love you," she said to him when no one was listening.

"Your mom loves me, and your dad approves . . ."

"My mother thought I was with Phil when she walked in the room."

Liam glanced over her shoulder. "I'll take whatever I can get. Thank you for letting me be a part of your life," he said before kissing her.

Damn, she loved this man. White picket fence, two point five kids kind of love.

She broke off their kiss and started toward the First Wives, who were all smiles. Avery took several steps and stopped. "Excuse me," she called out. "Can someone turn the . . . thank you." The music dropped again.

"Liam?" She turned toward him, hands at her sides.

He grinned like a fool.

"I've had enough time. The answer is yes."

Liam opened his arms and swooped her up. "Took you long enough."

He kissed her long and soft before slowly setting her down. From his pocket he removed a box, took the ring from inside, and slid it on her finger. "Marry me."

"I already said yes."

They kissed again, ignoring whistles and clapping from their family and friends.

"That's enough of that, son. Time for that later."

Avery grinned at her father's words.

"I should say so" was her mother's reply.

Liam opened his eyes a little wider as he stared down at Avery chuckling.

"I knew my parents would show up sometime."

He leaned in closer. "They're going to have to get used to me kissing their daughter." He placed his lips on hers. "Whenever, however, and wherever I want."

Acknowledgments

It takes a village to publish a book. This is the part where I thank my townspeople.

Jane Dystel, my brilliant agent, who I lovingly refer to as my pit bull. For all you do . . . thank you.

Kelli Martin, my developmental editor and dear friend. Good call on the Sheldon arc. Love ya, sista.

Maria Gomez and everyone at Montlake Romance who took my manuscript and made it a novel. Big hugs, big kisses . . . and even bigger glasses of bubbles to celebrate another one under the professional belt.

Krav queen of Santa Clarita, Bonnie Formia. Okay, you're not German, and you never made me do fifty burpees at the same time. But you did roll your eyes at me when I punched with the strength of a gnat, and you did nag me to join your group class. You've opened my eyes to krav and everything it can do to help me out of a crappy situation. Thank you, my friend.

Now on to Tanya.

As I said in my dedication, strong women fuel me. Anyone who reads my work can easily deduce that the relationships with the women in my life are vital. Men may come and go, but strong friendships between us ladies last a lifetime. You're one of the strongest, most beautiful, smart, funny, supportive friends I have the pleasure to call one of mine. Thank you, my friend.

I love you.

Catherine

About the Author

New York Times, Wall Street Journal, and *USA Today* bestselling author Catherine Bybee has written twenty-eight books that have collectively sold more than five million copies and have been translated into more than eighteen languages. Raised in Washington State, Bybee moved to Southern California in the hope of becoming a movie star. After growing bored with waiting tables, she returned to school and became a registered nurse, spending most of her career in urban emergency rooms. She now writes full-time and has penned the Not Quite series, the Weekday Brides series, the Most Likely To series, and the First Wives series.